LONG LIVE
GROVER
CLEVELAND

Robert Klose

LONG LIVE GROVER CLEVELAND

Robert Klose

MEDALLION
P R E S S
Medallion Press, Inc.

Printed in USA

32007 4139

For R.S.

There is a crack in everything
That's how the light gets in

— Leonard Cohen

I have tried so hard to do right.

— Grover Cleveland

CONTENTS

ONE	One man's vision
TWO	What the cat dragged in
THREE	A first walk and an honored guest
FOUR	The world turned upside down
FIVE	The provost's tale
SIX	A clock like no other
SEVEN	A chance meeting, bison, and something about mucus
EIGHT	Bella learns the truth
NINE	Small things
TEN	Luncheon of champions
ELEVEN	An emergency meeting and a budgie
TWELVE	A request, with kid gloves
THIRTEEN	A collegial visit
FOURTEEN	YaYa again, and Bella swallows her pride
FIFTEEN	A grand plan
SIXTEEN	A novel idea
SEVENTEEN	A walk in the woods and a surprise visitor
EIGHTEEN	The metamorphosis
NINETEEN	Brisco alone and a sexual consideration
TWENTY	Conversion
TWENTY-ONE	Aloha and a cerebral affront
TWENTY-TWO	Sanctuary and a dark cloud
TWENTY-THREE	The eve of convocation
TWENTY-FOUR	The greatest show on earth

ACKNOWLEDGMENTS

I am grateful to the following for their careful reading of the manuscript and their helpful comments: John Greenman, Christopher Mares, Deborah Rogers, Deb White, Tim White, and Mary Gardner. Likewise, I am indebted to my editor, Emily Steele, for her keen eye, attentive ear, and skilled pen.

ONE
ONE MAN'S VISION

Grover Cleveland College was dying. The faculty knew it, the staff knew it, and the students knew it. Only its president seemed oblivious to its impending evaporation.

Crisis was once again upon the school. This was an annual event. As Grover Cleveland College was almost exclusively tuition driven, faculty wouldn't know whether there'd be enough money for their paychecks until August, when registration numbers became better known. But this particular crisis had an unprecedented gloss to it: the end was indeed nearing.

And so coalesced, under emergency circumstances, a Convocation of Concerned Faculty—an attempt to

1

divine a course of action from tea leaves: the perceived eccentricities and wrongheaded policies of the school's current president, Marcus Cleveland, the culprit who had, in the minds of many, brought the college to the brink of oblivion—and in record time.

While the faculty listened to Professor Brisco Quik, their self-appointed leader, rave about the sinking ship, President Marcus, a rotund man with a bushy mustache and wearing an old-fashioned suit, was trying to remove two bison from a glade in the campus forest. He pulled, pushed, and cajoled the mammals, fiddling while Rome burned, his tasseled loafers covered in mud.

In the meantime, amidst the hubbub and calamity, the doomsday clock—that grim sentinel hovering over the campus like the eye of a cyclops—ticked.

Grover Cleveland College had appeared, as if by Immaculate Conception, in the wilds of Maine just as Vietnam had begun to get on people's nerves. It had been the brainchild of Cyrus Cleveland, uncle of Marcus and first cousin once removed of the late president's nephew. Cyrus was a ferocious pacifist and wanted to create a haven for young men seeking coveted college deferments from the draft.

Cyrus was as surprised as anybody when a thousand men and a handful of women enrolled in Grover Cleveland College that first semester. The school, at that point, consisted of a large, Victorian-style house with sagging rooflines, a smaller frame structure, a few cabins, a pigsty, and an old barn with attached silo. Army-surplus Quonset huts had erupted over the years as additional classroom space. Students lived in the cabins, the basement of the Victorian, tents, and the pigsty, which also housed the student union. Some students boarded in private homes in the surrounding villages.

To meet demand, classes were held from sunup until late into the night. A small army of faculty members— many of them also seeking refuge from the draft—had been hired on the fly.

In short, Cyrus, with all the aplomb of a magician pulling a rabbit out of a hat, had slapped together a college. The war that he so hated turned out to be the engine of Grover Cleveland College's success, and Cyrus found himself secretly rooting for the collapse of the Paris peace talks. He was eternally grateful for the tenacity of Ho Chi Minh and the determination of Lyndon Johnson—that randy bastard—to win an unwinnable war. Providentially, Johnson's mantle was later assumed by the sainted Richard Nixon, whose election and illusion of some variation on the theme of victory guaranteed a fight into the long, dark political night and a bright future for the college.

Those were the halcyon days. There was a certain romance about a college operating on a shoestring, with students sitting on lobster crates and hay bales as they listened, stoned to the gills, to similarly stoned faculty employing the poetry of Rod McKuen as a weapon of insurrection against the imperialist, hegemonic government of the United States, the instrument of Satan for those who believed God had a nemesis. Surrounded as they were by wilderness, black bears, moose, and communes dedicated to the production of dream catchers and dried fruits, it was easy for students and faculty to believe Grover Cleveland College was an island of truth, Eden, Atman, Brahman, Asgard, the cat's meow. And slowly but surely the world without, in a very real way, adjourned from heart and mind as Grover Clevelanders tucked ever more deeply into their books, theories, and cannabis and accustomed themselves to the austerities of paying handsome tuition to a school that heated its buildings with wood, drew its water from a well, and offered only one degree: the Bachelor of Human Experience.

Cyrus Cleveland, as gangly and disarticulated as Ichabod Crane, presided over this glorious conglomeration of decrepit buildings, wild-eyed faculty, outlandish courses (Christ as Communist, The Lighter Side of Mao), draft dodgers, and potheads. It didn't matter that Grover Cleveland College was not and had no illusions about being accredited. The students came. In droves. In beat-up Volkswagen Beetles, paislied minibuses and death-defying Corvairs. Some arrived on foot, others on bicycles. Some fell upon the college by accident while hiking in the woods and decided to stay.

And then, at the very height of this onrush, Cyrus had his greatest coup, a sort of ersatz for accreditation but much better, much more symbolic. Cyrus Cleveland, exploiting political connections that went back to the Depression-era days of his father, a notorious rum runner, got hold of the brain of Grover Cleveland, salvaged for posterity from the autopsy of the largely forgotten president. Once he had secured it, he slunk back to Grover Cleveland College like a thief in the night, in a pounding rainstorm, with thunder drumming the hills and lightning splitting the heavy summer air. A group of students seeking extra credit constructed a shrine for the relic, a lump of fat and connective tissue about the size of a cantaloupe. The ex-president's neurons lay in state in a glass jar, on a catafalque, in the pigsty. An eternal flame was ignited, and a student was assigned to solemn—if somnambulant—watch.

The late president's brain was a sort of punctuation mark on the college's growth and progress. It arrived just at the institution's high point, with classrooms bursting at the seams; a steady flow of tuition dollars, which made for a contented faculty; and alumni remitting cash to the alma mater that had kept them out of harm's way. The Brain also became a minor point of cultural interest, like the Corn Palace or the World's Largest Ball of Twine, attracting the curious, Cleveland biographers, the president's descendants, and native Hawaiian recidivists wishing to honor President Grover Cleveland for courageously opposing the annexation of their once-independent homeland.

But happiness is a vacuum inviting catastrophe. Just as things were going swimmingly for Grover Cleveland College, the draft ended. As if a button had been pushed, student enrollment collapsed. Not only did applications slow to a trickle, but many enrolled students packed their Beetles and left, sometimes without so much as formally dropping their courses. But this was only the beginning of hard times. Not long after the inactivation of the draft, the unthinkable happened: the war ended.

Cyrus was in his office at the top of the grain silo when he heard the grim news. Furiously winding his hand-cranked television, he watched as Richard Nixon, looking as if he'd just swallowed a particularly tasty canary, announced, "We have peace with honor."

"Peace?" screeched Cyrus. "Honor?" He threw himself into his swivel chair, his head dipping into his hands. "Half a million troops!" he hollered at the talking head in the boob tube. "We could have gone on forever."

And then he wandered to the window and surveyed his school, his creation, the fruit of his aspirational loins. Everything seemed so still. So quiet. A few barefoot students in ragged jeans shuffled across campus. One— the current sentinel of the Brain Shrine—was zonked on the threshold of the pigsty. Worse, the eternal flame had gone out because nobody had paid the gas bill. But the sight that made his heart sink was the small, dark line headed away from campus and down the road to town like marching ants. But they weren't ants. They were students. And they weren't coming back. The great rout was underway.

What could he do? Upgrade the facilities? Get another brain? Start another war? Hopeless, hopeless. Falling into one of the sloughs of despondency to which he was prone, Cyrus dragged his lanky frame down the winding stairs of the silo and over to the Brain Shrine. Except for the snoring student on watch, he was alone.

"What should I do?" he voiced, as if trying to communicate with the inert organ. "Tell me what to do."

But the noble presidential synapses had long since ceased to fire, and The Brain remained plump, pickled, and unresponsive.

Through sheer force of will, Cyrus girded himself and managed to keep the school on life support for ten more long years, during which student numbers, although trending steadily downward, achieved the occasional modest bump. Cyrus knew exactly how to get blood out of a stone. He took to shaking down alumni who'd met with success but conveniently forgotten the haven that helped them keep their heads down long enough to make that success possible. In a sort of protracted mania,

Cyrus invaded boardrooms and family rooms of Grover Cleveland College graduates, ranting until they coughed up cash. Beyond this, he exhausted his own small fortune until the school seemed to be running on little more than the memory of adequate funding. Inevitably, though, having run the decade out, Cyrus collapsed from exhaustion, the pilot light of hope barely flickering in his rheumy eyes.

It is a truism that state of mind influences state of body. As if having no choice, Cyrus crawled into his bed, intending to never rise again. Such was the fickle nature of his leadership. But he was not without sympathizers. Worn-out hippies from Khamigar, the local fruit-drying commune, tended him with dried figs and apricots— not with any hope of inducing a miraculous recovery but merely out of compassion and, yes, gratitude for keeping them alive during the conflict in Indochina when they had been Grover Cleveland students.

The scene was quite beautiful. There lay Cyrus, drawn and ashen, propped on multiple pillows, his long gray ponytail draped about his neck and flowing down the front of his dingy nightshirt. Despite his sunken cheeks and sallow countenance, an inner light still shone, as if he were able at this final juncture to savor all the good he had done.

And yet his head could not rest easy—literally, for under his pillows lay a toxic document that Cyrus had struggled to pretend didn't exist. It was, in fact, so radioactive with import that he'd not made its existence known to anyone. In tandem with the great student rout, it had been delivered by a special courier who then beat a manic retreat to his idling vehicle before roaring off whence he had come, as if he couldn't bear any proximity to the document's contents.

While the thing throbbed beneath his head, giving him not a moment's peace, the Khamigar hippies continued to minister to him, angel-like, while the faculty, staff, and a coterie of students formed a slow procession up the silo's spiral staircase. They, too, had reason for gratitude. Cyrus's vision had enabled them to carve out decent lives, to pursue their academic interests, to raise children with names like Butterfly and Hotep, who frolicked barefoot in the woods surrounding the campus and bathed naked in a nearby stream. Not a bad legacy for a man who was so thoroughly shunned by his colleagues at the accredited institutions.

What frustrated and disappointed the employees, however, was that Cyrus didn't seem to have anything to say to any of them. It was as though he'd lost the ability to speak.

But that wasn't it. The question was, what more could he say? Grover Cleveland College, by virtue of its existence, said it all.

It was at that very moment, when the throng hovered uneasily about the all-but-dead man, that a complete stranger appeared on the scene. He was portly, with a decent head of brown, pomaded hair brushed straight back, a prominent nose, and a bushy, overgrown mustache. This middle-aged man wore a baggy, pinstriped suit with stiff lapels, which he straightened as he huffed and puffed his way up the silo. He apologized as he pushed past faculty, staff, students, and alumni waiting to pay their respects. Sensing his right of way, everyone dutifully parted for him.

He finally arrived in the death room, where silence reigned. The visitor walked to the side of the bed, said "Uncle," and laid a fleshy hand against the cheek of his fading relative. "Dear man," he said with a compassionate smile, "I'm here."

Cyrus opened his eyes and frowned. "It's about time. Lean in."

The visitor inclined an ear to the paper-thin lips that fluttered with every breath. The onlookers strained to hear the communication. All they were able to make out were the listener's periodic grunts of comprehension. But now and then an audible syllable bubbled up from Cyrus, and it wasn't long before everyone divined that the visitor was to be the new president of Grover Cleveland College. This took everyone by surprise. They'd assumed that Cyrus, in dying, was taking the school with him.

Finally, the large man stepped back and watched a white-robed woman from Khamigar administer one last, tentative bite of dried apricot to Cyrus, whereupon the old man closed his eyes and transitioned to spirit.

Many faculty and staff felt oddly cheated that Cyrus hadn't said good-bye. But his end was not bereft of drama. No sooner had Cyrus passed than their attention was drawn to the new president.

He pulled up a sleeve and slipped an arm under his uncle's pillows, where he fished around for a few moments before exhaling, "Ah!" He retrieved a thick gray envelope and, without a word, quickly deposited it in an inside pocket of his jacket. Then he turned and addressed the room for the first time. "Does anyone know where my office is?"

There was, then, reason for hope, and everyone began to unpack their bags. It seemed that a resurrection was afoot.

Nothing in Marcus Cleveland's aspect, personality, or presentation augured a bright future for the college. At the poorly named Greeting Meeting, held in the large conference room of the Victorian, faculty and staff managed to muster a modicum of attention, hope, and expectation, but Marcus dashed all of these within the first five minutes of his little speech. He spent the first three of those minutes struggling to identify the assembled by name, but he'd mistakenly been given the list of emeriti, several of whom were dead. And so the long moments wore on.

In an attempt to recover his decorum, Marcus put the paper down, smiled inanely, and asked, almost rhetorically, "Can anyone tell me what the main issues were at your last meeting?"

After a few moments of awkward silence, Bella Proins, the heavyset executive aide and adjutant for administration, cleared her throat. "Three years ago the campus was finally wired for electricity. A committee was formed to identify the best location for a vending machine." And then, after a pause, "For soda pop."

At first Marcus thought he was being led along. He glanced about the room and decided to yield the benefit of the doubt. Striking a tone of earnest concern, he prompted, "And?"

Bella clutched her pearls and moved her ample body uneasily in her seat. "I'll defer to the chair of the committee," she said with a sick smile, nodding to Brisco Quik, veteran professor of political science and teller of war stories.

Brisco seemed taken by surprise. He normally wore a fixed expression of anxious concern. But the sudden attention seemed to momentarily bewilder him. Nevertheless, he pulled himself together, rubbed the back of his neck, and drew himself out of his seat with all the aplomb he could muster on short notice, as if he were preparing to make a statement for the ages. "We're about to make our final recommendation," he said, straightening up and smoothing his polo shirt over his paunch. "We'll have it on your desk by the end of the week."

Marcus nodded appreciatively. Treading carefully, he probed, "The student union is in the pigsty?"

Bella acknowledged that it was.

Marcus's mustache rose with his smile. "Then let's put the vending machine there."

Bella scribbled a furious note to that effect, while there ensued a low moan from the others seated.

Marcus was not an academic, but he was astute in his way. He had never run a college. In fact, he'd never gone to college. He had sold used cars in Jersey City for two long decades, making Salesman of the Year eight times. He knew how to read people. And he was honest. When he told a customer he'd given him his lowest price, he meant it. And when the customer said, "Well, I'll just have to pass," Marcus offered a smile that complemented the twinkle in his deep-set brown eyes and said, "I understand. Come back if you're still interested." In other words, the customer walkaway had no effect on Marcus. He let them go, then waited. They almost always came back, and Marcus, because he was true to his word, always said, "Sure, that price is still good. Come into my office and have a cup of coffee while we settle things."

The thing was, Marcus had been happy selling cars. He liked people. They fascinated him. He'd often thought if he weren't a used-car salesman he could easily spend his life sitting in a sidewalk cafe in some large city, watching people come and go and conjecturing about their lives: Where were they off to? What did they do? Did they like their work? Did they love? Were they loved by others? In a sense, the dealership had been his cafe, a place where Marcus could observe and, best of all, interact with people. Rather than a business, he approached selling cars as an art, or perhaps a form of therapy, an attempt to match the car to the buyer with the end of helping the customer feel good about himself. Many a time someone would come in with his heart set on a four-door sedan but leave with a convertible, because Marcus had sensed and fulfilled the patron's unspoken longing to, for once in his life, cut loose. All the customer needed was a little push, and Marcus was happy to administer it. And he felt a pervasive, gentle warmth when the transaction was completed and the customer drove off in his new purchase, completely satisfied.

The great irony was that the owner of the dealership, Mr. Harlen Bell, had never liked Marcus, for reasons, if indeed reasons existed, he himself might not have been aware of. But an observer of the interactions between the two men might have concluded that the culprit was Marcus's chronic politeness, which threw Harlen Bell's character into stark relief. An old-school mercantile tyrant, Mr. Bell had been a personal friend of Henry Ford and shared many of the old master's suspicions about people based on presumption and sentiment rather than anything evidential. It would be unfair to say Harlen Bell, like Ford, was an anti-Semite, because in fact he was a broad-spectrum bigot, finding fault with Poles, blacks, Italians, the Irish, and even—based upon a single interaction involving a Rambler station wagon—the Montenegrins. Fortunately, he didn't prowl the selling floor, where his prejudices and uneven ways would have disaffected the clientele posthaste.

But damn!—could Marcus sell cars. There had been many days when Harlen Bell wanted to let him go, but just as the ax was about to fall, Marcus would—well, there was the time when he quietly communicated that he'd firmed up a contract with the Jersey City Police Department to provide them with new cruisers and Harlen Bell, blindsided by visions of green, erupted, "Marcus! Friend! Pal! Salesman of the Year!" And there would follow the warmest period of grace and bosom fellowship for a week or two before Harlen Bell returned to the native stream of his character and went grimly snuffling about for an opportunity to number the days of Marcus Cleveland.

And how often did he come so very close to doing the deed. The scene was a repetitive one. Marcus would be summoned to the old man's office, where the rail thin Harlen Bell hunched, insect-like, rolling his hands incessantly, his white eyebrows grown out to prehensile proportions, like antennae. Behind him, leaning against the wall, was the large white clock that had blown from the roof of the dealership in a windstorm, emitting its loud, wooden tock! second by second, as if counting away what remained of the old man's life. Into this scene Marcus would enter, and Harlen Bell would unlink his hands and generously indicate the chair in front of his desk. Marcus would assume the pose of a schoolboy sitting before the principal, his hands clasped between his knees, awaiting judgment.

"Marcus, you've been here a long time—"

"Yes, Mr. Bell," Marcus was quick to agree, having heard this preamble on numerous occasions. "Long enough to make Salesman of the Year eight times."

At which point Mr. Bell found himself struggling for the upper hand. "Yes, yes. And your timing in the matter has always intrigued me."

Whereupon Marcus, unbidden, would take that as his cue to reveal—for the umpteenth time—the secret of his success. "I like to give the customers not just what they want but sometimes what they don't know they want."

Harlen Bell shifted in his swivel chair. He didn't like philosophy and moved quickly to clear the air of it. "What I'm saying," he chopped with a practiced hand, "is that's all well and good, but—"

"Are you disappointed with the police department contract? Should I have tried to sell them more cars than they needed or asked for?"

"No, no, it's not that," insisted Harlen Bell, blinking madly, as if battling a sand storm. Throwing himself back in his chair, he regarded Marcus with a cold eye. He took in the great, grape-shaped bulk of the man, his crude, dark suit from the time of John Philip Sousa, and his shoe-brush mustache that fell down over his mouth like a curtain.

There! That's it, then, thought Harlen Bell. *Maybe that's what I don't like about the man. How do I know he's not talking about me beneath that mustache? And at this very moment, when I'm trying to be fatherly with him. The gall!* Harlen Bell felt the tension of prejudgment rise in him like a storm tide. *Who does this bloated anachronism, this tintype of a man, think he is? He believes he's a success, but his Vaseline ways with customers won't work on me. And sooner or later the customers themselves will catch on and he'll drive us all to bankruptcy.*

"Now, Marcus," he said firmly, "the time has come—"

"Speaking of time," Marcus interjected ever so deftly, "it's almost twelve thirty. Do you remember reading, some seventeen years ago, about Hippolit Krzyzanowski, the dock worker who rose to the presidency of Harborside International?"

Harlen Bell's head swam. What was he talking about? And what was this strange foreign name with all those syllables? "I don't think I—"

"Mr. Krzyzanowski, if you recall, fathered

quadruplets. The children are now seventeen. He wishes to buy each of them a new car. Cadillacs, I believe. I'm meeting with him in five minutes."

There she was, then, materialized before Harlen Bell's very eyes—Helen of Troy. "Marcus!" he whooped, levering his chair forward. "Friend! Salesman of the Year! Cadillacs!"

"Thank you, Mr. Bell. "I'll go now and take care of Mr. Krzyzanowski." And off he went to do what he did best.

One wonders why such a gentle, good-natured man had never married. Marcus led a deeply self-examined life and often asked himself this question. He liked women, but the closer he drew to them, the wider the chasm grew. It was like the paradox of light velocity: it was impossible for a solid object to achieve because as it approached light speed, it became infinitely dense. Thus, Marcus Cleveland found himself alone, with no companion except his cat, Pacer, and not much of a life outside the dealership, which seemed to color his entire view of the world.

On Sundays he would go to the Y, change into his bathing suit, and sit at the edge of the pool with his small feet dangling in the water—looking like a perfectly contented Buddha—for no other purpose than to observe the bodies of women. But because he'd concluded he'd never enjoy their company, much less their touch, he regarded them as he did the cars on the showroom floor, noting make, model, and design and admiring

20

the craftsmanship of it all. Then he'd go home to the silence and austerity of his small apartment over Perlman's Hardware Store to enjoy the comfort of a good book, a cup of steaming rose hip tea, and a purring Pacer curled in his lap.

An outside observer would conclude that Marcus was a happy man, the picture of contentment. But life does not abide calm waters for very long. Turbulence, either imposed or self-inflicted, is the natural state of the species. One evening, just as Marcus came to a particularly interesting plot turn in his book, just when he was savoring the halfway point of his cup of tea, and just when Pacer was nestling deeper into his lap, the phone rang.

Marcus sighed, smiled, and shook his head. He put down his book and his tea, set Pacer on the floor, and hoisted his bulk out of his easy chair, lifting the receiver just before the answering machine had a chance to engage.

A voice began to bark. "Marcus! I know you're listening. Say something."

Marcus didn't recognize the voice. A disgruntled customer? Not likely. He'd never had one of those. But if this was the exception, he'd make things right. He'd take the car back, no questions asked, in the interest of customer satisfaction and a return to a life devoid of ripples. He pressed the receiver to his ear and meekly responded, "Yes? I'm here."

"This is Cyrus. I'm calling from my deathbed. Time

is short, so shut up and listen."

As Cyrus began his monologue, Marcus struggled to recall the speaker. Because the tone was so familiar, he assumed he was a relative. And then—ah!—the oblique family connection sparked to mind. Marcus remembered an uncle who'd fled to the woods of Maine, where he'd opened some sort of school.

Marcus listened so intently, in absolute silence, that Cyrus, after ten minutes of soliloquy, finally paused for breath and demanded, "*Hello?*"

"Yes, Uncle."

Cyrus resumed his screaming and general complaining.

Marcus noted key words and strung them into a chain of meaning. *President. College. Nixon. Mess. Vietnam. Death. Successor. Brain. Pigsty.* "But Uncle," he said during an ebb in the torrent, "I'm not an academic. I sell used cars."

"Perfect!" Cyrus fell into a vicious coughing fit. After recovering, he went on. "This is your chance to make something of yourself. It's not every day that a college presidency is dumped in a man's lap. If you can sell cars, you can run a school. Believe me. You'll control the purse strings, and that's all you need to know. We cannot let this dream die."

"I'll need time to think about it," said Marcus, amazed he was even considering such an unexpected and, in his mind, inappropriate offer.

"Time? I'm dying. If I die before you say yes, the faculty will pick this place apart like a pack of hyenas. Even the doorknobs aren't safe. I need to know new leadership is en route."

Marcus thought about the dealership. He was happy there, despite the periodic tension with Mr. Bell, which he'd learned to navigate like a tanker in shoal waters. Why should he leave? But then again, he was one of several salesmen and would probably not be missed. Besides, rumor had it that the dealership was slated for closing due to cost cutting in the American automobile industry. Should he stick with it out of loyalty? Or was it time to jump from a burning building? Was his uncle's summons a once-in-a-lifetime opportunity? Was duty calling? Could he really run a college? He'd read many books, more titles than most people had forgotten. And he'd always been interested in the history of his ancestor, the late President Grover Cleveland. Wouldn't this be a way to honor his legacy of leadership? By becoming a leader himself?

Marcus seemed to have arrived at the threshold of the door to which his reasoning had led him. "Yes, Uncle."

And that was that.

All that remained was to screw up his courage to confront Mr. Bell and tender his resignation.

Tock!

Marcus stood before Harlen Bell's desk because the old man hadn't proffered a seat. In fact, not having summoned Marcus, he wouldn't even look up at him. "Yes, yes," he said as he scribbled away at some papers, the victory flush of the four Krzyzanowski Cadillacs having already dissipated. "What is it now? Can't you see how busy I am?"

"I find it necessary to leave."

The old man's head snapped up, his eyebrows bobbing. "W-what?" *What kind of perfidy is this? Is he attempting to rob me of my opportunity to fire him?*

"I've found another position."

Tock!

Whatever walls surrounded the small, scheming mind of Harlen Bell came tumbling down until not one stone was left upon another and abundant light poured in. "Marcus! Why are you standing? Have a seat!"

In an instant, all the facts, figures, and balances of the business marched before Harlen Bell's mind's eye. *My God, this man is the life ring who's kept us afloat on the black sea and not the red.* "Is it money?" he begged, gulping the word.

Marcus, now seated, knotted his hands and nibbled his lips. "No, no, Mr. Bell. Nothing like that."

"But you've found another position." Harlen Bell's pale face now flushed bright red. "Who's trying to take you away from me? Friend!"

Marcus stared blankly at his agitated, soon-to-be ex-boss. Both men hovered in the ether of silence for a long moment.

Tock!

Marcus wasn't good in confrontational situations. As for Harlen Bell, he'd parried with the best of them but was totally unmanned when the other person wasn't saying anything.

Tock!

Marcus cleared his throat. "It's a college."

"College? Colleges don't sell cars. What are you talking about?"

"I'm to be the president of a college."

Harlen Bell cackled. "You must be joking."

But Marcus shook his head, reflecting that he'd never in his life told a joke. "I have to go now. I want to thank you for everything you've done for me."

You're damn right! Harlen Bell thought. Every cell of his body rebelled at this unfair turn of events. But he hung fire. "Marcus," he said unctuously, his hand slithering across the desk toward his ungrateful employee.

Tock!

That last tock seemed to take Mr. Bell by surprise, and his anger ebbed. "Well," the old man said, withdrawing his hand. "I suppose I should be grateful you're not going over to the competition."

"I wouldn't do that. I've been happy here. Very happy."

In a transitory moment of sentiment, Bell channeled a very tiny, almost nondescript, better angel of his nature. "I think it's traditional for you to be awarded a gold watch. But as you know, times in this business are hard."

"I don't expect a gold watch. I wouldn't know what to do with it."

Tock!

Harlen Bell turned and, for the first time since the thing blew off the roof, paid heed to the massive white clock, six feet in diameter. "Here." He got up and stretched his arms around the monstrosity. "Take this. To remember us by."

Marcus pitched in to muscle the clock around the desk.

"Good-bye, Marcus." The old man didn't extend his hand. Deep inside he was chuckling—that clock had never kept time. In fact, despite its incessant tocking, the hands moved grindingly slow. It was an appropriate parting shot for someone who also seemed, in Harlen Bell's mind, to be stuck in time.

"Good-bye, Mr. Bell. And thank you." Marcus rolled the clock out of the office.

Behind the closed door, Harlen Bell stood by the window, then sank into his chair. It had taken many years, but he'd done the thing he always said he'd do. He'd gotten rid of Marcus Cleveland. No one was going to say Harlen Bell never finished what he started.

But a college?

Two days later, Marcus was on the Greyhound to Maine, a state he knew nothing about, except that it was cold, remote, and abutted Canada.

"Did you see how he circumvented the authority of the committee?"

Brisco Quik had been the last faculty member to achieve tenure before Cyrus abolished it in his bid for absolute control. As such, he felt he had nothing to lose by being the school's loose cannon, and venting every concern, real or imagined, that came to mind. Brisco didn't trust administrators, period. He regarded them as a different species. "They're like hostile extraterrestrials," he liked to say. "They strip a school of its resources and then move on."

"The faculty took great care," he continued, red-faced, "to appoint a committee to decide the vending machine question. And in one fell swoop, this pompous, bulbous cat lover"—Marcus had brought Pacer to the meeting and had set him on the lectern—"comes in and usurps the committee's authority. I move for a vote of no confidence."

If he'd phrased it differently, everyone might have

sympathized with his indignation, but several cat lovers on the faculty were put off by his deprecation of the species. Thus, the general sentiment was to give the new president some latitude. "After all," said Diane Dempsey, associate professor of English, "he's only just arrived."

Brisco didn't give the other faculty members a chance to concur. He was a square man with a bull neck who took up a lot of space, and he used his intimidating presence to his advantage whenever the opportunity arose. Standing in front of the room before his colleagues, he looked wall-like. He ran a hand down his face. "I have a bad feeling. The man doesn't seem to know anything about running a college. He's a used-car salesman, for God's sake. He came storming in here and took over the vending machine question as if he were parking a truck, not caring what he backed into. I don't think he has any respect for faculty at all. And why should he? We rolled over and played dead." He took a deep breath. "And what about that clock? It's leaning against the silo like a piece of junk."

Diane, sitting bolt upright as always, was unmoved. Her aspect was austere and weathered, but this crust belied a keen and attentive mind. "I don't like any talk of death," she intoned, antiseptically. "Especially since student numbers are still coming in. We don't know what the coming year will hold."

Pete Blatty, a small, lean, large-knuckled man who

taught music, was inclined to see both sides of every coin. "Well, I can see Brisco's point. We need to be careful. On the other hand, maybe it's best to wait and see what this new guy has for a game plan."

Brisco rolled his eyes. "Wait and see?" he said, feeling increasingly isolated in front of the room. "No need. I can tell you what he'll do—what new college presidents everywhere do. He'll reorganize, whether we need it or not. It's all about his résumé."

"Oh, let's not put the cart before the horse," Diane said, slicing one hand in front of the other as if she were interpreting for the deaf. "No one knows what he's going to do."

The clutch of adjuncts, who formed their own little unit in a distant corner of the room, swung their gazes from Diane to Brisco, as if they were watching a tennis match.

Brisco focused on Diane. "Whether we need it or not," he repeated. "I'll put money on it."

"Can we move on?" Jim Burns said. The tenured biology professor attended faculty meetings only occasionally, because he was totally absorbed by the book he was writing on the nature of mucus. It was his job to wait until arguments became obtuse, repetitive, and entangled, at which point he'd erupt, "Can we move on?"

Brisco now felt surrounded. He spun on his heels, almost losing his balance. "Oh, I didn't see you, Jim. Do you still work here?"

"Are you trying to belittle me?" Jim asked dryly, his long face seeming to grow even longer under the burden of the insult. "Because if you're trying to—"

"Nobody's trying to belittle you," Diane interjected, bringing a thumb and index finger together. "Nobody's trying."

Brisco shifted gears. "Did you see the way that cat crouched there on the podium? Like it was ready to pounce on anyone who said a discouraging word. It didn't meow; it growled, like a dog."

"I'd just as soon listen to a cat as to a college president," said Dan Stupak of biology, pulling his pipe from his mouth just long enough to eject his riposte. Dan was an almost perfectly ovoid man from whose head the hair had long ago departed. For these reasons, his students had dubbed him The Egg. He was playing the peacemaker in his indirect way. He was also reflecting the fact that he was a cat lover whose house was infested with the beasts. "By the way, what was that envelope business when Cyrus kicked the bucket?"

"Dan!" exclaimed Diane Dempsey. "Show some respect. I mean, 'kicked the bucket.' Please!"

Brisco fell silent. Having found not a single ally among the faculty, and with the new semester about to commence, he was, like everyone else, beginning to feel resigned. But Dan's comment about the envelope renewed his interest. "Yeah, that baffled me too. What the hell was in that envelope? Was it a will or something?" He appealed to Hattie Sims, the source of campus innuendo and occasional insider information. "Any ideas?"

All heads turned to the secretary, who drew strength from the attention. "Not yet," she grudgingly admitted. "But give me a little time."

Frannie Moore, presiding over the faculty and staff assembly, took advantage of the lull. Throughout the meeting, the mathematics prof sat at a table in front of the room, small and unobtrusive, with not a hair out of place, her short, delicate legs dangling like a child's. Because she spoke so seldom, her words usually carried great weight. She cleared her throat, which was enough to garner everyone's attention. She looked from face to face with a beguiling expression of abject warmth, as if she were about to say good-bye forever. "We do have some good news. Some very good news."

"It's about time," said Brisco, throwing himself into a chair and rubbing the back of his neck.

Frannie ignored the comment. As a mathematician, she knew there were unwavering laws, and one of these laws was that her own consistency of tone was key to her influence among the faculty. "We are getting a visitor from the National Endowment for the Arts." She paused to give the room time to take this tidbit in. "He's going to recognize us for the fine work done by Grover Cleveland College Press."

"Splendid," cheered Vikram Chabot. The diminutive, round-shouldered history professor was the director of the money-losing press. He was distinguished by a red eye that had hemorrhaged while proofreading unsolicited manuscripts. "The publicity could raise the profile of the campus, bringing more students in. And God knows we could use them."

"This is nice," said Pete Blatty, looking around the room for approval. And then, fixing on Brisco, "Isn't it?"

"Yes, Pete," Frannie volunteered, nodding with her eyes closed, "it is. Our new president will, of course, be at the reception on Friday. This award will be a nice way to kick off the new semester, and it will, as Vikram indicated, give us some good, and much needed, publicity."

That said, the meeting adjourned.

Brisco stormed out, with Pete on his heels all the way to the Victorian.

"Well, that meeting was a bust," said Pete. "The vending machine issue is still open. Should I ask to put it on the next agenda, Brisco?"

But Brisco retreated into his office and slammed the door. He hadn't noticed Scott Ott, professor of sociology, slinking down the hallway, hauling a toolbox, seemingly in a great hurry.

THREE
A FIRST WALK AND AN HONORED GUEST

Marcus didn't perceive any animosity or opposition from the faculty. In fact, he thought his presentation—excepting the enumeration of dead emeriti—had gone quite well. "Didn't it, Pacer?" he asked as the feline rounded its back under the stroke of his meaty hand. A final meow affirmed for Marcus that he was, indeed, on the right track.

He'd taken over his late uncle's office at the top of the grain silo. This was not his wish, however, because it required that he climb ninety-two steps—an exhausting task for a man of his girth and unfitness. He'd approached Hattie Sims, his personal secretary, about office space closer to the surface of the earth, but she'd slowly shaken her head, gazed at him in utter disbelief, and appeared to generally regard him as a representative of a more primitive, perhaps extinct, culture.

"President Marcus," she'd intoned, striking a pose that bore the slightest hint of defiance and establishing the form of address that would be used henceforth by all, "space has always been a problem on campus. If I were to move you, I'd have to move somebody else, and then somebody else would have to move, and then . . . Well, do you understand what I'm talking about?"

Marcus hovered before her, shifting his weight from one tasseled loafer to the other. "I understand."

But he wasn't sure he did. He was just yielding the response he'd always used when a customer said, "I think I'll pass on this vehicle."

"Anyway," said Hattie, implying she had more important things to do, "Mr. Hutchinson is coming today. He'll be arriving at ten."

Marcus searched his memory for a Mr. Hutchinson. Finding nothing, he peeped, "Who?"

Hattie rolled her eyes. *First the daring request for another office, now ignorance about an important guest from Washington*, she thought. *Is this guy really going to lead Grover Cleveland into the future?* "Hutchinson. From the NEA. I've ordered finger sandwiches for the ceremony. I put the info on your desk." She sniffed about, as if she smelled something awful.

Marcus nodded, smiled inanely, and left it at that.

"Jesus!" yelped Hattie. "What on earth…?"

The sudden pounding on the silo wall had given her a start.

Marcus went to the window and stared sidelong from it. "Ah, Professor Ott—I think that's his name—is already on the job."

"What job?" asked Hattie, nonplussed that something was happening on campus of which she was unaware. She walked to the window, overcoming her discomfort at standing so close to Marcus. "What is he doing? He's scribbling across the wall like a monkey."

The scene was a complicated one. Scott Ott had rigged an elaborate block-and-tackle device, as well as a congeries of ropes, pulleys, and pitons with which he hoisted himself to the top of the silo, where he was swinging side to side and up and down, pounding away with a hammer.

"He'll kill himself," fretted Hattie, although she quickly considered that if Scott Ott fell to his death, she'd be the first to know and to have the privilege of spreading the awful news across campus.

"Oh, he assured me he would be okay. I trust the man. He spoke with such confidence."

Which, as the rest of the faculty saw it, was Scott Ott's problem. In fact, they referred to him as OK Ott because of his willingness to take on any task at any time, whether he knew what he was doing or not. He was an inveterate tinkerer, more suited to puttering than to sociology. But he was unevenly gifted in this regard, and although the faculty huffed and sighed about him behind his back, they also knew he was indispensable. Every one of them had benefitted from his sometimes successes with photocopiers, telephones, and squeaky hinges.

"He was the first to greet me when I arrived on campus," said Marcus. "Do you know my shoes made a type of *weesaw* sound when I walked? I didn't, but Professor Ott noticed and said he could fix them. And by jingo, he did. Isn't that wonderful?"

"Yeah, spectacular." Hattie craned her neck. "It looks like he's going to haul something up there."

"He is." Marcus chuckled. "It's a gift for the campus."

"A gift?"

"Yes. Just keep your eyes open."

Keeping her eyes—and ears—open was Hattie's stock in trade. She retreated from the window and gathered up some papers from Marcus's desk. "I need to do my campus errands." She locked her gaze upon a thick gray envelope on the desktop. It was the one Brisco Quik had asked about and whose significance she was intent on divining. She licked her lips.

"You inspire me," said Marcus, stirring Hattie from her trance. "I think I'll go out myself. Take a constitutional, get the lay of the land."

Having said this, he followed Hattie out the door and began the long descent.

It was a hot late-summer day, with a warm breeze and clear skies in which a host of swallows dipped and swarmed. The maples in the surrounding woods were already tinged with gold. With Pacer at his heels, Marcus walked about campus, around the barn, then on to the Victorian, where most of the faculty offices were located, and thence to the small frame house that harbored the business office and its long-suffering staff. He continued around the cabins, the Quonset huts that housed most of the classrooms, the log structure that constituted the library, and finally the pigsty.

"There," Marcus said, as if he'd just performed a heroic deed. He stood in the great heat of the day, perspiring through his baggy suit while Pacer meowed mournfully and rubbed up against his leg.

It was at that moment that Marcus noticed the Brain Shrine, although he had no idea what it was. He walked over to the simple structure, made from discarded bricks, and entered the recess. There, in a heavy glass jar, swam the twin hemispheres of his ancestor in a greenish fluid. Marcus squinted to read the plaque:

Here reposes the brain of President Grover Cleveland, most capable of the unknown presidents. Twice elected, he championed Hawaiian independence and died a Democrat. Conveyed to this college through the ingenuity of Cyrus Cleveland.

"Well, there," said Marcus as he studied every sulcus and convolution of the organ.

Pacer leapt onto the catafalque and scratched at the depository.

"No, no, that's not respectful." Gently removing the cat, Marcus found he was actually taking strength from the knowledge he could access such a relic. "I feel a link," he said to himself. "And a debt of honor."

Marcus eventually emerged from the shrine to find Hattie running toward him while trying to keep her tower of hair in place. "Where have you been? Mr. Hutchinson is here, in the Victorian. I've brought the finger sandwiches! Everyone is waiting for you."

Marcus had forgotten about the finger sandwiches. He hoped they were the little triangular ones from which the crusts had been removed.

Hattie all but dragged him by the hand to the Victorian, where he found the faculty, a few staff members, and a dozen or so wan-looking students huddled about a tall, distinguished-looking, carefully groomed man in a charcoal-gray suit and red tie. An American-flag pin adorned his lapel. He extended a hand and said in a mellifluous voice, "David Hutchinson. It's a pleasure, Mr. President."

Marcus instinctively thrust out his hand, but he stared dumbly at the visitor for a few moments before realizing he himself was the president in question. "Oh, yes." He glanced about the room at stares that were, by turns, angry, bewildered, and astonished.

Pacer meowed loudly as he circled his master's legs.

Brisco Quik leaned toward Diane Dempsey and whispered, "See? I told you. The cat's in charge."

Mr. Hutchinson hovered expectantly, holding a finger to his nose as if being accosted by an offensive odor.

"Er, well," Marcus began, wondering what exactly this meeting was all about—he hadn't looked at the briefing Hattie had left on his desk but sensed this was no time to start asking questions.

Bella Proins sidled up behind him, fussing with her pearls. She'd been one of "Cyrus's girls," a Grover Cleveland graduate who'd never left the campus. She'd made herself omnipresent, on a volunteer basis, fetching coffee and running paperwork for Cyrus and faculty, until it was presumed she actually worked there and was placed on the payroll, becoming, in time, Cyrus's loyal mud hen, reporting to him every whisper she gleaned from the ranks of faculty and staff. To show his gratitude, Cyrus had leapfrogged her from gopher and mole-in-chief to executive aide and adjutant for administration, to the resentment of the faculty.

Now, with a change of presidents, Bella was on thin

ice, not knowing if Marcus, this new man, would, as Cyrus had, consider her indispensable. If he didn't, what on earth would she do? The only other job she'd held was as an hourly wage earner at DeMonier's Chicken Farm in South Millinocket. She had, by hand, sliced the throats of countless thousands of birds. Wearing oversized rubber gloves, she dunked the carcasses in scalding water to soften the feathers for removal before gutting them and repeating the process with the next bird. The thought of returning to that chapter of her life was repellent in the extreme and was enough to keep her eyes front and forward.

Marcus continued to stammer. Bella pushed her massive bosom into his back and whispered, "Thank him for the honor."

"I thank you for this honor," Marcus erupted as he grasped one of his stiff lapels in an attempt to strike a statesmanlike pose.

That was all it took. Mr. Hutchinson, still struggling with that odor, launched into his prepared speech. "The National Endowment for the Arts has sometimes been criticized for paying too much attention to the big. Big universities. Big names. Big projects. But my being here is testimony that we do not overlook the small. In this light, Grover Cleveland College has not escaped our attention. Why, just the other day I was chatting with my wife, Amana, and do you know what she said?"

The assembled leaned forward in anticipation of some

revelation, while the politically adept Mr. Hutchinson prolonged the moment for dramatic effect, looking from face to face, a finger raised as if he were about to select a soul for human sacrifice.

He finally continued, "She said, 'Lub'—that's her pet name for me—'I read a wonderful book this summer about blackflies. Did you know that they have a culture all their own? Maligned, cursed, and swatted, they actually have a unique system of communication, a unique ecology, a unique history.' Well, when she told me this, I decided to investigate to see who the publisher of this book was. In fact, I read the first chapter myself. And you know what? It was wonderful. It was like having a blackfly of my own, and I began to sympathize with them. And then the NEA discovered—"

At this point Marcus, feeling Bella's proximity, leaned his head back and asked out of the corner of his mouth, "What's he talking about?"

The rest of Mr. Hutchinson's speech could be summarized as "etcetera, et al, and so you see."

In the interim, Bella had neatly brought Marcus up to speed on Grover Cleveland College's reputation as a onetime center of research on the hated blackfly. Marcus immediately sensed what he needed to say. After the applause for Mr. Hutchinson had ebbed and he'd handed Marcus an inscribed plaque, Marcus cleared his throat. "I thank you for this honor. In the name of the college."

Tepid applause.

Bella stepped out from Marcus's shadow and directed everyone to partake of finger sandwiches and coffee. The faculty and staff swooped upon the food like starving refugees while Marcus lingered on his spot, admiring the plaque.

Bella placed a hand on his arm—but gently!—and said, "It was a wonderful speech, Mr. President. Wonderful."

Which immediately led Marcus to wonder whose speech she was referring to—his or the visitor's. Bella smiled at him and hobbled toward the refreshments but not before whispering in his ear, "Your shoe."

Marcus looked down and noticed he had stepped in shit.

FOUR
THE WORLD TURNED UPSIDE DOWN

"**G**oddamn it, I told you so!" roared Brisco Quik, drawing himself up in a major display of puffery, his hair gone wild as he pounded the conference table with a fist the size of a rump roast. He glared about the room, at every face in turn, as if anointing them with his ire. "Didn't I tell you? Didn't I?"

Diane Dempsey looked weary. Not only had the photocopier gobbled up her syllabus, as if disapproving of it, but there had been a disturbing accident on the approach road to the college that very morning. At last, at long last, the new vending machine had been on its way, but the delivery truck had hit a moose. At high speed, the vehicle had struck the large bull in its hindquarters. The animal had whipsawed around the truck in a seemingly impossible manner, impaling the vending machine with its antlers. And now Brisco was on the warpath because, well, it was true: President Marcus was going to reorganize.

Pete Blatty, characteristically, chose precisely the wrong moment to try to smooth things over: just when Brisco was in no mood for making peace. "Well, maybe we should wait and see what happens."

Brisco turned on him like—well, like a moose struck in the hindquarters by a delivery truck. "Wait? Do you know what reorganizing means? It's a synonym for downsizing. And control. And do you know what downsizing means?"

Pete nodded and swallowed audibly. His classes had the smallest enrollments in the school. Nobody was interested in martial music of the Gilded Age anymore. "Well, maybe you're right, Brisco," he said. "I see what you're talking about."

"You're damn right I'm right," barked Brisco with finality. He looked at Pete as if he'd redeemed at least one soul. "And don't make me tell you what this means for our adjuncts." He zipped a finger across his throat.

The adjuncts in the back of the room drew together like baby chicks huddling for warmth.

Hattie Sims sat there like an android, her large pupils darting like the components of some infallible machine, not missing a thing. Her perm—a high mound of broad waves—was welded in place by an exuberance of hairspray, making her head look enormous. A fan of outspokenness, she couldn't help but look on with admiration as Brisco took charge of affairs.

"I'm with Brisco on this one," said Dan Stupak, holding his pipe and examining it. "My bio courses are doing okay. I remember when Cyrus reorganized. I had to take on more work for no more pay, teaching extra lectures while still being responsible for supervising the adjuncts he hired." After a pause, he added, "If it ain't broke, leave it alone," in a tone suggesting he had just coined the expression.

"If it ain't broke, break it," countered Brisco. "That's always been the philosophy of the administrators."

Dan rapped his pipe on the table. "Hear! Hear!" he said, egging Brisco on to see how far he would go.

Frannie Moore cleared her throat. As she was head of the assembly, it was incumbent upon those gathered to pay attention to her. "I'd be interested in the numbers."

"What numbers?" Brisco asked, tapping the table.

Frannie lowered her voice to the point where she was almost inaudible. "The student numbers," she said, barely rippling her lips.

"Oh, I forgot. Your field is math. Well, what do the numbers have to do with reorganization?"

Frannie moved her small hands before her on the table, as if arranging cookies on a tray. "If the numbers are good, we can argue that reorganizing at this time would be tampering with success."

Brisco threw her a condescending smile, as if she were a child included in adult conversation out of kindness. "Frannie," he said, making a heroic effort to be gentle, "when have student considerations ever stopped a president from improving his résumé at everyone else's expense?"

"The numbers are rising."

Silence.

Everyone turned to Hattie, who was sitting there, gazing into the distance like a sphinx. "The numbers are rising," she repeated. "Someone ask me why."

The faculty hated it when the secretary played this game. Hattie always seemed to have proprietary tidbits of information of interest to everybody, but she wouldn't give them up until the faculty all but begged her. And in Hattie's view, it served them right for always talking around her and pretending she didn't know squat just because she didn't have a college degree.

Dan smiled. "Okay, Hattie," he said without taking the pipe from his mouth. "I'll bite. Why?"

Dan hadn't groveled, but Hattie was in a generous mood. "Prurient interest," she said cryptically, pleased with herself for using a word she'd learned that very morning from the crossword in the local paper, *The Crier*.

Brisco hung his head. "What the hell is that supposed to mean?"

Hattie didn't like profane speech. She wouldn't stand for it, except when she herself used it in the heat of gossip. So she waited, bottling the information up inside herself like a sneeze she was determined to suppress, holding it close, until the faculty just couldn't stand it anymore.

"Hattie," Frannie prompted almost in a whisper, "please."

"Well, okay then," said Hattie, still looking hurt, unsure whether they were deserving. "I took it upon myself to get some publicity for the college. I called the city desk at *The Crier* and told them all about the new president and how he was a legacy, a direct-line descendant of the late, great President Grover Cleveland. It was picked up by several New England newspapers. I can't believe you didn't see it."

The faculty members looked at each other, abashed. None of them read *The Crier*, not since, eight years ago, it had published a reader's letter suggesting that, with Vietnam behind them, and a not particularly distinguished faculty or diverse curriculum, there was no longer a reason for the college to exist. Hattie held up the newspaper in a schoolmarmish manner, as if she were about to commence a lecture on the virtues of print journalism in a democracy. "I also sent dispatches to all the press and educational outlets I could find. Do you know there are over a thousand?" she preened as the faculty moved uneasily in their chairs, those know-it-alls who never, not once, recognized her on Secretary's Day. Not even a potted plant or box of chocolates.

"Can we move on?"

Jim Burns stirred, waving his hand in a breezy manner, as if bored by the whole business.

"It's not time for that yet," said Brisco. "Go back to sleep, Jim."

"Now you listen . . ." growled the biologist, wagging a finger.

"Boys!" Diane clipped. "Hattie's talking."

Hattie liked that. The corners of her mouth drew up in a self-satisfied smile.

"OK, then," said Brisco. "The numbers are up. So why is the new president reorganizing?"

Hattie's gaze ran back and forth. She didn't want to admit she didn't know, so she decided to gamble. "There's that envelope in his office. The one he dragged out from under President Cyrus's pillow. I think that has something to do with it."

"Something?" Brisco echoed, raising his hands.

"I've said my piece. We're on an upswing." And then, darkly, "At least for the moment."

"Be that as it may," said Brisco, "there is no rest for the weary. We must remain vigilant and kill this thing, this reorganization, before it sprouts wings. The enemy is at the gate, and we must man the ramparts. I'm open to suggestions."

Mindful that the college had been founded in a time of war, during which Brisco himself had served, he favored military language. This rankled the rest of the faculty, none of whom had served in either war or peace.

Brisco looked around the room. Hector Lopez, the Spanish prof, moved his mouth, but nothing came out. One of Grover Cleveland College's few exotics, this man with the thick mane of auburn hair and high, rounded cheekbones wore an expression of chronic worry that detracted from his Latin good looks.

The others thought long and hard, until Pete Blatty, of all people, came up with an idea. "If the president wants reorganization, it's going to be hard to stop it. But we can slow it to a slog. In other words, he can't have vivace, but we can give him andante."

Frannie nodded with deep feeling but only out of respect, because she had no idea what Pete was talking about.

But Brisco was intrigued. "Spit it out, Pete. Without the music metaphors."

All eyes turned to Pete, which put him on edge. But he was center stage now, so he had to go on. "We want to impede the process? It's easy."

"Yes?" prompted Brisco.

Pete raised his hands. "Form a committee. Tell the president we think his idea is a good one. That we're on his side. So much so that we want to take the lead."

Brisco threw his colleague a sly smile. "Are you suggesting . . . ?"

"Yes. Remember the vending machine?"

"Why, Pete," said Brisco, "I didn't think you had it in you."

"Better yet," Dan Stupak said, "my advice would be to form a committee whose charge would be to select a committee to examine reorganization. Or best of all, turn the whole thing over to the Committee on Committees. That's where all the unmatched socks go."

Brisco glowed. "Can we concur that the question of reorganization should be turned over to the Committee on Committees?"

"Brisco," Frannie admonished, "you have to make it a motion."

"Oh. I move that we turn the president's proposal for reorganization over to the Committee on Committees."

"Second?" Frannie said.

Dan Stupak raised his pipe. "I second it."

"Any discussion?"

There was none.

"All those in favor?"

A sea of faculty hands went up, excluding the adjuncts, who had no voting rights and whose input was limited to timid nods of concurrence.

"Opposed?"

No one.

"So moved."

"Can we move on?" asked Jim Burns, looking weary.

Brisco turned his gaze to the biologist. "Yes, Jim. Now we can move on."

In the meantime, Marcus was ensconced in the silo, reading—no, devouring—the book he'd received as a gift from the secretive Council of New England College Presidents: *The Handbook of College Reorganization— How to Feather Your Own Nest & Prepare for a Snappy Exit*. He congratulated himself on his powers of concentration despite Scott Ott's continued pounding on the outer wall of the silo, punctuated at intervals by a metallic hee-hawing.

"Interesting, interesting," mused Marcus as Pacer dozed in his lap. But the nest feathering and snappy exit ideas weren't what intrigued Marcus. It was the chapter on cost cutting. The idea, according to the author, was to cut costs in a radical fashion but not so radically that students deserted the school. However, the loss of some faculty was always a good thing, because the ones who stayed on were willing to put up with almost anything, grateful as they were for not being axed.

This is where Marcus sensed his initial assessment of the book had been premature. "This part isn't so wonderful," he confided to Pacer as he scratched the appreciative feline behind the ears. "I don't want to fire people. No one at the dealership was ever fired. What would Mr. Bell think of such behavior?" But he liked the cost-cutting idea in principle.

In every system—every system—there is waste. Like a cancer, it must be cut out. Cut it out!

"Think of all the good things we could do with the savings."

There was a knock at the door. Marcus looked up.

There, wheezing, with one hand on her heart and the other against the doorjamb, was Bella Proins. "Whew, those steps are a doozy." She straightened her dress and attempted a smile.

Marcus returned her smile. "Has anyone ever thought about an elevator?"

Bella wanted to roll her eyes, but there was too much at stake for her to be cynical, at least at this juncture while she was still assessing the new president and needed to be well thought of for the sake of her job. And so she played her cards very close to her vest and said, "That is a brilliant idea. Absolutely brilliant. It's clear your uncle selected the right man for the job."

Pacer meowed, as if to second a motion.

Marcus raised his eyebrows in an attempt to prompt a more relevant response from his executive aide and adjutant.

Bella, ever so gently, informed the president that the fiscal situation at the school prohibited any capital projects. "At least for the moment," she was quick to add. "But we could always mount a campaign." After a few moments, she ventured, "Even a telephone in your office would be a nice touch. So we could ascertain your availability before . . . before making the long ascent." She cast a glance over her shoulder. "It would be convenient for the times when Hattie isn't at her desk."

"A phone, a phone," Marcus pondered, rubbing his chin. "Hattie Sims told me my late uncle took pains to avoid having a phone. He felt if all communication were in person, it would ensure that only the serious-minded got through to his office."

Bella forced a smile. "I see." And then her ears perked at the banging on the silo wall, which immediately found a slot on her mental agenda. She had, of course, noticed Scott Ott and the contraption dangling on the outside of the silo, but she'd get to that later. For the moment, it was important to stay on task. There was a new president now, and inroads to excavate.

Marcus shifted gears. "How did the faculty take the news of the reorganization I proposed? Were they happy?"

Bella searched Marcus's face for evidence of irony. But no, he was serious. He actually seemed to think the faculty would whoop to the cause and bear him out on their shoulders. "Well, Mr. President, you know the faculty is a very diverse group and they like heated discussions, so—"

Marcus frowned. "So they didn't like it?" His hand wandered to the thick gray envelope and reposed upon it.

Bella immediately recognized it as the mysterious packet he had withdrawn from beneath Cyrus's death pillow. But she'd pry into that later as well. For now, it was important that she give the new president her undivided attention.

She smiled in silly embarrassment, her blue eyes softening as she crept ever closer to the new leader. "Mr. President—"

"Please call me Marcus."

Bella felt a frisson of triumph, as if she'd surmounted a crucial obstacle on the path of ingratiation. "Marcus," she murmured, savoring the name. "I'm afraid the faculty doesn't use the word *like*."

Another banging, followed by a harsh "Hee-haw."

Marcus tipped his head and raised his eyebrows again. "They don't?"

"Er, no. They feel . . . Well, they feel if they say they like something that comes down from the top, they're giving in to administration."

"Hmm," said Marcus, looking down at Pacer as if seeking a witness to his bewilderment. He raised his head and leveled his gaze at Bella. "Speaking of administration, I read that colleges have something called a provost.

Is this so?"

Once again, Bella was aghast at the man's ignorance, but she soldiered on. "Yes, Mr. Pr—, er, Marcus," she said, blushing, "we have a provost, but he doesn't spend a lot of time out and about."

Marcus stared unblinkingly at Bella. "Is that so?"

Bella nodded cautiously.

"Well, I understand the provost is the chief academic officer. I would like to speak with him. Can you tell him to come up to see me?"

Bella yielded a sick smile. "I'm afraid the provost doesn't do stairs."

Marcus took a moment to ponder this. "He doesn't?"

"Hee-haw!"

Marcus looked toward the window.

"No." Bella now felt herself to be in competition with the racket outside. "In fact, if the truth be told, he rarely does level land."

"Meaning?"

Bella clutched her pearls. Her feet ached from so much standing, but there was no seat in the room other than the one Marcus was sitting in, so she shifted her weight. "Well, you see, the provost is rather reclusive."

"Reclusive."

"Yes. He lives behind the pigsty."

"Lives?" Marcus had discovered that small investments of words yielded wholesale returns of information.

"In the old woodshed. He built it with his own hands when he realized he needed to be alone if he wanted to be a productive member of the campus community. It suited him so well he decided to spend most of his time there."

"The old woodshed."

"Yes."

"Well," said Marcus, with finality, as if he had reached a momentous decision. "Then I think there's no other option than for me to go see him."

Bella beamed. "Oh, Marcus. Brilliant!"

"Hee-haw!"

Bella's glance flew to the window.

Marcus was pleased with himself and his ability to take command of a situation. But he was only reflecting an epigram he'd read in *The Handbook of College Reorganization*: *Even when you don't know what you're doing—act!* "And now to another matter." He petted the gray envelope.

Bella's pulse quickened. She leaned toward Marcus, as if attracted by a strong magnet. *Is he about to admit me to a confidence?* she wondered.

Marcus withdrew his hand from the envelope. "Please see about purchasing a couple of bison."

Bella swallowed a gasp. "Bison?"

"Yes," said Marcus as he placed Pacer on the floor and struggled to his feet. "It's time to reduce costs. That lawn-cutting machine is always going out there, making a terrible racket. Think of the gas, the upkeep, and what-not. Let's get rid of it and let bison roam the campus. Don't you think that's a good idea?"

Bella didn't know what to think, except that livestock would be a sickening reminder of her former life at the chicken farm. "Well, er, Marcus, I suppose it is, yes. I'll start inquiring right away."

Marcus rubbed his hands together. "Good, good." He got up and walked to the small window. Standing there, looking down on the campus, he realized this was something his uncle must have done many times. He considered that his tenure as a college president thus far had been successful. There was the initial move, the meeting with the faculty and staff, the NEA award, and of course those little crustless sandwiches, which had been delicious. And now the bison. He turned to Bella, who was still hovering. "I think that's it for now, Executive Aide Proins."

"Bella. Please."

Marcus smiled. "All right, then. Bella." He watched as she turned to go, hobbling toward the stairway after taking one last, furtive glance at the gray envelope.

"Are you injured?" he inquired.

Bella turned and made puppy-dog eyes at him. "Truth to tell, Marcus, with every step I take, it's like stepping on a knife." And then she whispered, as if the subject were a delicate one, "Plantar fasciitis."

"You poor thing," said Marcus, though he'd never heard of plantar fasciitis.

Bella closed her eyes and nodded. She made for the door to begin her slow descent to ground level.

Marcus watched her back and, for the first time, noticed her figure, which he found rather comely. Very full. Very, very full. But pleasing to the eye. And he wondered, *Is she married? Who is she, really?* He made a mental note to embark upon an exploration.

But for now, he fingered the envelope and sighed. Once Bella was gone, he said aloud and plaintively, "I've taken little steps. But the big question still lingers: What am I going to do?"

At which Pacer let out a mournful moan, perhaps the feline version of *I don't know.*

FIVE
THE PROVOST'S TALE

The provost, Jiminy Schmitz, was following everything from his peephole in the woodshed. He was a small, unshaven man with wild salt-and-pepper hair, who walked, slightly bent, on uneven legs. Jiminy had the uncanny ability to discern a situation from the way other people moved about, and the expressions on their faces. He had observed Brisco tearing across campus, leaning forward with that angry mask that had frozen into a grim rictus. And the diminutive Pete Blatty, clutching his books to his chest like a schoolgirl, stumbling behind Brisco, feeding on his approbation. And Jim Burns, who always looked like he was out for a stroll, with one hand sunk in a pants pocket and his long face angled skyward, seeking respite from his ridiculous work on mucus. And Hattie the snitch, jockeying for advantage and favor as she scurried from one office to the next, no doubt to make the residents beg for the gossip she harbored.

And now he took in a new scene: a large clock being winched up the side of the silo. This was the handiwork of Scott Ott, who was suspended near the top of the structure by some sort of Rube Goldberg contraption of ropes, harnesses, and pulleys. Very puzzling, perhaps even propitious. Jiminy scratched his beard. But it was something new, and he felt his skin tingle with intense interest. He chortled as he rubbed his hands together. The slight, weedy man clopped over to his hot plate and shuffled his pan of sizzling sage potatoes.

There was a knock at the woodshed door. "Jiminy," sang Bella. "Are you in there?"

"Where else would I be?" he snapped.

"Can I come in?"

"How can I keep you out?" rasped the provost as he lifted a potato from the pan, gave it a cooling shake, closed his eyes, and landed it reverently on his tongue, as if taking communion.

Bella pushed the rattly plywood door open and stepped inside. "Can I talk to you?"

"Make it quick. Can't you see how busy I am? Ha!"

Bella smiled weakly. Jiminy was the least busy man

on campus, a true believer in the autopilot theory of running a college. He considered the faculty perfectly capable of developing new courses, expunging old ones, and determining core and general education requirements. Why on earth would he want to leave the woodshed to deal with any of that?

Bella always felt uncomfortable visiting Jiminy. She wondered if it elicited gossip. The thought of trysting with him made her blood run cold. (Well, not exactly. She supposed if she had to, if he had any real power, she would lie back and think of the chicken farm.) But there were times when she had to consult him in person. There was no other way. The provost had no phone or any other means of distance communication. In the early days of the school's existence, he had been a dashing, outgoing man, square jawed, clean shaven, with flowing blond hair. He had lived in town where he'd kept an enviable flower garden and scanned the obituaries in his free time for eligible widows. He had also had a stirring singing voice and, during Maine's recurring January thaws, was often heard crooning, "It Might as Well Be Spring."

So what happened? Jiminy was a potter by training. He'd been up late one night with some of his students, during those heady days of the Vietnam War when all was well in the world of Grover Cleveland College, making the mother of all bongs. After it cooled, he stuffed it with Chingada Magnum from Paraguay and, essentially, blew his mind. He was found in the Brain Shrine in a paroxysm of ecstasy, smoke flowing from his ears. It was then that he abandoned his cozy home in town and built the woodshed, where he took up a troglodyte's existence.

"Jiminy," Bella fretted, "Marcus wants bison."

"Who?"

"Marcus. The president."

The provost scratched his head, his bony hand disappearing in the mire. "The president? Of the United States?"

Bella clasped her hands. This was going to be difficult. "No, Provost, the president of the college. Marcus Cleveland."

"Huh? Cleveland? You must mean Grover Cleveland."

"No, Provost. You see, Cyrus died . . ."

"Died?" Jiminy's eyes became moist. "*Sic transit gloria mundi.*" Then he pulled himself together. "Oh, well."

"Provost," said Bella patiently, "this Cleveland is one of Cyrus's relatives. He's come to run the college."

Jiminy's head cleared. "Oh. Yes. I've seen him walking about. Heavyset fellow. He seemed lost."

"Actually, he's not a bad man."

The provost's eyebrows took flight. "Who said that he was? Did I?"

Bella realized the question was an earnest one. "No, Provost. You haven't even met him yet."

"Oh. Well, I suppose I should."

"He's in the silo. I told him you didn't do stairs."

"Good girl!"

Bella winced. The word *girl* had been banished from campus during an effusion of feminist sentiment. Even newborn females had been referred to as baby women. But at the moment Bella didn't want to open up another can of worms. It was going to be difficult enough to address the question of the bison. "I need some advice."

Jiminy stroked his beard and gazed at Bella with hooded eyes. "Advice is easy to give but difficult to make relevant."

Bella sighed. *Now what on earth is that supposed to mean?* It was at moments like these that Bella felt the weight of her office. A new president, the faculty in disarray, an erratic student population, an absent provost, not to mention the issue of the vending machine. And now bison. How would she ever keep the college together? And if she didn't? The thought of returning to the chicken farm made her heartsick.

The provost had returned to his sage potatoes. "What's the situation with the vending machine?"

"It was on its way, but the delivery truck hit a moose and the moose hit the vending machine."

"Tragic." Jiminy shook his head.

"Yes, but the Vending Committee is taking a look at the situation."

"Good, good. And reorganization? How's that going?"

Bella was pleasantly surprised that the provost was aware of the reorganization. It was a small indication of his contact with reality. "Well, um, the first step has been taken. The president has informed the faculty of his intentions. Hattie told me—"

"Hattie? That old bogus?"

Bella had to tread carefully here. She was closely allied with Hattie, who was her dedicated mole, reporting back to Bella on every word spoken at campus meetings. "Hattie will outlive all of us," sang Bella cheerfully in an attempt to lighten the mood.

"Unless someone murders her," said Jiminy in his own merry tone.

Bella felt an unaccustomed shiver of compassion for the scarecrow of a man shuffling about his monk's cell in his threadbare jeans and T-shirt, seemingly lost in the small space. "Are you feeling all right, Provost?"

Jiminy struggled to focus on Bella. "It's in here." He tapped his temple with a bony finger. "I think the problem lies in my amygdala. It's the seat of passion, you know."

Bella swallowed and took a step back, her apprehension bubbling to the surface. She quickly turned to go but then remembered her purpose. "Provost," she said, facing him again, "what about the bison?"

"What about them?"

"President Marcus wants them."

"He wants bison? Check with Zev Osnoe in Lagrange.

He's got them." And then, after a pause, "And don't say I never did anything for you."

Bella beamed and backed toward the door. "I won't, Jiminy. I won't ever."

She stepped out into the day, closed the door behind her, and inhaled deeply of the fresh, fresh air. Her gaze was captured by the clock being hoisted up the silo. *What on earth?* she mouthed.

Scott Ott waved down to her.

Bella barely managed to return the gesture. She didn't like the idea that there was a pie on campus unadorned by her finger.

SIX
A CLOCK LIKE NO OTHER

y the end of the day, the deed was done. The great, white, wooden clock—lately of Bell's Auto Sales in Jersey City—was firmly installed at the top of the silo, presiding over the college. Its loud Tock! drew all attention to the thing, and by sunset the campus community had gathered to stare at it, as if summoned by a deity in need of propitiation.

"My God, my God," moaned Brisco through gritted teeth, shaking his head, his arms crossed over his chest.

OK Ott was still aloft, rappelling and scaling in turns, making final adjustments. At one point, he landed on the clock's face and looked to be plastered against it.

To Diane Dempsey, the scene was reminiscent of

Ahab's last moments as he rode Moby Dick to perdition.

"It's quite a clock," remarked Pete Blatty innocuously, crouched alongside Brisco.

But when the political science professor lowered his gaze on Pete, the latter pivoted and asked, "Isn't it?"

"You tell me."

Jim Burns sauntered over, whistling, his hands in his pockets. "Something new, eh?"

"There's always something," Brisco said.

"'From the stink of the didie to the stench of the shroud,'" quoted Diane Dempsey. When nobody commented, she appended, "Robert Penn Warren."

But Brisco continued, "What the hell happened to the hour hand?"

It was true. The clock had only the long minute hand, which, despite the tocking, didn't seem to be moving. The hour hand lay bent at the foot of the silo.

Hattie Sims, standing next to Brisco, hunched her shoulders and rubbed her upper arms in the chill air. She fleetingly laid her head against his arm, but he shook her off. *What was that about?* he wondered and peeped at Hattie, who examined him with the softest of eyes.

Everyone watched as Scott Ott rappelled down the silo as smoothly and briskly as a spider emitting silk. He landed squarely on his feet and, with superhero panache, threw off his safety harness. It was an amazing feat for a fifty-eight-year-old man who chain-smoked and sang the praises of tequila. Good genes had left him fit, looking younger than his years with a boyish shock of still-black hair dangling over his forehead. He walked away from the silo to join the crowd in staring up at his handiwork.

Frannie Moore, diminutive beside him, was quickly enveloped in cigarette smoke. "Oh, Scott," she said, waving it away.

Brisco tapped Scott on the shoulder. "Is that thing even running?"

Scott pulled a fresh cigarette from his pocket and lit it off the glowing stub of the one that plugged the corner of his mouth. "Yeah, but dead slow. The prez knows it, and when I told him I could jimmy with it to bring it up to speed, he told me to leave it alone. That's the way he wants it."

"The way he wants it?" Jim Burns exclaimed. "How slow is it running? I mean, the thing is ticking. You can hear it from here to Bangor."

"Please don't exaggerate," said Diane, feeling slighted that no one had congratulated her on the Warren quotation.

"Geez, Diane. A little hyperbole to make a point, okay?"

Brisco grunted. "People! Is everyone missing the forest for the trees? Hasn't anyone thought of asking why the damn broken thing is there in the first place?"

"Not broken," said Frannie so softly that she might have been talking to herself.

Hattie's ears perked up, and Bella's followed suit. The allies moved closer together and seemed to be sharing a common thought: someone on campus knew something they didn't.

"Okay, Frannie," Brisco prompted, "what are you trying to say?"

All eyes were on the president of the Faculty Assembly, staring down at the woman so sparing of speech and countenance. She took a moment to savor the sense of control and then displayed a small notepad and a pencil. "I've been doing some calculations, observing the movement of the minute hand as a function of elapsed time."

"So in other words, you've been watching the clock," Dan Stupak said around the stem of his pipe.

Frannie firmed her lips. "Yes."

"Well?" Brisco said.

"That minute hand is moving. But slowly. I noted where it was three hours ago and compared it to where it is now. I've extrapolated its rate of movement and come up with a figure."

Brisco threw his hands out imploringly.

"At this rate, the minute hand will make one circle of the clock in exactly one hundred days."

A murmur circulated among the assembled.

"That's"—Brisco fluttered his fingers before his eyes—"the end of the coming semester. You're telling us this good-for-nothing clock is not even going to tell us the time? It's just going to tell us when the semester is up?"

"To the day," confirmed Frannie.

Scott Ott took a drag on his cigarette and blew three perfect smoke rings. "That sounds about right."

Brisco turned to him. "When did the hour hand fall off?"

"Collateral damage," said Scott. "While I was hauling the clock up the silo. But when I offered to replace it, the prez said not to worry about it, that it would be a more potent reminder the way it was."

"A reminder?" Brisco said. "Of what?"

OK Ott shrugged and returned to the base of the silo to clean up his things.

Bella was taking all this in, not missing a syllable. There were now two campus mysteries confounding her—this strange, slow-moving clock and Marcus's thick gray envelope, toward which he seemed to display some degree of affection. Could the two be linked in some way? Invoking the diligence she'd shown at the chicken farm, she girded herself to tackle the challenge of solving these puzzles. She glanced up, and her gaze met Hattie's. Could she be making the same connection? Bella had to consider this possibility and the need to stay one step ahead of the secretary. There must be no confusion about who was working for whom.

"One semester. I don't like it," Brisco said, which

didn't surprise anybody, because there wasn't much Brisco did like. "Is it a coincidence that we have a new president, he installs a clock, and it's going to take precisely one semester for that hand to make its circuit?"

"Maybe it means something terrible is going to happen at the end of the semester." Pete Blatty wrung his hands. "I can feel it. It's like a . . . a doomsday clock." And then, noticing everyone staring at him, he appended, "I mean, don't you think so?"

No one was willing to comment on something that smacked of lunacy. Pete found himself in the uncustomary position of having had the last word, his comment having been greeted with silence.

The sun slid off below the tree line as evening drew on and the temperature sank. The crowd broke up and diffused across the campus.

Brisco sank his hands into the pockets of his chinos, and he turned toward the Victorian. But before he'd gone five steps, he was seized with the impulse to stop and look back.

And there she was. Hattie. Staring dead at him. Her expression blank.

SEVEN
A CHANCE MEETING, BISON, AND SOMETHING ABOUT MUCUS

Two bison grazed placidly on the green in the center of campus while a stark figure in an oversized Carhartt work coat pedaled his beat-up Schwinn toward the Victorian. Henny Spox sat in the saddle, gripping the handlebars with firm assurance as his white, fighter-pilot-style helmet with green visor reflected the late-summer sun. He slowly rode past Brisco Quik and Pete Blatty, neither of whom acknowledged the professor of mathematics.

If there was such a thing as having a reputation beyond Grover Cleveland College, then that was what Henny Spox had. Since 1956, he'd been working to solve a mathematical stumper—the Wahazy Continuity—which had first raised its head and demanded notice in fifteenth-century Budapest. The thing was, Henny seemed to be making progress. Every time he progressed one step farther down the line of his equation, a paper resulted, and he'd put in a request for travel money to present his findings at the annual conference of the International Society of Mathematical Quandaries. But such requests were always denied.

"It's not easy to say no," the late Cyrus Cleveland had frequently declared as he pushed papers around on his desk, pretending Henny wasn't standing before him. But it was actually very easy to say no. Cyrus had never been a fan of math and didn't see its value in promoting the interests of students on the lam from the draft. He would just as well have stricken it from the curriculum since, as he put it, it was a nuisance subject that kept more students from graduating than it advanced. The other faculty members were equivocal about it, but Henny Spox was not. At meetings where the abolition of math was discussed, he'd rise, straighten up, and make a speech consisting of the most exuberant alloy of run-on sentences and jargon but with such power that, by the time he finished, no one dared push the motion forward for fear Henny had said something that might involve their salaries. And so the matter was invariably dropped.

However, the faculty felt compelled to do something about their mad professor, this pretender, this tall poppy, this crab consistently trying to climb out of the bucket. And so they did what came naturally: they ignored him.

In fact, one day Jim Burns, who was chairman of science and math—he resisted being called chair ("I am not a stick of furniture!" he had declaimed during one faculty meeting)—put out the word that any mail addressed to Henny should be discarded. This was because he himself was intent on being the first crab out of the bucket with the book he was writing on mucus. However, his attempt to block Henny's mail frightened Bella, of all people, who was no stranger to intrigue. She'd gazed at Jim and said, "I can't do that. It is plainly against the law." And so Henny's mail continued to flow unimpeded.

As Henny sailed majestically on toward the Victorian, he rubbernecked when he noticed two large, grazing bison. What he didn't notice was another large figure, lost in thought, straying into the orbit of his bike. It was inevitable that these two planets would collide.

Just before Marcus was knocked into the hedgerow of *Rosa rugosa* fronting the Victorian, Pacer sprang from the path. And there Marcus lay, clutched by the shrub's countless thorny canes.

For his part, Henny Spox also lay perfectly supine, gazing skyward, his helmet intact.

The minutes dragged on, and then serendipitously both men sat up at the same moment and looked at each other.

"I-I'm sorry," managed Henny. "I thought I saw buffaloes."

Marcus began to pull the canes from his clothing. "You did, my friend. Timmy and Boss."

Henny focused on the big man. "I'm sorry I hit you."

"It's nothing," said Marcus, unruffled by it all. "There are worse ways to meet, I suppose." And then, after a pause, "Aren't there?"

"I suppose so," said Henny, and the two men smiled at each other.

They chatted amiably for the next five minutes, during which Henny learned the identity of this pleasant fellow.

"You know," said Marcus, "I've seen you tooling about campus on your bike. Very, very healthy, I must say. It's made me consider that we might pursue a personal fitness initiative. Call it Health Helps or something like that. Do you think the faculty would go for it? Staff and students would be included, of course."

Henny was greatly pleased by this new president, if only because he was being acknowledged by him. Few on campus, save the students, had spoken to Henny in years, and the emotion of the moment put him at a loss for words. All he managed was, "I think it's inspired."

Marcus smiled, as if Henny were representing the collective affirmation and wisdom of the faculty. He sensed the beginning of a friendship. "Well," he said as he struggled up from the *Rosa rugosa*, "I'm on my way to see what the faculty are up to. I'm sure they'd appreciate a visit."

And with that, the two said their good-byes and Henny watched Marcus ascend the front steps of the Victorian and disappear inside.

Marcus still didn't know his way around the building. He wandered like a child on his first day in a new school, dipping his head about with his hands knotted behind his back. He had a friendly greeting for everyone who passed.

When Hattie Sims emerged from an office, moving at mach speed, she almost ran into him. "President Marcus," she exclaimed as she clutched a pile of folders to her breast, "what are you doing here?"

"I just had a very interesting run-in with . . . Well, I didn't catch his name." Marcus rubbed his chin. "Well," he said, looking up at Hattie again, "he was a very interesting man. On a bike."

Hattie pursed her lips. "Henny Spox."

"Spox. What an intriguing name."

"Yeah. Very intriguing. Anyway, do you need help? You look lost."

"Just wondering what people are up to."

Hattie jerked her head toward the door across the hall. "That's Professor Burns's office. He's in the middle of research for a book he's writing."

"A book!" Marcus said with glee. "A book is being written on campus?"

"Why not? That man is always writing books. Someday, you just watch, he's going to get one published."

Marcus half expected some detail to follow the word *published*, but there was nothing.

In fact, Hattie didn't know what Jim was writing about. She was simply passing on received wisdom, and the word *research* had a nice ring to it, making her feel she was part of a bigger picture.

"Well, you've piqued my curiosity," said Marcus, well pleased. "I'll have to go in."

"Yes," said Hattie, already moving on to her next labor. "You'll have to."

Marcus tapped on Jim Burns's door. Nothing. He knocked a little harder.

"Who is it?"

"It's me."

"Oh," sneered Jim, addressing the door. "Then I'll have to let Me in."

Marcus took this as an invitation. Opening the door and stepping inside, he beheld the picture of austerity, an office bereft of adornment. There was an old oak desk, a chair, and a bookcase with maybe five volumes, the other shelves vacant even of dust. From the ceiling, however, hung a small, desiccated starfish on a string.

Jim was seated at his desk, scratching on a yellow legal pad. "Well, hello, President Marcus," he clipped, making an effort to throw the man a cursory glance as he scribbled away.

"I hope I haven't caught you at a bad time." Marcus lingered near the desk. There was only one other place for a visitor to sit, a sort of camping stool, but Jim didn't trouble himself to offer it. "I ran into Hattie Sims in the hallway," Marcus said. "She told me you were writing a book." This last sentence bore a distinct crescendo, as if he were taken by the idea that human beings were capable of such endeavors.

"Yes. Must publish or perish, you know." Jim said this without a hint of irony, because he was the only one presently at Grover Cleveland College who'd ever published anything—a pamphlet on local freshwater invertebrates—and the others who hadn't obviously hadn't perished. The now-celebrated blackfly book had been the baby of a former professor who, despite this triumph, had indeed perished—from extreme old age. No, *Publish or perish* did not rise to letterhead status at Grover Cleveland, where a more fitting slogan might have been *Breathe or perish*.

"Can you tell me what it's about?" Marcus asked with childlike curiosity.

Jim shrugged, as if it were all the same to him. "It's

called *Mucus and Its Precursors*."

Marcus stood there with his hands behind his back, still smiling amiably, although he now wondered if Jim was pulling his leg. "M-mucus?" he finally managed, moving the word about in his mouth as if tasting it.

"Yes," said Jim, examining Marcus's face for the least sign of skepticism or mockery. "No one's ever written a book on mucus, and I want to be the first." In a moment of self-indulgence, he pulled an envelope from his desk drawer. "I already have a letter of interest from a publisher," he said before slipping it back into its place.

"Why, that's wonderful!" cheered Marcus with genuine enthusiasm. "Absolutely wonderful. Another first for Grover Cleveland!"

Jim continued to examine the president. What was he talking about? Had there been other firsts at the school? Did Marcus know that the contract was with Grover Cleveland College Press, which, like the school itself, was hanging on by its fingernails? Would he think this somehow devalued his work? Would he be accused of inbreeding?

"I also have a cover blurb," Jim volunteered. He pushed a sheet of paper at the president.

Marcus fetched his glasses from his breast pocket and read it: *This is destined to be the definitive work on the subject of mucus.* Jim didn't bother to mention that his colleague, Dan Stupak, had written the blurb, under duress, since Dan didn't have even a fleeting interest in, or appreciation for, cellular secretions.

No matter. Marcus smiled broadly when he read the blurb. "Wonderful, wonderful," he repeated. "Maybe your book will win a prize."

Jim firmed his lips and squinted. Again, was he being mocked? But no, Marcus's praise seemed earnest.

"Are you ready for the students?" asked Marcus, segueing smoothly from mucus to pedagogy.

Jim shrugged. "I've been teaching for twenty-five years. If I'm not ready by now, I'll never be." He glanced at a small pile of yellowed, tattered notes at the far end of his desk. He'd put them together at the outset of his teaching career and never deemed it necessary to revise or update them.

"Yes, yes, I suppose you're right." Marcus rubbed his chin. "Now, Professor Burns, are there any issues on campus you think I need to address?"

Jim turned his eyes heavenward for a moment and then leveled them at Marcus. "Do you mean aside from the vending machine?"

"Oh, I heard about the moose accident. Very unfortunate. So close and yet so far. Do you think we'll get a machine before the start of the semester?"

Why is he asking me? Jim thought. "I don't know," he said, waving a hand in the air. "Have you asked the Vending Committee?"

"No. Not lately."

"They've been at it for eight years."

"I shall ask them, then," concluded Marcus with authority. "In the meantime, good luck with your very interesting research."

Again, Jim searched Marcus's face for any inkling of condescension. Finding none, he still felt the need to make a statement in his own defense. "Some of the humblest creatures and substances in the world have changed the course of history. The Black Death was caused by a bacterium. All organic chemistry is based on the carbon atom. And without mucus, there would be no humanity."

Marcus felt tears well. He couldn't keep his hands from coming together in a round of applause. "By gum, you're the man for me. At those moments when my spirits flag, I'll think of you, Professor. You're an inspiration to us all."

Jim Burns couldn't help but be moved by the president's generous words, although he wondered, *Is he talking about me?* And then he recalled an event from the previous day. "President Marcus, that clock—"

"Ah, you noticed."

Jim Burns sniffed. "It could hardly be missed. And that tocking."

"It is loud, isn't it?" said Marcus. "But I think it's important that we're constantly aware of it."

"How could we not be? If we're not seeing it, we're

hearing it."

"I will explain everything when I address the faculty."

"Address us?" said Jim.

"Yes, very soon. I don't want to lose touch with you good people."

It occurred to the biologist that Marcus was already out of touch, but he only nodded dumbly.

Marcus left the professor to his labor. As he stepped back out into the day, he considered that only some minutes earlier he'd been struck by a bike and was lying in thorns. But now he was celebrating, in his heart, the forward momentum of a clearly gifted faculty member who'd help put the school on the map and perhaps avoid an unhappy fate. He clapped his hands and shouted, "Good!" At the same moment the bison bellowed, as if concurring with the heartfelt sentiment of their benefactor.

EIGHT
BELLA LEARNS THE TRUTH

Bella Proins bustled about campus, wringing her hands and generally bearing the weight of the world on her shoulders. The students were coming, and nobody seemed prepared. The president was out and about, Hattie was nowhere to be found, there was no money to pay the faculty, there was still no vending machine, and those two bison were grazing, scraping, and moaning as if they owned the place. And then there was that clock, that envelope, and the prospect that the two were related. But Brisco Quik had butchered the moose that had destroyed the vending machine, so at least there was meat to spare in the freezer of the dining commons.

The thing was, Bella had gone to great lengths to find those bison and had succeeded in bringing them to campus despite their protestations—she had thought only donkeys could kick and buck like that—but nobody, not one person, had deigned to thank her. Did they think she'd materialized those animals out of thin air while lying on a chaise longue dipping her hand into a box of chocolates? On the contrary. She had worked with that awful, lurching Zev Osnoe and his dirty fingernails to negotiate a reasonable price and then arranged to have the animals delivered.

Bella wondered, as she frequently did, if it was all worth it. And then, as always when she took time to collect herself in such moments of stress and self-pity, she recalled the chicken farm and immediately gave thanks to the powers that be that she was where she was. Yet she was still haunted by the suspicion that, under the new president, she was no longer the linchpin of Grover Cleveland College. Until she'd achieved that assurance, her position was tenuous, and just as fast as one could say *poultry*, she could be back in a bloody apron, rubber gloves, and paper bonnet, processing chicken carcasses, some still twitching.

It was unfair; the very idea that she could be released at the whim of the president. Faculty could be tenured. The only way to get rid of such professors, if they didn't leave of their own volition, was to murder them. But she could never aspire to those ranks, not with her Bachelor of Human Experience degree from Grover Cleveland College. Well, there was more than one way to entrench oneself.

Bella stopped in the middle of her labors to gaze up at the grain silo. She wanted to visit Marcus, but she needed to gird herself for the long ascent. She wondered what the president thought of her. Had she noticed something in his eye, a glint of something more than simple compassion perhaps, when she told him about her plantar fasciitis?

Bella slipped into the pigsty and sought out the ladies' room. She was alone. She stood before a mirror and, hands on hips, dipped from side to side, examining herself. *Ach, when did I become so round?* she thought. *I look like a Russian nesting doll.* But she considered that the comparison was accurate. *There's a girl in there. Svelte. Spry. Impish.* There was no reason she couldn't have all sorts of girlish feelings. But the question still interposed itself: Did Marcus feel anything for her? Could he feel anything?

The door flew open, and Hattie Sims all but fell into the restroom. "Bella! You scared me."

"I scared *you*?" rejoined Bella, crossing her arms over her bosom as if she'd been caught in a state of undress. "You almost made me jump out of my skin." Bella had indeed been frightened, but she acknowledged the need to temper her every comment with a soft edge. Hattie was, after all, her undercover cop, her third ear, her conduit for information regarding campus business conducted in her absence.

"Listen," said Hattie, lowering her voice, "the students are on their way, and nobody seems to be running the show. Least of all the president."

Bella's impulse was to leap to agreement, but she stifled herself, ever mindful that information must flow only one way: from Hattie to her. It was important that she remain a free agent, play her cards very carefully. In no way could she afford to even suggest President Marcus was not on top of things. But neither did she want to appear oblivious to reality. So she chose a middle path. "We've been here before. It seems every September starts like this. We'll pull through. We always do."

Hattie threw her a wry smile, perceiving with the pinpoint accuracy of the born busybody the truth of the matter. "He's nice in his way, isn't he?" she ventured.

Bella blushed. Hattie was digging her nails in, but the feelings her probing elicited were not unpleasant. "Well . . . I believe in giving people the benefit of the doubt."

Hattie leveled her gaze at the executive aide. "Doubt?"

Bella had stepped in it, but she quickly extricated herself. "No doubt." She forced a smile. "How about you?"

Hattie chuckled. "Me? I'm full of doubt. Loads of it. Enough to spare. You want some?"

Bella drew back. Talking with Hattie was like tossing a ticking bomb back and forth. Now the thing was in her hands, but rather than continue the play, she threw it into a ditch. "I am a woman of great faith. Every day is an up day for me. The sun will always rise in the morning."

Hattie cackled so mercilessly that she might have been heard outside the pigsty. "Bullshit. That's just plain bullshit, and you know it."

"If you're going to use profanity—"

"Oh, Bella, please!"

The executive aide firmed her lips. "I'm going up to the silo. Is he in?"

"Yes, he's in. What's going on?"

"Going on? Just administrative matters."

Hattie nodded. "You mean the gray envelope."

"What gray envelope?" Bella snapped too quickly.

Hattie's smile was arch. She left Bella without another word and sauntered into a stall.

Bella glowered. She felt as if she'd been plucked. On the way out, she troubled herself to turn off the bathroom lights.

Hattie wailed. Before the door closed, she screamed out, "There's no toilet paper in here!"

Bella had no time for reconsideration. Her plantar fasciitis had gotten so bad that she was limping cruelly, pumping her arms to propel herself along. As she drew past the campus green, Timmy clopped toward her, snorting steam. Bella pumped her arms with even more fury to put some distance between herself and the beast.

She ran into Brisco Quik, who was standing at the edge of the green, staring at the bison. "Hello, Professor Quik. Busy?"

Brisco gazed past Bella at Timmy. "Why the hell did he do this?" he asked miserably. " We need students, not livestock."

Bella, ever vigilant, was skilled at deflecting harsh commentary. "I understand that the students are on their way. They'll start to arrive tomorrow."

Brisco ignored the comment. He was still looking at the bison. Timmy and Boss had reunited and were bumping against each other, their flanks making dull thuds every time they met. "It must be love."

Bella's eyes widened. "What did you say?" Had Hattie divulged something? Oh, God.

Before she could make some feeble reply, Brisco went on. "Does he know these bison are a mating pair?"

Bella stood down. She turned her head toward the animals and smelled the sodden mustiness of their coats, which were swarming with flies. "Do you think so?"

Brisco threw her a doubtful look. "Bella, didn't you notice one of them is a male?"

Bella blushed deeply. It had never occurred to her to conduct a physical examination of the animals. But should she have? What difference did it make that there was one of each? Just then a cry went up from Timmy, a deep, reverberating moan of raw, mammalian vigor as the animal scraped and kicked the ground with its forehooves. Bella watched Boss trot away from the anxious bull.

"Bella."

She turned to Brisco again. "Y-yes?"

"I wanted to mention something to you. Something that's the concern of your desk." A beguiling smile. "I mean, aside from livestock."

Bella darkened but quickly regained her composure and threw Brisco a receptive look.

"Do you know Frannie Moore is parking in the handicapped space in front of the Victorian?"

Of course Bella knew. She had authorized it. But confidentiality concerns prevented her from elaborating to parties without a need to know. "Yes. I gave her the placard."

"Well? She looks perfectly healthy to me. And to everyone else, I might add."

"Professor Quik, you know I can't tell you the nature of her disability."

"Aha. So it is a disability."

Bella pursed her lips.

"Well, whatever it is, I've watched her. She springs out of that Volkswagen like she's fleeing a burning building. I don't see why she has to park at the doorstep."

"I can't tell you," said Bella coyly. Like Hattie, she thrilled to the sensation of knowledge withheld.

"Then I consider it my duty to find out. And by the

way, do you know anything about this clock business?"

Here Bella could be more forthcoming. "Not a thing. I was taken by surprise like everybody else. I'm going up to see President Marcus now. I'll make a point of asking him about it. Rest assured I'll share everything I learn with the faculty."

Bella forced a smile, hoping her candor had won her some points with the influential professor. But Brisco left it at that and walked on.

Bella pumped her arms again and headed for the silo, and not a moment too soon, because Timmy was once again approaching, snorting with blunt, unbridled ardor.

In the meantime, Marcus sat at his desk in the grain silo, his chair turned toward the window. He was still feeling stimulated by what he'd learned from his visit with Jim Burns. *What had the biologist said? Something about the humblest creatures and substances in the world having changed the course of history? What an incredible thought! Truly inspiring. That's what we need more of on this campus: more incredible thinking. More inspired thinking. Could there be a better formula for salvation?* He rubbed his hands together.

His joy would have continued unabated if not for a knock.

"Come in!"

The door creaked open, and there stooped Bella,

hanging on to the knob. "Oh, Marcus," she sighed, as if exhaling her last mortal breath.

Marcus brought his great bulk to his feet as quickly as possible, knocking his chair over. "My goodness!" He hurried to Bella. "What's wrong? Here. Let me help you."

But where would he help her to? He held Bella's arm, waltzing her around his office in a futile search for a place for his executive aide and adjutant to rest. "Hattie!" he finally called out.

Hattie didn't have far to travel because she'd just completed her own ascent and was still on her feet. She entered to find Marcus and Bella hanging on to each other.

"Quick," said Marcus. "A sofa! A couch!"

Hattie thrust her hands onto her hips. "Well, where am I supposed to get a sofa? And even if I could, who's gonna drag it up all those steps?" As she said these words, she luxuriated in them. Could there be better payback for being forced to sit in a dark stall without toilet paper?

Bella threw Hattie a pathetic look, like a dolphin slowly dying on a beach.

Hattie rolled her eyes. "Well, all right, then. Put her on the floor."

Marcus brightened. "Of course." He lowered his burden. "Don't worry," he said as he got to his knees. "I'll stay with you until you feel better. Do we need a doctor?"

Bella cupped Marcus's hand in both of hers, then

squeezed. "No doctor," she said in a low voice filled with emotion. "You will do."

Marcus looked down at her and was seized with a feeling of inexpressible tenderness. He smiled and breathed, "Bella."

Recuperation was swift. Bella was soon respiring normally, and both she and Marcus were sitting on the floor with their backs against the front of his desk.

"Marcus," she began, "do you mind if I ask you about that clock?"

"You preempt me," he said, smiling. "I was just about to tell you about it."

Bella searched his face, but all she could read there was an abiding kindness, a sweetness that, she was convinced, arose from his core. "Is it good news?"

Marcus hummed. "I suppose it's a matter of how you look at it. Have you noticed how slowly the clock's hand moves?"

"Yes. Professor Ott said you wanted to leave it that way."

"Correct. Do you know how slowly it's moving?"

Bella knew the answer to this as well. "Professor Moore said the hand will take exactly one semester to circle the clock face."

"Correct again," said Marcus, as if he were grading an oral exam.

"But why?" probed Bella, continuing to run her gaze

over Marcus's face.

"Brace yourself. I'm afraid the news is dire."

"Marcus!" Bella gripped his arm.

"Are you aware of a gray envelope on my desk?"

"A gray envelope?" echoed Bella, not wanting to yield any inkling that her eyes had recorded every detail of his office.

Marcus glanced up at his desk. "My uncle Cyrus conveyed it to me."

"You mean . . ."

Marcus nodded. "Yes, on his deathbed, from under his pillow. I opened it that evening and, well, let me tell you, it was a great blow, especially as I was just starting out in this job. Can I tell you, in all confidence, that upon reading it I considered taking Pacer and boarding the next bus back to New Jersey?"

"Marcus! What was in it?"

Marcus swallowed hard. "I fear we're living on borrowed time. Uncle Cyrus left the school in terrible debt. The bank has given Grover Cleveland College exactly until the end of the current semester to get our financial house in order and catch up with the mortgage payments we owe them."

"And if we don't?" Bella asked as a small army of chickens danced before her eyes.

"Then," said Marcus, still holding her, "we all go back to where we came from, and I presume nature will reclaim this campus, or some large, rectangular store will be erected here."

Bella let out a gasp. "Where we came from?"

"Keep this to yourself for now. I intend to inform the faculty, since we're all in this together."

"But . . . the clock. Did you mean it to—?"

"No. It's pure coincidence that it will take a semester to go around once. It makes me think there is a higher power guiding affairs at our dear school. Let's hope it's on our side. But I thought the clock would be a reminder to all of us to pull together in looking for solutions to our difficult situation."

Bella was speechless. She placed a hand over her heart as Marcus helped her to her feet. She couldn't even find the words to say good-bye but simply limped out the door, closing it behind her.

Hattie was sitting at her desk and threw Bella an expectant look.

"You heard?" asked Bella.

Hattie nodded.

"Then the cat is out of the bag."

Hattie nodded again. "You mean the lid has been taken off hell. Wait 'til Brisco Quik gets wind of it."

Brisco, still fixated on Fannie's handicapped space, was in Pete Blatty's small office in the Victorian, venting. He never expected much in the way of commiseration from Pete, but the musician was a good sounding board and sometimes stumbled upon a useful suggestion.

"Yes. Frannie," he said as Pete sat with a sousaphone wrapped around his body. "She's disabled now. That's what Bella says. Do you think she's disabled?"

Pete tilted his head. "Well, maybe she's disabled in a way that we can't see."

Brisco huffed. "Of course she's disabled in a way that we can't see. If we could see it, it wouldn't be an issue."

Pete was quick to nod. "Right, Brisco. I see your point."

Brisco threw Pete a patronizing smile. "I know you do, Pete. I can always count on you."

Pete extricated himself from the sousaphone. And then something occurred to him. "Brisco, talk to Jiminy. He'll know what to do."

Brisco's whole aspect changed, becoming brighter. He laid a hand on Pete's shoulder. "You know, Pete, that's not a bad idea. Jiminy won't stand on ceremony. He's the one who told me about Cyrus's final illness, organ by organ."

Brisco lit out from the Victorian and hurried toward the woodshed. Along the way he ran into Hattie.

"Brisco," she said as she drew unusually close to him, "you're not going to believe this—"

"Not now, Hattie. One war at a time."

Just as her heart was quickening, she watched his

retreating back. "Who said anything about war?" she shouted after him. "What I have to say is important!"

A wisp of smoke curled from the chimney of the woodshed. Brisco knocked and was greeted with a harsh, croaking bid for him to enter. Jiminy stood barefoot beside his white enamel cook stove, stirring something in a large aluminum pot.

"Lobster?" quipped Brisco as he closed the door behind him.

"No, not lobster. Keep guessing."

Brisco had not meant his little joke to be preamble to a game. "I give up."

Jiminy slowly shook his head. "That's the problem. You give up too easily. Everyone here gives up too easily."

"Jiminy," said Brisco in a pooh-poohing way.

"Poetry," said the provost out of the blue.

"Jiminy?"

"Come here."

Brisco drew up to the cook stove and beheld a pot of boiling papers. "What the hell is that?"

"I told you. Poetry. I've been writing it for forty years, and you know how many I've had published?"

"You mean, aside from the ones that appeared in *The Grover Rover*?"

"The campus paper doesn't count. The answer is zero. Nada. Zilch. I used to think I could feed myself by writing poetry. And you know something? I was right!" The provost daintily grabbed hold of a sodden page, pulled it from the pot, shook it out, and pushed it into his mouth. "Ah," sighed Jiminy after swallowing. "Puree of villanelle."

Brisco wanted to avert his gaze but continued to focus on the provost. "Look, Jiminy, I have a question about Frannie Moore."

"A woman of few words. But not a bad math professor. You know, people make the mistake of referring to math as a science; but it's not. It's a language. Maybe that's why Frannie doesn't say very much. Because most of us don't speak or understand her language. Remember how Cyrus wanted to dump math from the curriculum? He hated math. But Henny Spox—"

"Jiminy," Brisco interrupted, making fists by his sides to keep from strangling the provost, "I'm curious why Frannie Moore has a handicapped spot."

"That's an easy one," said the oracle. "She's handicapped."

"Is she really?" asked Brisco, ignoring Jiminy's attempt at repartee.

"According to the letter of the law," said Jiminy absently as he continued to stir his verse.

"Jiminy?"

The provost turned and looked at Brisco. "The law states that a disability is any condition that prevents one from carrying out a major life function."

"I don't understand. Do you mean she can't skydive or pole vault anymore?"

Jiminy made a clicking sound. "That's funny. The answer is that she's unable to conceive."

Brisco smiled, thinking Jiminy must be kidding. "Are you—?"

"Serious? Yes. She got the report last week. She's infertile."

"And she gets a handicapped space for that?"

"Reproduction is a major life function, wouldn't you say?"

"The world has gone insane. Well, I'm not going to stand for this."

"Nor should you," said Jiminy as he devoured another page of his life's work.

"Thanks for the info," said Brisco and stormed out, having plopped another dollop of concern onto his already full plate.

When Brisco emerged from the woodshed, he saw it—a streamlet, a wavelet of figures flowing onto campus in crummy cars, on bikes, and on foot. Some were rangy, others mangy. The new ones had stars in their eyes; the returnees looked resigned. *So soon*, said Brisco to himself.

Spoiled by three months of summer repose, he once again had to face the reality of teaching. As he stood observing the returning students, someone sidled up to him and said, "Professor Quik?"

Brisco turned and recognized a student from the previous semester, a towheaded teen with the palest blue eyes. He'd already forgotten his name.

"Professor Quik," repeated the lad, beaming with the enthusiasm of the high-achieving young scholar, "it's good to see you again. Over the summer I was thinking about poli-sci every day. Do you have time to discuss the inevitability of a three-party system in the United States?"

The boy's question paralyzed Brisco. He tried to move his lips, but nothing came out. It was true, then. School was actually starting. Brisco felt his heart sink. And then, after a moment's consideration, he smiled. This wasn't just a student standing before him. It was his paycheck. "Y-yes," he blurted. "I have time."

NINE
SMALL THINGS

The annual rite of student return was always something to behold, like a run of smelts to a familiar stream. The students seemed to ooze out of the surrounding woodlands, as if from the earth itself. Onto campus they drifted—life being pumped into the carcass that the college became during the summer, when faculty turned their concerns to other matters and pedagogy at Grover Cleveland went into stasis.

The faculty couldn't help but get caught up in the activity. Brisco Quik planned to teach a new course, The Declining Talent Pool in College Administration, which the catalog described as "exciting." Diane Dempsey would teach her regular fall course, Emily Dickinson: No Need for a Boyfriend. Pete Blatty finally had to give up Martial Music of the Gilded Age due to student disinterest—only one soul had registered for the course. To compensate for this loss, he was given an extra section of The History of Rock and Roll, a perennial favorite at Grover Cleveland. Jim Burns dutifully began to prep his bio labs, but he resented having to turn his attention from his mucus book. Dan Stupak had gained fifteen pounds over the summer due to general inactivity, which enhanced his ovoid proportions. He was unimpeded by this development and soldiered on as he prepped his own bio labs and got ready to teach his stock course on the neurology of Grover Cleveland's brain.

No one knew if Frannie Moore enjoyed her new parking privileges, because hers was the perfect poker face and, being from the Midwest, she didn't talk about herself. If she knew Brisco was on the warpath about her handicapped space, she hadn't confided this to anyone. This small woman simply went about her business arranging things in the math lab and silently dreading the remedial work on exponents, which drove so many students to despair.

Hector Lopez had no trouble filling his Spanish I class, but his problem was intractable: his Uruguayan accent made it difficult for the students to understand what he was saying, and any attempt to teach his course at least partially in Spanish met with insurrection in their ranks. And so he muddled along, struggling in front of the class to pronounce *error*, which came out as *errrr*, while his charges corrected his English, as if he were the student. The result was that little got done and certainly little Spanish was learned, except for the oft-repeated *chicas calientes*, uttered by his young *varones*. An added complication was that Hector was cursed with sexual paranoia and believed the females in his class were plotting to seduce him in exchange for passing grades. Truth to tell, he was sorely tempted to give in, but the fear of losing his teaching position kept his passions at bay.

Scott Ott was slotted to teach Death and Dying in Maine, in which no one saw the least irony, given the college's tenuous existence. Scott had taught this course, in addition to his stock Intro to Sociology, for nine years now, so little preparation was necessary—and a good thing, for he had long ago lost his notes and his eternal tinkerings with the nuts and bolts of the campus left him with little time to draft them anew.

This left the adjuncts, who scavenged the surviving sections of bio and chem labs and English comp, which were also teetering on the brink of cancellation due to the shrinking student population.

Despite this flurry of activity, registration forms, for some reason, had never appeared in Henny's mailbox, and someone had carefully and diligently lined out geometry in each and every copy of the current schedule of courses. But Henny was nothing if not prescient. He'd preemptively placed an ad in the "Welcome Back!" edition of *The Grover Rover*:

Students! If you want to take geometry, consider yourself in the course. Spox admits you!

It worked, and Henny shuffled into a room with twenty-one warm bodies seated at their desks.

As for the students, they were thrilled to see bison on campus. They wrote home to friends and family, who came out to the school in droves to see if it was true. Timmy and Boss became the centers of attention, and a movement got under way to make them the new mascots.

As Marcus looked down from the silo on the swarm of students and those connected to them, his heart warmed. "Well," he said as Hattie laid a stack of papers on his desk, "that's quite a crowd down there. Is it always like this at the beginning of the school year?"

"Only when we have bison," she said dryly. "Brisco Quik is here. He's on a tear. He wants to see you."

Marcus turned from the window. "Oh. Tell him to come in."

Brisco entered, still catching his breath after the long ascent. "I need to tell you," he gasped with a hand plastered to his chest, "faculty are up in arms because you've removed the phones from their offices."

Marcus looked pained. "It was a difficult decision, but I didn't do it only to save money. It was a way of bringing us closer as a community."

Brisco looked stupefied. "Excuse me?"

Marcus's face glowed as he rose from his chair. "I'm replacing the faculty and staff phones with a buzzer connected to a campus loudspeaker. From Hattie's desk, we will be able to signal individual faculty and staff members when a call comes in for any of them. Then they can use the common phone in the pigsty. That way, the phone will be a gathering place and spontaneous interactions can erupt. Everyone will have a special buzzer number. Dan Stupak, for example, is number twelve. You, Brisco, are number thirteen."

"Thirteen?"

"Yes," said Marcus, his enthusiasm unabated. "If a call comes in for you, Hattie will buzz thirteen times."

"Thirteen!"

"Yes. And the beauty of it all is that when you retire, we will also retire your number."

Brisco's expression intensified. "Just out of curiosity, what number is Bella Proins?"

"She's number two. As you may have heard, she has special needs now. Her foot has been giving her terrible trouble." Marcus caught himself and paused. "Oh. I wasn't supposed to tell you that about her foot. Something about confidentiality."

"Number *two*?"

"Yes. To make it easier on her. Her condition has preoccupied her so much that she doesn't have the time to drop everything to listen for a higher number."

Brisco suddenly felt the thrill of inspiration. "I'm glad you raised this subject, President Marcus. I've just been given a devastating diagnosis myself."

"My boy!" exclaimed Marcus, his face filling with concern.

"Yes," said Brisco, hanging his head. "It's a very difficult thing to talk about."

Marcus planted his knuckles on his desk. "But you must, my boy. You must. I want to rally the troops on your behalf. We're family, you know."

"Well, that's really decent of you, President Marcus. All right, then. I've just learned that I'm . . . Well, how should I phrase this?" Brisco feigned deep embarrassment. "President Marcus, can we just say I'm no longer the man I used to be?"

Marcus's eyebrows arched. "You don't mean . . ."

Brisco nodded. "And as you know, reproduction is a major life function."

"Say no more," said Marcus, waving a hand. "You shall have a placard. The problem is, there aren't that many handicapped spaces on campus." He thought for a moment, pinning a forefinger to his chin. "I have it! You shall have Bella's space. Despite her bad foot, she still gets around, so I wouldn't say she's not completely unable to perform a major life function. Unlike you."

"Thank you, President Marcus," said Brisco, feeling the intense heat of victory. "I'm overwhelmed."

Marcus quickly dispensed a placard from his desk drawer and, with a heavy black marker, wrote Bella's space number in. He then took Brisco's hand in both of his. "And if there's anything else I can do for you, you'll let me know, won't you?"

"I will."

As Brisco made his way out the door, Hattie signaled to him and whispered, "Did he say anything about the clock?"

Brisco looked genuinely pained. "No. Maybe I should go back in and ask him."

"No!" commanded Hattie. "It means he doesn't want faculty to know yet."

"Know what?" Brisco drew closer to Hattie, thankful a desk was interposed between them.

Hattie cupped her hands around her mouth. "Remember what Professor Blatty said about it being a doomsday clock?"

Brisco gave a cautious nod.

"Well, it's true. This school has a semester and then . . ." At this, she drew a finger across her throat.

"What are you talking about? We've been living semester to semester since I got here."

Hattie fanned the air while shaking her head. "Those were false alarms. This is the real thing. Remember that envelope from under President Cyrus's pillow?"

"Yes. So?"

"It was a last warning from the bank!"

Now Brisco grasped everything. "My God, who else knows about this?"

"Just Bella and me. And now you." In a flash, Hattie reached across her desk, wrapped her arms around Brisco's neck, and pulled him in for a stiff kiss. "There," she said with a note of triumph as she released him. "Fair trade for what I just told you. I was entitled."

The kiss did nothing to temper Brisco's surging rage. He immediately rattled down the winding staircase of the silo. At the halfway point, he ran into Bella, who was on her way up, pulling herself along the railing, favoring her pained foot.

"Oh, hello, Professor Quik. Is President Marcus in?"

"Oh, he's in," said Brisco, furious Bella knew about the school's execution date and kept it from the faculty. But he decided to hang fire for the moment, knowing forbearance could prove an invaluable tool in luring prey into the snare. "And you know something? It's just like you said. He's not a bad guy at all. Look. He gave me this." He held up the placard.

Bella looked dazed. "Isn't that my space number?"

"I think so. I'm afraid I'm not a well man, so President Marcus wanted to make things as easy as possible for me. I wish I could tell you precisely why, but you see, confidentiality prohibits me." And with that, Brisco resumed his descent, with Bella still clutching the railing.

When Brisco emerged into the light of day, he was immediately confronted by the sight of Timmy rutting. The large bull was scraping the ground and moaning dolefully while Boss seemed to be ignoring him. Finally, Timmy began to romp, tossing his head about and snorting steam. The ring of onlookers—students, parents, and hangers-on—widened their circle, many looking wary of Timmy's erratic movements.

Brisco's delight at his placard had been short-lived, usurped by Hattie's devastating news that within a semester he might have to look for real work. He was so beset with anxiety that the very thought of teaching seemed like a distraction from the emergency state of affairs that now reigned on campus—still unbeknownst to the other faculty. But what could he do? For now, the classroom called. Concepts in Political Discourse was his walk-in course that demanded almost nothing of him but his physical presence. It was his Garden of Eden course, his perfect world. The discussion themes simply suggested themselves, and Brisco was a master at keeping the ball of conversation rolling. He looked at his watch and marched off to meet the new students.

The class met in one of the three Quonset huts behind the Victorian. The arching steel structure had been subdivided into five neat little classrooms. When Brisco walked into his, he found twelve students sitting at their desks, quietly expectant. Brisco still didn't know what he wanted to talk about, so he effectively turned the business over to the students by asking, "So what is of political import at Grover Cleveland at the moment?"

If they only knew! he remarked in his aching heart. The students, as usual, threw him blank stares. When he met their gazes, they looked away. Finally, as a young woman raised a can of Diet Coke to her lips, Brisco seized the moment. "Ah! Good. You had to buy your soda off campus. But why? Can anyone tell me?"

A sweet-faced boy with a mop of red hair raised a tentative hand. "There's no vending machine on campus?"

"Excellent," said Brisco, and the discussion took wing from there.

Fifty minutes later, the ordeal was over.

As Brisco hurried back to his office, one thought echoed in his mind: *Only fifteen weeks to go until the end of the semester. Only fifteen. And what then? Oblivion.* He now had the sorry job of divulging the significance of the ticking silo clock to his colleagues.

In the meantime, Marcus alighted from the silo to take his daily walk about campus. This time he found himself milling among students and visitors who'd come to view the bison. None of them knew who he was, of course. And why should they? He was just a heavyset man with a thick mustache and a baggy suit, meandering about with his hands behind his back, leaning slightly forward as if inspecting the world nose-first.

The bison had settled down again and were grazing contentedly in the center of campus. They were accomplishing exactly what Marcus had intended them to: the grass would never again need to be cut with machinery, as the two animals ate ceaselessly. In fact, the grass was now so short that here and there the field was going bald, the bare, brown earth already showing through. Of course, this might all be moot in a few months, should the great rout of the campus take place, whereupon nature would reclaim what was, in the beginning, hers.

Marcus still couldn't get Jim Burns's mucus research out of his head. What was it he'd said? About the simplest, humblest things on the planet having vast import?

As Marcus was contemplating this, Henny Spox rolled by on his bicycle. "Mr. President," he breathed as he came to a squeaking stop and raised the visor of his helmet.

"Please. Marcus," said the chief executive.

"Yes. Marcus." Henny's dew-lapped face drew up into a broad smile, revealing the teeth of an exhumed corpse.

"It's good to see you. How are your classes going so far?"

"Well, I have only the one this semester. I spend most of my time at my research."

"Research!" Marcus echoed, pleased once again with the creativity and diligence of his faculty.

"Yes. I've got that ongoing Wahazy Continuity equation. But I also have a more practical, applied project. What do you know about nanotechnology?"

Marcus hung his head and rubbed his chin. "Nano, nano . . ." he repeated to himself, like a mantra. Finally he looked up. "Well, nothing registers. Wasn't there once a car called the Nano? But I suspect this has nothing to do with what you're studying, does it?"

The mathematician smiled generously. "No, I don't think so. My nanos are so small it takes a microscope to see them. They're tiny machines that can be injected into the body to do all sorts of work."

"Machines! Tiny, you say?" And Marcus smiled broadly because, well, there it was again, the idea that little things could make big changes in the world. "Please tell me all about them."

"It's really fascinating," Henny said, anxious to share his ideas, because nobody at Grover Cleveland ever asked him about his work. "You probably know that certain fungi produce powerful pharmaceutical compounds. Some of these drugs are quickly metabolized by the body and are therefore weakened before they can exert their effects. I'm trying to design nanobots—tiny robots—that will hand carry fungus spores to the sites of disease and seed them there, where they can release their products in situ. Like little farmers planting their crops."

Marcus struggled to get his mind around the concept. He didn't understand most of what Henny had said, but the mathematician's words contained pleasant poetry, and Marcus liked it. "Fungus. Of all things." In a whisper laden with hope, he asked, "Is there money in it?"

"Well, maybe someday."

Marcus's mood ebbed. "Oh. Might that someday be within a few months, by any chance?"

"I don't think so." Henny hadn't taken Marcus for a man who placed a lot of emphasis on profit. "But I suppose the unexpected can always happen."

"I find your work fascinating nonetheless. I applaud you."

A lump rose in Henny's throat. "Thank you. If you like, I can show you my work sometime."

"If I like! Of course I would like."

Henny could scarcely believe his ears. Before Marcus, the last time he'd mentioned his work to anyone, it had been to a faculty member, and that person had troubled himself to stifle a yawn before walking off.

"I wonder if you'd mind presenting your research to the faculty and staff at the welcome-back luncheon tomorrow."

If not for Timmy's full-throated bellowing in the background, Henny would have offered a cry of thanks. As it was, all he could do was nod in gratitude as Marcus walked away, muttering "fungus" under his breath. "Of all things."

Marcus continued to the edge of campus, where the pine forest began. Now that he had fungus on his mind, it seemed serendipitous that he should immediately encounter it. There, on the ground before him, coming up through the needle litter, was a lovely, creamy-white mushroom. "Exquisite," said Marcus as he bent down. On closer examination, the thing looked quite phallic, and Marcus blushed. But there was also something otherworldly, veil-like, and incipient about it, as if it'd been freshly set there by the hand of God.

"Careful."

Marcus gave a start. He straightened up and came face to face with Dan Stupak, The Egg, standing there in a crisp white shirt and red suspenders, one hand planted in a trousers pocket and the other supporting a stark black pipe wedged in the corner of his mouth, the smoke wreathing about his bald head. "Careful," he repeated. "That's a poisonous one. It's called the destroying angel."

"Angel?" echoed Marcus.

"Yes. Of all the misnomers. It's one of the most deadly mushrooms on God's earth."

"You don't say!"

"I do say." Dan moved closer and hovered over the mushroom. "Very disarming, isn't it, considering its beauty?" he said without emotion. " But I wouldn't even handle it without gloves."

"Aha!"

"I'm a mammal man myself, but I think I'm really a frustrated mycologist. I find these things fascinating beyond words."

"You don't say."

"I do say. It looks so delicate, so pure in its whiteness. And that veil. Like a young, blushing bride."

Marcus found himself moved by the poetry of it all. He stared down at the destroying angel as if he expected it to perform a dance, or take flight.

And then, without warning, Dan Stupak lifted one of his stumpy legs and brought his foot down on the mushroom, taking pains to grind it, slowly and deliberately, into the earth whence it came.

Marcus was dumbfounded. "But why—?"

"Don't worry. The mushroom is just the part you see. It's like an iceberg. Most of the thing is below the surface. No harm done." Having said this, Dan waddled away, puffing contentedly on his pipe.

Marcus looked down at the flattened white mass,

for which he felt an acute sense of loss. Flies had already alighted on it. *How quickly death gives way to life*, he thought and then turned from the unpleasant scene and continued on his way.

As Marcus returned to campus, he caught sight of Bella limping along, pumping her arms. That indefatigable woman! His heart accelerated as he beheld her. He'd never felt this way about a woman before. In fact, he'd never felt much in the way of deep affection for anybody. People were, to him, simply people, deserving of kindness and respect, but he sensed this only as an inclination and, intellectually, knew it to be correct. But to feel something like a magnetic pull, or a powerful wind driving him toward Bella, well, this was something entirely new. And for a man of his years! Sexuality, on those rare occasions when he actually thought about it, had always been as academic as collecting beetles. If he'd been asked about his own orientation, Marcus would've had to say asexual. How could one feel what one didn't feel? But now! What was this eruption of heat? This suppuration of tension? Was it something he had suppressed all his life? Was it an abnormal development, like a tumor? Would it go away? Or was it symptomatic of a new life's spirit that, for one reason or other, had lain dormant until now?

Bella caught sight of Marcus, changed course, and limped toward him.

Marcus didn't attempt to meet her halfway. He

couldn't. He was anchored in place. Paralyzed by his infatuation.

"Marcus," she sighed when she finally reached him.

"Bella," said the president. "You're always working so hard."

Thank God someone noticed, thought Bella. "I had a longer-than-normal walk this time. Professor Quik claimed my parking place, and I had to take a spot near the pigsty. Way over there." She pointed theatrically, as if she were indicating the location of India.

"Yes, that's so. I'm afraid the poor man has been given a devastating diagnosis. Devastating."

Bella searched Marcus's face for evidence he might be willing to divulge the nature of the affliction. But his narrow eyes, all but obscured by his bushy eyebrows, betrayed nothing. "I see," she finally said, even though she didn't see at all and was deeply frustrated by this turn of events. She prided herself on knowing everything that occurred on campus. *Everything.* But here she stood, ossified and powerless. She realized she would have to deputize Hattie Sims to do the dirty work for her.

"How are preparations coming along for the welcome-back luncheon?" asked Marcus.

Bella reluctantly joined the new theme. "Very well. I've ordered the fruit plates and the cold cuts and cinnamon buns. Coffee and juice too. There should be something for everybody."

Marcus raised a finger. "You didn't forget those little crustless sandwiches, did you?" he asked, like a child seeking to insure that there was tinsel for the Christmas tree.

"I ordered them too."

"Cut on an angle?"

"Of course. Just the way you like them."

Marcus's smile hefted his mustache, compressing his eyes into almond slivers. "Dear Bella," he pronounced. "Good Bella. Sweet Bella."

The executive vice president melted under the coos, like a puppy having its tummy rubbed. "Marcus," she exhaled. Collecting herself, she continued, "Please don't think I'm being parsimonious, but is it wise, in this financial climate, to go through the expense of the welcome-back luncheon? I mean, in light of what you told me"—she glanced across campus at the doomsday clock, whose minute hand had departed the twelve and was now coursing, slowly but inexorably, along its fateful circuit—"that every penny counts. Doesn't it?"

"Dear Bella, even a doomed world deserves a rose, don't you think?"

Bella's eyes filled with tears. "Of course," she said, searching about for a tissue. "You're so wise."

"My motive is not only to feed the faculty and staff. My heart is heavy. The time has come to bring everybody on board."

Bella nodded. "Of course."

The two stood looking into each other's eyes for the longest moment. Marcus felt a desperate impulse to reach out and take Bella's hand. But the weight of his office—and his inexperience in such matters—held him back. Still, he wagered that she would be receptive to such a gesture. The day would come. The presidency of a college promised not only the opportunity to remake an institution in accordance with one's vision, but also the possibility of one's self being recast by the serendipity of human interactions, not the least of which was the tickle of love.

TEN
LUNCHEON OF CHAMPIONS

"**Y**ou had no right to keep such a thing to yourself," Brisco scolded Bella, who stood before him, a martyr, allowing his rhetorical blows to fall upon her.

Bella knew Brisco well enough to understand he had only so much wind, and sooner or later he'd blow himself out and everything would return to the status quo of a low hum of resignation and static calm, punctuated by eruptions of indignation.

Of course the current crisis, she had to admit, might constitute an exception to the familiar pattern. As she stood at the edge of the commons with Brisco, the doomsday clock was in her line of sight, its relentless tock reminding her that the second that had just passed propelled them that much closer to their dissipation as an institution of higher learning. And then? Already her dreams—or nightmares—were filled with images she constantly labored to disperse. The way things were going, she wouldn't be surprised if old Mr. Demonier himself, fresh from the chicken farm, arrived on campus, opened the door to his pickup, and yelled, "Get in!"

"This involves the entire campus community," Brisco said. "It was nothing less than selfish of you to think it was a private matter."

Of course, Brisco had no idea what Bella thought, because she hadn't communicated her thoughts to anyone. In fact, she didn't know what to say or who to talk to. In that sense, yes, she was being selfish, because, again, she harbored a craven fear of what would happen to her—and nobody else—should the worst come to pass.

Timmy ambled toward them. Bella wondered why Timmy always turned his attention to her, as if she were the obvious alternative to Boss.

"Bella!" growled Brisco. "Are you listening to me?"

She refocused. "Believe me when I tell you, Professor Quik, that I myself was only recently told about the clock and the letter and the . . . the one semester we might have left."

"If that," Brisco rushed to add, which comment was punctuated by a solid, cutting *tock*!

Bella sighed. "I think all your questions will be answered at the welcome-back luncheon. Please give the president a chance."

Brisco was somewhat mollified by Bella's willingness to take the full brunt of his bluster without offering any resistance. The bison were almost upon them now, and Bella was the first to step away. "I really have to go. Your concerns have been noted."

Brisco took pains to head in the opposite direction, even though it took him away from where he wanted to go. He was suddenly mindful he was guilty of the same thing he'd accused Bella of: keeping explosive information to himself. But the welcome-back luncheon beckoned, which would give him a chance to prepare the faculty before the president dropped the bomb.

In the meantime, Hattie Sims was in the woodshed with Jiminy Schmitz, trying to cajole him into attending the luncheon. "They'll be expecting you!" she chastised as she pulled his arm.

The provost yanked away, refusing to abandon his cot. "Leave me, woman!" He strained to recall one of the verses he'd consumed during Brisco's visit, the one about the timeless art of seduction, but it eluded him. He had thought eating his work would endow him with a sort of genetic memory of its contents, but the act had produced the opposite effect, inducing amnesia about everything he'd written.

"Provost Schmitz! Jiminy! They'll expect you to say something." Hattie finally released him and took a step back, looking down at the Robinson Crusoesque figure curled in his simple bed, a bearded, disheveled man with wild hair and mania in his gray eyes.

"Who's the president?" he finally asked.

"Cleveland," said Hattie, realizing they'd walked this path before.

"Grover?" asked Jiminy, his face awash in consternation. "How can a man function without a brain?"

Hattie redoubled her efforts to get the provost to his feet. "No, not Grover," she said as she finally managed to haul what was left of Jiminy out of bed and lift him to a standing position. "Marcus."

"What about reorganization? How's that going?"

"Now you're talking." Hattie moved the mass of wiry hair from the provost's face. "That's what you want to think about. Courses. Students. Reorganization." She added, "You're the number-two dog."

"I am? What about Bella?"

Hattie clucked her tongue. "She only thinks she's number two."

"Aha." Jiminy's eyes glinted. "I can't go. I've ordered a parakeet. It's being delivered."

"What are you talking about?"

"A parakeet. I'm told they're good company."

Hattie made Jiminy presentable and coaxed him out

into the sunlight, where he threw his hands before his eyes. She immediately bumped into Bella, who was on one of her innumerable errands.

"Hattie, I'm glad I ran into you." Bella nodded at Jiminy as Hattie held him by the arm. "Hello, Provost Schmitz," she said, mustering an ingratiating smile.

As if by telepathy, she conveyed to Hattie the need for privacy. Hattie received the signal loud and clear and thrilled to the prospect of a deposit of proprietary information. "Now, Provost," she said as she turned him around, "that's the Victorian dead ahead. You just keep walking straight and follow the smell of coffee." She gave him a little shove, as if launching a toy boat on a small pond. Jiminy stumbled off, bandy-legged, but generally maintained his trajectory.

Hattie turned to Bella. "Okay, shoot," she said, licking her lips.

"It's a small thing," said Bella, trying to turn the thermostat down on this particular intrigue. "I just need to know something I'm supposed to know anyway."

Hattie squinted. "That's double-talk. Just let me have it plain as day."

Bella put all her energy into maintaining her smile. "I just need to know the nature of Brisco's disability. You see, President Marcus gave him a dedicated parking space—"

"You mean your space," Hattie interjected with joy,

knowing that voicing this put her one leg up on Bella, who blanched at being trumped. "And he never cleared it with you."

"I wouldn't phrase it quite like that," said Bella, her smile now frozen.

Hattie loved—literally *loved*—this! There she was, a secretary, giving an executive aide the hot foot. "Well . . ." She hesitated, as if contemplating a monumental undertaking. "This might be something I can help you with."

Bella *knew* this was something Hattie could help her with, because word had spread that Hattie's wandering eye had settled on the political science professor. She also knew there would be a price, which was, of course, what Hattie was waiting for. "There's talk of just-cause protection for staff members. That is, for certain staff members."

Hattie's ears perked up. Just cause was like tenure— she'd never be fired, couldn't be fired, short of committing mass murder or embezzling precious tuition money. But then again, she knew she was so valuable, harbored so many secrets, and had been there so long, that firing her in any case would be like the school's shooting itself in the foot. So she held out for more. "I don't think so," she said, examining Bella for soft spots. "I feel that I'm already secure. At least as secure as one can feel in a burning barn. What I'm saying is, this handicapped thing seems like small potatoes compared to the pickle we're in, doesn't it?"

Was Hattie accusing her of being petty? Just because the school was facing a terminal calamity didn't mean it should cease to function on a day-to-day basis. What was it Marcus had said? Something about even a doomed world needing a rose? Well, this information was her rose, and she would have it.

Bella focused on Hattie again and shook her head slowly, as if dispelling a mist of misunderstanding that hovered between them. "Then what do you—?"

"A special parking space of my own would be nice. And I want you to create a new one right next to Brisco's."

Now Bella tried to turn the tables. "Why so much concern for something that won't matter in a semester's time?"

Hattie's answer was immediate. "I want to go out in style, with a little more respect than I have now."

Bella knew she was being wrung out like a washcloth. But what could she do? In any case, ultimately, she wanted her space back because she, too, was interested in respect and appearances. She decided to grant Hattie her wish, but when Brisco was exiled to the campus periphery again, well, what was it Hattie had said? That she wanted a space next to his? Well, then, she would have it. "Done."

Hattie smiled. "Okay, then. I'll get back to you."

At the welcome-back luncheon, the grand dining

room of the Victorian already buzzed with faculty and staff. All the goodies were arranged on side tables. Platters of cold cuts and cheese, fresh rolls, and magnificent salad and fruit bowls were flanked by a broad sheet of cinnamon buns and cookies. Dominating the display was a ziggurat of little crustless sandwiches, cut on an angle.

Brisco arrived and immediately tried to corral his colleagues so he could unburden himself of the grim news of their collective fate. But he was upended from this business when Jiminy entered the room and all heads turned in his direction. The provost was accustomed to such attention. He nodded sagely and raised a hand in mock papal blessing as well-wishers among the faculty and staff gravitated to him.

Brisco had no choice but to follow suit and eventually succeeded in extricating Jiminy and moving him away to a relatively quiet corner of the room. "Good to see you, Jiminy."

"Yes. Yes, it is. Bring me a fruit plate, will you? No pineapple, though. It has an enzyme that irritates my gums."

Brisco hurried to the spread and quickly assembled a small plate of oranges, apples, and grapes, which he delivered to the provost.

Jiminy straightened up as if receiving a gift of state. "So tell me the news. Are we reorganized yet?"

"Jiminy," said Brisco darkly, "reorganization may be irrelevant."

"Irrelevant? How so?"

"We did vote to turn reorganization over to the Committee on Committees. It will take an archaeologist to dig to the bottom of that mess. But, Jiminy, we have a much bigger problem now, one that is rendering the reorganization moot. But maybe I'm making assumptions. Surely President Marcus told you."

Jiminy chewed nervously on a tuft of his beard. "Please don't give me bad news," he pleaded.

But before Brisco could begin to explain, silence fell over the room.

Marcus walked in, with Bella limping at his heels. He received a few nods, which he immediately took for approbation. "As you were, everybody." He caught sight of the crustless sandwiches and immediately made for them. "Small things," he said under his breath.

After devouring five of them, Marcus realized there could be no further delay. It was his bitter duty to convey the darkest of news to faculty and staff. He walked to the head of the room. This time he felt well prepared because he'd just finished the chapter in *The Handbook of College Reorganization* that focused on persuasive speaking, emphasizing a president's need to speak with confidence, even when he knew little about the topic in question. *Take command*, the chapter affirmed, *and they will follow. People want to be led.*

"Colleagues," Marcus pronounced and then glanced

about the room to make sure everyone knew whom he was addressing. Without a single note, he went on, the words filling his mouth as if heaven-sent. "We are off to a good start, I would say. We have already cut costs, and student numbers are up. The combination of these two things has pushed us in the direction of a balanced budget. You have been working so hard. Our diligent admissions department visited homeless shelters and prison release programs to convince people that what was lacking in their lives was not money or success or a job or even happiness, but a college diploma. The result has been a spike in our student population, which you have handled magnificently. Timmy and Boss have also done their share, I'm happy to say. For the first time, we have tourists on campus, and when they leave, they spread the word about all that Grover Cleveland has to offer. I know some of you have been irritated by the removal of the phones from your offices. But I have also observed the increased interactions among you as you patiently wait your turns at the community phone in the pigsty. Think of this common resource as the equivalent of drawing water from the village well."

In the audience, Hattie Sims, who had slipped in unnoticed, was looking not at Marcus but at Bella, who stood just behind the president. When their eyes met, Hattie squinted and slowly shook her head. Both of them knew how tenuous the concept of a balanced budget was at Grover Cleveland. Always based on projected revenues, hope of solvency was inevitably shattered when struggling and disillusioned students began to pull out mid-semester and a promising fall gave way to an anemic spring. Further, Hattie realized that the dragnet the school had laid for new students—from the homeless shelter, prison, and mental health institution—had snared precisely those least likely to stay.

For his part, Brisco was aghast at this speech. *What is he talking about?* he thought. *When will he tell us the truth?* He quickly glanced at the faces of his colleagues— placid, receptive, collected. *If they knew what I know, they'd be up in arms!*

Marcus continued in stride, finding that making a speech wasn't such hard work after all. In fact, it was rather pleasant and effortless. As long as one kept opening one's mouth, words continued to fill the cavity. When he bumped up against the issue of the vending machine, he paused and reached out to his listeners, because chapter seven of *The Handbook of College Reorganization* had talked about making one's audience a partner in one's ideas, lest those ideas fail and one is forced to shoulder the blame alone. "Where do we stand on this, Professor Moore?" he asked, settling his eyes on the math professor at the far end of the room.

Frannie picked up the beat. "The vending machine? The Vending Committee is looking at a new vendor."

Brisco wanted to leap onto the table, expose the emperor's nakedness, and shout *"Sic semper tyrannis!"* But he found himself almost paralyzed with—what, fear? Unable to rise to the demands of his indignation, Brisco, for the first time in his life, was faced with the realization that whatever courage he possessed seemed beyond his reach. And once the faculty found out he'd known about the school's death date? Well, he'd tried to gather them before Jiminy walked in, hadn't he? And he'd tried to inform Jiminy before Marcus arrived. He could always cite these attempts in his own defense.

Marcus nodded toward Frannie, well pleased with her report. "Initiative!" He speared the air with an index finger. "That's what I like. Great things are happening at Grover Cleveland. And now I have a surprise for all of you. To demonstrate what I mean by *great things*, I'd like one of our distinguished faculty members to give us a synopsis of his most exciting research."

This took Jim Burns by surprise. He hadn't expected Marcus to highlight his work. Maybe he had been mistaken about the guy all along. Well, if he wanted a presentation, Jim was happy to oblige. No one had asked him about his mucus research, but here, presented to him on a silver platter, was a chance to deliver a report wholesale to a captive and well-fed audience.

But as Jim rose, Marcus continued, "Professor Spox, would you please come up to the lectern?"

Jim fell back into his seat like a sack of bricks, stupefied and embarrassed.

What is this? wondered Brisco, now tied in emotional knots. *What about our crisis? That clock is ticking, damn it!*

Hattie pleaded silently, *Brisco, say something!* She had been watching him and noticed his crimson shade and the bulging vein in his neck. She felt the most powerful impulse to go over to him and rub his back but was afraid if she touched him, he'd explode.

Henny was seated alone, pecking at a cherry Danish that had bled into a bone-white slice of cheese. He was flanked by empty seats, forming a cordon of antipathy. When he heard his name mentioned, he blushed and looked sheepishly about. Then he got up and made his way to the head of the room, nodding from side to side, acknowledging the nonexistent peer approbation.

A collective groan rose from the faculty. But as soon as Henny arrived at the lectern, there was a sharp flutter of applause from one member, Jiminy Schmitz, who seemed electrified by the prospect of a professional presentation from someone he had thought long dead. The others had no choice but to follow suit, but the applause was so fleeting that by the time Henny raised his hand to calm it, there was only silence.

"As you know," he began, taking a deep breath.

No sooner had he exhaled than there was a heavy thud at the door.

Bella was about to signal to someone to see who it was, but Marcus touched her arm. "Let it be. The door's unlocked. Let's listen to Henny."

"*Nano*. A powerful word for such a small thing. And, being so small, I've given them small tasks that may have great import for human medicine. In fact—"

Thud!

The crowd turned toward the door.

"Let it be," Marcus said to the assembly. "The door is unlocked. Please go on, Professor Spox."

"In light of inconclusive analyses of dubious parameters, I have been inclined to hedge my bets using the Paternowski Theorem of inhibition of nonorganic functionality in organic media, which states—"

Thud!

The door splintered, and a cry broke out as Boss thundered into the room with Timmy on her heels. They headed straight for the luncheon spread, moaning and plowing through tables and chairs. Henny gripped the lectern like a captain steadying the wheel of a ship as faculty and staff fled the scene, looking for any avenue of escape. Marcus tried to calm the crowd, but the situation was beyond repair. Only Jiminy retained his place, picking at his fruit plate while watching the scene with intense interest. This was the first time Marcus noticed him—a bony wisp of a man with fantastic, unkempt hair which was one with his long beard.

While the bison settled to graze on the overturned breakfast spread, Marcus went over to Jiminy and took a seat next to him. "I don't think I've had the pleasure," said the president, wondering who this stick figure could be. *Perhaps*, he thought, *he's one of the new students admissions recruited from the homeless shelter.* Marcus asked, "Have you registered for your program of study?"

Jiminy examined Marcus in wonder. "I'm your provost," he said, his voice filled with emotion. "Or so I'm told."

"You don't say! I had been told I had one." After a pause, he inquired, "Do I need one?"

Jiminy shrugged. "No one's ever asked that question before. But I know I can't be fired, because I'm also tenured faculty."

"Fired! Why would I want to fire you?"

Jiminy's gaze wandered for a moment before coming to rest on Marcus again. "I don't know. But presidents move in strange ways."

Both men were distracted when old Stash Zakraski, the school's custodian, arrived with a push broom to corral the bison and shoo them out of the Victorian. He looked unaffected about it all, having long ago acknowledged the idiosyncrasies of academics. The two beasts, however, wouldn't budge from their feast, so Stash began to work around them.

"I think we should go and let Stash do his work," Marcus suggested. "It's a shame because I had so much more to tell the faculty."

"I think your speech was brilliant. I could have listened to you for hours."

"Could you have? I thank you for that. My only sadness is that the news I didn't have an opportunity to share would have been so hurtful."

Jiminy's small eyes darted back and forth. He recalled that Brisco had wanted to tell him something about a problem. He mumbled, "Sadness?"

"Yes." Marcus led the provost past the stubborn bison and into the open air. "Since you're my provost, you really should know. But first things first. I heard from the Faculty Assembly that my proposal for reorganization, although not received with joy, did inspire them to have the Committee on Committees expedite things. I ask you, has a college president ever had such a wonderful faculty to work with? The book I'm reading warned me that I would be opposed at every turn, but I've found just the opposite. In any case, since the committee is so eager to assist me, I've decided to speed things up by initiating an immediate provisional reorganization that will remain in effect until the committee finishes its work and formalizes it. But remember"—Marcus winked—"mum's the word for the moment."

Jiminy stared up at Marcus with a look of utter perplexity. Tentatively, he raised a crooked finger and pressed it to his lips. "It seems to me there's more to say."

"Ah, yes," sighed Marcus. "I was getting to that. I suppose you're aware of the clock on the silo."

"Yes. But I think it's running a little slow."

"Not slow enough, unfortunately. We have less than a semester to come up with a rescue plan for our dear school, or the bank will move in and dispose of what's left of us. My reorganization is more of a consolidation to save some money or at least set an example for others to think of ways to save. But I'm afraid we can't save our way out of our crisis. We need new thinking, and I'm . . ." Marcus took a deep breath. "To tell you the truth, Provost, I am wracked with doubts about my ability to lead."

Jiminy was uncharacteristically at a loss for words. He reached back in his memory for some fragment from his now-extinct writings that might be of help. An epigram, perhaps? But all he could come up with was, "I have complete faith in you."

Marcus was immensely moved by Jiminy's sentiment. "That's so considerate." He placed a hand on the provost's shoulder. "I think we'll make a great team. In a short while, I'll tell you a little more of my plan to unite the faculty." He ambled off toward the silo to begin the long ascent to his office to ruminate in peace.

Jiminy commanded his thin legs to do their duty and get him to Brisco as quickly as possible. *Mum* may have been the word, but that wink had been ambiguous, and Jiminy, in a moment of lucidity, decided to err on the side of self-preservation. From long experience he knew that, although he, as a tenured faculty member, couldn't be fired, there were other ways to dispose of the unwanted or unneeded. If his days at Grover Cleveland were indeed numbered, he wanted to go out under his own power.

ELEVEN
AN EMERGENCY MEETING AND A BUDGIE

Panic.

Brisco marched from office to office, rallying the troops with the news that Marcus had failed to deliver at the luncheon. Most reacted as if they'd just received a terminal diagnosis. Hector Lopez immediately began to pray, promising to amend his life if only this cup would be taken from him. Frannie Moore gasped and took a mental inventory of every detail of her well-appointed office. She tenderly noted every photo and potted plant and the elegant lines of her ergonomic chair, as if the room were destined to become a museum reflecting her last moments on duty. When Brisco broke the news to Dan Stupak, the biologist had a spastic involuntary response and bit the stem off his pipe. Jim Burns leapt to his feet and gathered his manuscript to his chest, in the manner of a man rescuing it from a conflagration. Pete Blatty's eyes welled, and he instinctively reached out for an embrace from his sousaphone. Only Diane Dempsey appeared quietly accepting. She closed her eyes, nodded, and seemed to fall into a trance.

The faculty—utterly, completely, inextricably dependent upon the school—were perfect symbionts, like those deep-sea invertebrates that couldn't exist beyond the warmth of oceanic steam vents; their entire worldview was colored by their interactions and preoccupations within their static bubble. With the possible exception of Diane Dempsey, who had always thought herself too good for the school, they couldn't conceive of the end of Grover Cleveland College. Where would they go? What else could they do? Was the old, cynical adage true—that those who can't do, teach?

As coincidence would have it, when Brisco burst into Scott Ott's office, the latter was reading a newspaper article about a taxi driver in the Bronx who had a PhD from Caltech. The headline: "Jobless Physicist Drives the Night Shift."

Brisco had made his frantic rounds and was satisfied that the faculty, at long last, had roused itself from what he'd always seen as its fundamental apathy. His anger mingled wildly with a thrill of vindication. Now that he had everyone's attention, he designed to bring all of them into the same room to create the synergy and riot mentality they'd need to spearhead what he saw as the necessary counteroffensive to save the school.

But, damn it, he had a class to teach. In his fever to leap into the breach, he'd forgotten about his—or any other—students.

Bitterly, reluctantly, he gathered himself, grabbed the latte he'd been drinking, which was the last thing he needed, and hurried off to Quonset #2 to confront Concepts in University Governance.

Brisco impressed himself with how smoothly he shed the armor of the righteous warrior and donned the phlegmatic, measured demeanor of the senior academic. He leaned back against his desk and, latte in hand, gesticulated grandly as he struggled to get on top of his subject, which had to do with the exploitation of adjunct faculty to lower overhead costs. As he took in the twenty or so undergraduates seated before him, he considered that by the end of the semester they'd be sent packing. In this light, he wondered if it was worth it to even go on with the lesson. *Does one plant crops when one knows that drought or catastrophic flooding is imminent?* He asked himself whether he should tell the students what was afoot or aspire to normalcy to delay panic, which could exacerbate matters if it resulted in a general rout of the student body.

Five minutes into his lecture, and these ruminations, Jiminy scratched at the door. With the glass perfectly framing his manic face, he looked like a man trapped in a chamber slowly being bled of oxygen.

Brisco excused himself, not ungrateful for the interruption. "Continue the discussion," he directed his students as he set his latte on the desk. "Consider, er, the question of why university governance is a concept. Form small groups and let me know what you think."

Brisco ambled out the door. "What is it?" he asked Jiminy. "You look like you're having an asthma attack."

"You will too," gasped Jiminy. "He's using the nuclear option."

Brisco screwed up his face and shook his head. "What are you talking about? Who? What?"

"Reorganization!" yelped the provost, leveling wild eyes at his colleague. "He's doing it."

Brisco's expression begged clarification. He thought Jiminy must be losing his mind. "What do you mean? We turned all that over to the Committee on Committees. Anyway, what I wanted to tell you at the luncheon was that reorganization is now the least of our worries. The college itself is on the brink of collapse."

Jiminy waved a thin finger at Brisco, who was a good head taller than him. "I know. He told me. But he's imposing an interim reorganization. To take effect immediately. I don't know how he even knew such a thing was possible. It must be that book he's reading. Or maybe Hattie is advising him. She's very sly, you know. Just this morning she tried to seduce me."

Brisco looked into the distance. "Assemble the troops. In the dining room of the Victorian. Get Hattie to help you. We need to sort this out. And we all need to be on the same page."

"But that's a disaster area. The bison—"

"Precisely. It will be the perfect metaphor for what that crazy used-car salesman is doing to this school."

Jiminy's bout of lucidity abated. "Very interesting," he said, and then added the cryptic note, "If you fight this battle, there will be a great victory."

Brisco took inspiration from this counsel and set off for the Victorian. He didn't worry about his class, knowing full well that college teaching was the only business where the customers—the students—rejoiced when product wasn't delivered.

Once Jiminy had contacted his share of the faculty, all of them either canceled classes or closed their offices to attend the emergency meeting. Hattie had just about finished sweeping her portion of the campus, propelling them toward the Victorian. Jim Burns was the last of the herd, but this was propitious because it would give her a few moments of privacy to excavate the information Bella had commissioned her to gather. Despite their occasional friction, no one was closer to Brisco than Jim, so he was the mother lode, all right. Still, Hattie felt a tinge of guilt. Now that her eye had settled on Brisco, she was uneasy doing anything that might spoil her chances with him. On the other hand, it was only information—and information that Bella, in any case, was routinely entitled to.

Hattie entered Quonset #1 and immediately heard a commotion coming from Jim's classroom. The door was open. She peeped in and beheld a general state of distress.

"I do not accept it!" cried a thirtyish, ill-shaven man in torn jeans, standing next to his desk, apparently pleading with his classmates. "Jesus Christ is my Lord and Savior!" He wagged an accusing finger at Jim. "For what you have taught here today, you shall be damned to the everlasting fires of hell!"

Jim was sitting at his desk, twisting a pen in his hands and looking pained. "Now, now, evolution is not an assault on your faith. It's just a way of describing how the living world changes over time."

But the man would have none of it. He turned toward his classmates and, with a broad sweep of an arm, said, "It's better at the shelter. They have normal courses there. Typing and cooking. None of this godless shit mess. Who's with me? Let's get out of here!"

Jim watched helplessly as six other students joined the rabble-rouser and marched out of the classroom. He rubbed his forehead to forestall a gathering headache.

The period mercifully ended, and Jim collected his fragile notes as the remaining students streamed past his desk.

After the room had emptied, Hattie ambled in. "Well, I see it was a hot time in the old town tonight."

Jim threw her a helpless look. "Where do these people come from? Did you hear that guy condemn me to hell? All I did was mention Darwin."

"Yeah, in *your* mind, but in his mind you were trying to destroy his faith."

Jim's expression dropped. "I hope you're not making excuses for him."

"No, uh-uh. I'm here for another reason. A clerical one. Trying to account for the handicapped parking spaces on campus."

Jim shrugged. "What does that have to do with me?"

"It seems that Brisco got a space."

"What?" queried Jim as he snapped his briefcase shut. "Did something happen to him? I didn't know he was handicapped."

"I assume so. Only thing is, nobody seems to know the nature of his disability."

Jim shrugged again. "What about Bella? Ask her. I can't believe she doesn't know."

"Oh, maybe she does," fudged Hattie, "but this is an independent audit."

Jim shook his head. He didn't like intrigue. It distracted him from his mucus work. He realized there was no such thing as wading in quicksand—it was all or nothing. "Look, I don't know anything about Brisco and his parking space. But if Bella knows, then every *i* is dotted, right?"

Stalemate. But Hattie was actually relieved at her lack of success. Now she could be honest with both Bella and Brisco without alienating either. "Well, I guess that's about all the hay I'm gonna cut here." She turned to go, pausing only to inform Jim about the meeting in the Victorian. "You'd better hurry. You don't want to miss the fireworks."

In the meantime, the only two people oblivious to the alarm were Marcus and Bella. At long last, the right words had made their way to their lips as they reclined on a checked flannel blanket under a spruce bower in the Grover Cleveland Ornamental Garden, out of sight of the curious.

Bella swooned. Lying there, looking up into Marcus's eyes, she felt as if she were gazing back through history, through the long line of Cleveland men. She'd been in love before, but it had always been unrequited. She'd always been a window shopper for romance, always on the prowl for a bargain. But everything had been sold out or was simply beyond her emotional budget. What was it about her? Too fat? Too short? Too consumed by her need to be organized and to organize others? Who knew! But by the time she was forty, she'd come to that watershed moment in a single woman's life when the pilot light of childbearing begins to flicker and momentous decisions had to be made. For Bella, there had been a sweet edge to giving up. It meant being unburdened by the labor intensiveness of maintaining a girlish figure. It was a moment when the frustration of man-hunting gave way to the relief of accepting that it was no longer worth the trouble. That's when she turned all her efforts—heart, mind, and soul—to rooting herself as firmly and deeply as possible to her professional life at Grover Cleveland. The idea that she could have ever found a mate at the chicken farm was ridiculous. And here was the evidence of it: she was gazing into the pudding-brown eyes of the president of a college. A college! This had been worth waiting for, this resurrection of an aspiration she had left for dead.

"Bella," ventured Marcus, "what did you think when you first saw me?"

Bella's response was immediate. "I didn't have to think. You were my proof of the existence of God."

Marcus was dumbstruck by the power of this response. He found himself awash in heat and desire. "Oh, Bella! My flower!"

They clutched one another and kissed with the desperate abandon of teenagers. Under the bower. Illuminated by the late-summer sun. And oh, the sweetness of her skin!

In the meantime, faculty and staff had assembled in the remains of the Victorian's dining room. Stash was out with his broom, whisking Timmy and Boss across the commons and toward the edge of the campus forest, where they could graze on the understory. He hadn't finished his work in the dining room itself, so it was left to the faculty to right chairs and move errant dishware and utensils out of the way to create something resembling an orderly meeting space, which still stank of bison hide.

Brisco arrived with a watermelon he'd grabbed from the student dining commons, having long ago learned that a fed faculty was a contented—and pliant—faculty.

Frannie Moore cleared her throat to bring the room to order.

But Brisco rose behind her like a planet dwarfing its moon. "Not this time, Frannie," he said as he took control of the meeting. "This isn't a formal assembly. It's an emergency ad hoc meeting. Think of it as martial law."

Frannie's expression revealed deep hurt, but rather than give voice to such a feeling, she chose instead to melt into the gathering. When she wasn't sitting at the front of an assembly as its facilitator, she was the smallest of women, easily overlooked.

Dan Stupak removed his new pipe from his mouth long enough to pronounce, "I hope this is more action than talk. I was in the middle of a laboratory exercise on photosynthesis when Jiminy all but broke the door down. I thought the bison had come for me."

The provost sat alone in a corner of the room in his sorry tweed sport coat, nodding and mumbling. Now that he had initiated the alert, he was spent and lapsed into his customary role of muddled sage.

Brisco didn't mince words. "I've already spoken briefly with all of you. That clock is a fuse. It's counting the seconds until the final dissolution of the school."

A general ruckus erupted, which Brisco calmed by aggressively waving his arms in a warding off gesture.

"People!" Brisco commanded, "there's more. To add insult to injury, the president is imposing reorganization on us."

"Imposing?" said Hector Lopez. "What does that mean? Is that really a word?"

"It means," piped up Diane Dempsey, translating for the Spanish professor, "that we charged the Committee on Committees with studying the issue, but President Marcus has decided to bypass it." But this explanation only further confused Hector, who, that very morning, had been approached by a very *linda* female student asking if there wasn't *something* she could do to improve her Spanish grade.

Brisco nodded and grunted. "I couldn't have said it better myself, Diane."

This brought a slow smile of satisfaction to the

English professor's lips.

"How can he do such a thing?" asked Pete Blatty, already straining to excavate some middle path.

"To force us to cooperate," said Dan, his pipe clicking against his teeth.

"That's exactly it," said Brisco, launching a finger toward Dan. "What he's saying is that we are going to reorganize come hell or high water. So the committee had better act."

"Well," said Pete, "that does narrow our options. At least we know the committee can't vote against reorganization now."

Brisco ran a hand through his hair. "Sometimes, Pete, I wonder whose side you're on."

Diane seized her moment. "Now, now. Let's not talk in military terms. I mean, we can't divide ourselves into sides."

Brisco made a pleading expression. "That's very nice, Diane. You light the campfire while I get the marshmallows. Who knows the words to 'Kumbaya'?"

All heads turned toward Jiminy as he began to hum "Kumbaya," accompanied by a peculiar chirping.

"Brisco's right," said Dan, striking a thoughtful pose with his pipe. "Administration and faculty are traditionally on opposite sides of the fence. It's the nature of the beast."

"Before we begin in earnest," said Brisco, "does anyone have any preliminary questions?"

"Yes," sang Joe Dolch from chemistry. "When are

you going to cut the watermelon?" Joe was impatient at meetings. Chemistry was his bailiwick, but he'd learned almost everything else he knew from the Marx Brothers. He was still wearing his white lab coat, scratching his head. Flakes of dandruff dusted his black horn-rimmed glasses. "Seriously, though, where is Bella in all this? Whose side is she on?"

Diane tsked. "Side, side, side," she repeated as she looked down, shaking her head, as if wondering what to do with wayward children.

"You're repeating yourself, Diane," said Joe, wagging a finger at her.

Diane stared daggers at him. "You're trying my patience."

"I don't mind if I do. You must come over and try mine sometime."

Pete Blatty snorted at that one but quickly abandoned his smile when Diane glared at him.

Jiminy was now singing "Kumbaya," accompanied by the chirping.

"What is that chirping?" interjected Jim Burns, who'd just entered the room.

Brisco waved his hands in front of his colleagues. "Hello! Hello! Forget about sides. Forget about chirping. Remember me? I'm trying to make a point."

"Make your point, Brisco," said Dan. "We're listening."

"Thank you, Dan. Now—"

"I asked about Bella," Joe said.

But Diane, still seething from his sarcasm, broke in with, "Don't you see that Brisco is trying to say something?"

Joe drew himself out of his chair and turned toward the door, setting his lanky frame in motion. "I need some air. But why should I leave? If I do, you'll still be here, Diane."

Brisco began to plead. "Joe, no. Please sit down. We can't afford to lose anybody. We need all hands on deck."

Joe shrugged and resumed his seat. "I have chemicals that can't stay out on the bench for long, so we have to make this short."

"Can we move along?" Jim Burns prompted, waving a hand. "Please?"

"Someone's dying, my Lord—"

"Jiminy?" pleaded Brisco. "Can you keep it down a little?"

"Bella," repeated Joe. "I think it's a legitimate question."

"Okay, okay," said Brisco. "Let's talk about Bella. Does anybody know anything about her stand on reorganization? Has she said anything to anybody?"

Silence.

Slowly, cautiously, expectantly, heads turned toward Hattie, who drew strength from the growing anticipation in the room that she would know something, which of course she did. But such prized information didn't come cheap. *Why should I give away the store for free?* she thought. So she stretched out the moment, allowing the silence to fester. When the tension became too much for anybody to bear, she nodded.

"Kumbaya . . ."

Joe let out a breath. "Well, if somebody doesn't say something, I'm going for a bike ride with Henny."

"Do you want to know, or don't you?" said Hattie, fearful now of losing the attention she'd garnered.

"A penny for your thoughts," said Joe. "Or has the price gone up?"

"That's it!" Hattie slapped the table, got up from her seat, and backed against the wall like a fox cornered by baying hounds. "I may not have a degree like you all, and I might not have a nice office and tenure, and I can be kicked out at a moment's notice, but I'll have you know that I am S-M-A-R-T, smart. You think you know so much, but you don't. That's why I have to tie your shoes at these meetings. Well, I do know where Bella stands on this, and if you kept your eyes open, you would too. But, no, you're too wrapped up in yourselves down there on the low ground while I'm up in the silo seeing everything. And I mean everything."

Winded from this catharsis, Hattie tried to compose herself by primping her hair. Then she headed for the door, pausing at the threshold. She leveled her gaze at the gathering.

Silence reigned, except for Jiminy's low humming and the chirping.

"If you want to know where Bella stands," Hattie said, "think about where she lies. And the answer is flat on her back under Uncle Jumbo!"

Then she was gone.

No one said a word until Joe, ever ready to lighten the mood, said, "Well, she left in a huff. Or was it a minute and a huff?"

"I don't understand," said Diane, gazing into her hands. "What was all that business about lying and Uncle Jumbo?"

"Oh, Diane, you innocent," said Joe. "The horizontal bop? Hiding the pickle? You can't be *that* naive."

Diane had had enough and rigged for battle. "I'll grieve you for sexual harassment."

Joe cocked his head. "And I'll grieve you. Let's all have a good grieve. Unless you think that would be too grievous."

Brisco, who'd thrown himself into a chair, ran his hands up and down his face. "This is clearly the wrong time for a meeting. The school is dying, but it's not going to die this afternoon. Let's try this again tomorrow. Make it a working lunch."

"Someone's crying, my Lord—"

"What *is* that chirping?" asked Dan. "I'm not an ornithologist—mammals are my game—but I think it's a bird."

Frannie Moore cleared her throat. "Is that a motion,

Brisco?"

Brisco, without taking his hands from his face, said, "It's anything you want it to be, Frannie." And then, wearily, "Will someone make it a motion?"

Pete was happy to oblige. "I move that we meet tomorrow over lunch."

Frannie nodded. "Second?"

"Second," Diane echoed.

"Discussion?"

Nothing.

"All in favor?"

A sea of hands went up.

"Any opposed? No? Then it's unanimous. So moved."

Everyone left the room and returned to their affairs, leaving only Brisco and Jiminy behind. Finally, after some moments had elapsed, the provost asked, "When will the meeting begin?"

Brisco turned his head. "Jiminy, what was that chirping? It seemed to be coming from you."

The provost's eyes lit up. "Ah," he said. He reached into a side pocket of his sport coat and retrieved a small blue-and-white parakeet. "Look. He sings."

"That's nice."

"His name is Onan."

"Onan?"

"Yes. I call him that because he spills his seed."

TWELVE
A REQUEST, WITH KID GLOVES

Brisco had not been sleeping well since Hattie had placed her head on his shoulder as they watched the doomsday clock being installed. That gesture had been on his mind ever since but in a well-cordoned-off place, sequestered in a sort of mental queue for later consideration. Or so he thought. Every night, just before bed, the thing migrated out of its synaptic crevice and stood front and center. Intellectually, Brisco knew he didn't want anything more to do with women. He had forsworn them. Twice married, he viewed both associations as unqualified disasters. In those rare lulls of his harried life, he couldn't help but ask himself what had happened. In truth, he didn't know.

He'd married Jasmine, wife number one, when he was twenty-two. They got off to a white-hot start, sexually speaking, but the sex had created a kind of fog, obscuring fundamental differences they'd never gotten around to addressing. In the end, Jasmine told him he had a critical nature, and the next day she was gone. His last words to her were, "Critical? You're leaving me because I'm critical? You're just being obscure." Which begged the question, obscure about what? There must have been something else, something deeper. Jasmine protested that they could remain friends. But with no children to warrant joint decision-making and ongoing contact, there really was no reason to, as they say, stay in touch. She sputtered off into oblivion.

There followed a lull of ten years. Of solitude. Recrimination. Then came Wanda: brash, easily roused to anger, and, yes, critical by nature. "She reminds me of me," Brisco remarked in a quiet moment. Perhaps, then, he'd been looking for himself all along, and so, on the same night they first slept together, they decided to marry. Brisco considered that this would be a more lasting union than the one with Jasmine because, in this case, there was only a pilot light of sexual interest rather than the incandescence of passion, an academic exercise to see what might happen if two like people attempted, in Einstein's words, to make something permanent out of an incident. But lo! Wanda wandered off after scarcely a year. She'd found, she said, that Brisco's was a black-and-white world: you were either with him or against him. She attributed this to some dysfunction arising from his military service, where more than once he'd landed in the brig for failing to follow the orders of superiors he'd deemed idiots. It didn't help when, one night after a rare bout of intercourse, she asked for another round and Brisco replied, "That's all for now," as if he were dismissing a subordinate. As Wanda walked out the door, he tried to quantify his affections by shouting, "We did it more than some people!" As if he cared.

By then he was pretty much ensconced at Grover Cleveland College, teaching his two courses per semester and otherwise taking advantage of the generous—embarrassingly generous —vacation time with no expectation of publishing papers or doing research. But after Wanda left, he found that his prodigious energy, and his willingness to make mountains out of molehills, and his tendency to find personal offense where none was intended, needed constant feeding. He said yes to every committee vacancy, seized leadership opportunities as they arose, and became a general pain in the ass, as far as Cyrus was concerned.

And now he was tossing in bed, unable to sleep, unable to bring his racing mind to heel. While Jasmine and Wanda remained little more than question marks or footnotes in his life, Grover Cleveland College was as clear, as pronounced, and as real as the Rock of Gibraltar. He railed against it, faulted his colleagues for apathy or inactivity at every turn, and tore his hair out at the inanities of administration. All of this mania created an impression in the minds of fellow faculty and staff that he was a malcontent who believed he could've done better, only it was too late, so all he could do was project his own frustrations onto the school and anyone associated with it. He wondered how he, a man who prided himself on his decisiveness and ability to see through complex issues to the core, could ever tell them the truth without seeming sentimental or weak. He loved Grover Cleveland College. *If Hattie's truly interested in me,* he thought, *where on earth will I find the time for her? My God. Time.*

The only chance of getting a handle on events and plotting a rescue strategy for the school was to quell the squabbling faculty and get them to put their collective shoulders to the proverbial wheel. Diane Dempsey—organized, rational, and, in her way, influential—seemed like a reasonable place to start.

Diane was frantic, but it had nothing to do with the school's crisis or—what she took more to heart—the embarrassment she'd suffered from Joe's antagonism at that so-called meeting. She still wanted to grieve him but had become preoccupied with one of her students in English comp. He was one of those recruited from the prison-release program, but due to privacy requirements resulting from some arcane rehabilitative or therapeutic arrangement, no one would tell her what his crime had been. However, true to form, the students whose personal information was so assiduously protected by the college were not the least hesitant to publicly divulge the most intimate details of their lives, including their disabilities, home situations, infirmities, tics, neuroses, and sexual challenges.

And now she was sitting in her tiny office in the basement of the Victorian, staring apoplectically at an essay this student had written, titled "Why I Did It." The author was more than blunt about the fact that he was, of all things, a murderer. Well, she should have suspected it. There he sat, in the first row, with an unkempt black beard, his long legs stretched out like a tarantula's, his roving green eyes—not unattractive—ogling the young woman next to him as he raised his eyebrows at her in a lewd and presumptuous manner. And now this paper. Diane's blood ran cold. The man had killed another man—his friend, no less—by running him down with a rider mower. This student was serving ten to fifteen years for murder in the second degree, but he was allowed release time to attend class.

The second degree? Diane thought. *How could it not have been premeditated? Doesn't it take time to start the mower, put it in gear, and then drive it? Don't those things move at a snail's pace? Wouldn't that have given him time to reconsider what he was doing?*

Oh, what did she know! Both her parents had been tenured English professors—at good, accredited Boston colleges—and she, an only child, had grown up in a Back Bay townhouse fronting the Charles.

But here, now, sitting in her class, was a murderer. She was looking at a passage of his essay:

It was a simpel thing, relly. You get in the mowar, take ame, and driiive. Before you now it, yore man is down.

Ach, the spelling errors! Should she correct them? Would it aggravate him? Did it make any sense to correct the spelling of a murderer? But if she gave him an A for the paper to propitiate him, would he feel patronized?

The whole thing was a mess. How could she get on board Brisco's battlewagon when she had a murderer in class? And what about the novel she was working on— the novel that was going to be her ticket out of Grover Cleveland and into an accredited school, preferably back in Boston or at least as close as possible, where she could breathe Back Bay air again? She thought of her recurring dream—the one where she wakes and the finished novel is lying on her pillow. And then the stark realization that it was only a dream, followed by the drudgery of another English comp class, a collection of students who'd never read a book, couldn't even spell *grammar*, and habitually substituted feelings for facts. She'd once asked them to write a position paper on the probability of an extinction-level meteoric impact in their lifetimes, and most of the responses ran along the lines of what one young woman wrote: *It makes me sad to think a big rock could kill everybody, including children and dogs.* Did she really need a PhD for this? Were these students entitled to having their pitiful work assessed and taken seriously by a tenured associate professor? And now, to add insult to injury—a murderer!

Her poor novel. She'd sworn to write a thousand words a day until it was done. By that reckoning, she should have had a first draft after three months. But it had been eight years now, and she was only on page seventy-six. The writing still captivated her, though, and she even had a title: *A Second Chance for Kraken*, about a woman in Victorian Vermont, Mabel Kraken, who yearns to free herself from the social and domestic constraints on her life in Burlington and flee to the Caribbean, where she could live with abandon, selling tropical fruits on the beach. Diane had, after practically begging, gotten an agent in Portland to take a look at the first fifty pages. The agent's review hadn't been negative, but she did tell Diane she could not, in this day and age, avoid writing about sex. It had never occurred to Diane that a reader might be interested in the sex life of a Victorian woman in Vermont. But even if this were true, where would she start?

At that very moment, Brisco Quik and Joe Dolch were headed toward Diane's office. Brisco had cajoled Joe into making nice with the English prof. "We need order in the ranks," he instructed him. "We can't afford any rifts, Joe. Otherwise we play right into Marcus's hands. You know, the old divide-and-conquer strategy?"

"Leave it to me, boss." Joe squinted through his horn-rimmed glasses, doing his best gangster imitation. "I'm wise. I'm wise."

The two men were an unusual-looking pair as they moved across campus. Brisco was square and plodding, while Joe was tall and lean with unusually long, prehensile arms and joints that went every which way, as if his body parts had been sewn together from separate cadavers and then reanimated.

"We have to keep things quiet for now," Brisco said as they entered the Victorian. "Marcus's spies could be anywhere."

"That's not easy to say."

Brisco threw Joe a questioning look. "What's not easy to say?"

"'Marcus'es.' You know, 'Marcus's spies'? It's like trying to clearly pronounce the word 'tusks.' As in, 'We shot the elephant but couldn't remove the tusks.'"

"Oh, that's not hard." Brisco said, waving him off.

'Tusks!'

"Yeah," rejoined Joe. "But you must be from Alabama, where the Tuscaloosa."

Brisco didn't get it, so he dropped it. "Diane's touchy right now," he said as they paused before her office door. "She's been working on this novel and covets her quiet time."

Joe snorted. "She's been working on that book for years. All English profs are working on a novel. The paradox is, the more they teach freshman English, the worse their own writing becomes. It's like trying to inscribe slowly hardening concrete. Eventually the business comes to a halt and you're stuck teaching English comp for the rest of your life. And no novel as a booby prize."

"You're being cynical."

It struck Joe as a remarkable thing for Brisco to say, since he'd cornered the market on cynicism. "Well, maybe I am, but all English departments are dysfunctional. Why should ours be an exception? Don't you see why? Look. I'm a chemist. My work is like the kabbalah: mysterious, magical, full of unpronounceable terminology. It's like a club. If anyone wants to join, they have to take courses or at least read a hell of a lot. But English? Well, English belongs to all of us. The material isn't arcane like chem or bio; it's part of the common wealth. This means since the material isn't crazy, the teachers have to be. In English language and lit, the profs are the kabbalah."

Brisco looked at Joe in wonder. "I wish all of us had your flea's-eye view of the world."

Joe shrugged. "We just need to spend more time together, brother."

Brisco shook his head. "Let's go in. And please, Joe, your best behavior."

Joe crossed his heart and smiled.

Brisco knocked and nudged Diane's door ajar. She was sitting at her desk, her pen hovering above the murderer's essay, not knowing whether to write any comments which could be misinterpreted or to simply throw the thing away, tell him it had been lost, and offer him a B.

"Diane?" prompted Brisco in a singsong manner. "Knock, knock. Got a mo'?"

The English professor looked up and cast her pained expression upon the two men. "Oh, you're here too, Joe," she said with distaste. "I've decided not to grieve you. To do so right now would distract me from my novel."

Joe Dolch smiled. "Gee, that's mighty decent of you. How is that novel coming along, anyway? I've already created a dedicated space in my library, between *Jonathan Livingston Seagull* and Rod McKuen's *Listen to the Warm*."

"Joe," pleaded Brisco, gesturing for him to stand down.

Diane waved a tissue at him. "It's okay, Brisco. I've

learned how to deal with those who've never published a thing in their lives. I will not deign to descend to their plain."

Joe beamed. "That's beautiful, Diane. Alliteration and rhyme, all in one compact utterance. Have you ever considered writing?"

"Joe!" snapped Brisco.

Diane's smile bore a hint of emerging triumph. "For your information, I already have a number of prominent reviewers lined up. Here, take a look at this."

She retrieved a single sheet from her desk drawer and passed it to the two men, each of whom laid a hand on it and read:

To be reviewed by J.P. Hemcross, Hvers Whorgan, Toolie Greenleaf, Paul Custis, and Ort.

Brisco could sense Joe revving up for a clever comment, so he immediately interceded. "Best of luck, Diane." He handed the sheet back to her. "Actually, we've come with hat in hand. The school's death date is hovering over us like the sword of Damocles. And in the midst of the crisis, the president wants to reorganize us—a clear attempt to cut us down to bite-size pieces for easier handling when the end comes. We need your attention to detail and your capacity for language to help with the resistance."

Brisco couldn't believe he was actually saying this. His usual modus operandi was to be overbearing and demanding, taking faculty to task for their inertia. But here he was, the diplomat, trying to make nice with someone he'd never particularly approved of.

In any case, his ministrations seemed to be paying off, as Diane visibly softened and even threw Joe an indulgent smile. "Well," she said, "I think all of us got a bit hot back there at the meeting."

"Not me," said Joe, raising a finger.

Diane was unshaken. "Okay, Joe," she granted magnanimously, "not you."

"That's the spirit," said Brisco, throwing one arm around Joe's shoulder and fetching up Diane's hand.

"I feel a 'Kumbaya' coming on," said the chemist. "Where's Jiminy?"

Diane continued in her conciliatory vein. "Has anyone spoken to Hattie? She really blew up, didn't she? I still don't know what she meant when she said Bella was lying flat on her back under Uncle Jumbo. Who's Uncle Jumbo?" she asked as she looked from Brisco to Joe.

Struggling valiantly to suppress a smart-ass comment, Joe at last erupted with, "Why, I have no idea. Do we have an Uncle Jumbo on campus? And why would someone lie under him?"

Diane's eyes continued to plead for clarification.

"Oh, who knows?" said Brisco. "Maybe she was confused. But we'll have to bring her back into the ranks. She knows a lot and can be terribly helpful."

"Or terribly dangerous," said Diane. "So what's the next step?"

"We've got to reconvene," said Brisco. "Tomorrow. We can't let this thing get ahead of us."

"How's Jiminy doing?"

Brisco smiled. "He bought a parakeet, which is taking up a lot of his time. Otherwise, he's on board. He's the one who told me about the imposition of reorganization in the first place. We owe him a lot." He drew a folded piece of paper from his shirt pocket. "Diane, I'd like you to take a look at this. It's an outline for a plan of attack. Go over it, put your editing skills to work, and make it say what it must. Most of all, guard it with your life."

"Which is putting it pretty cheap," mumbled Joe.

"That's it!" Diane slapped the desk and rose from her chair. "I'm really going to grieve you now. So prepare yourself. And please don't darken my doorstep again."

"And I'll trouble you not to darken my towels!"

"Out!" Diane turned to Brisco. "I'll do this for you, Brisco, and for the faculty and the college, but when I find the time, I'm going to make it my life's work to have Joe fired."

Having said that, and seeing that Joe was still rooted in place, she pushed her way past the two men and stormed out of the basement.

Joe called after her, "That's just like you, Diane. Just when I tell you to go away, what do you do? You leave me!"

"Joe, you idiot," said Brisco. "You're working against us. I wish you knew when to keep your mouth shut."

"Aw, boss," said Joe, resuming the vernacular of a thug. "She ain't gone on the lam. She's just coolin' her fans. She'll be back and make a great moll. You'll see."

Brisco shook his head. "Let's get out of here."

As the two men left the building, Joe asked, "Did you get a load of that list of reviewers for her book? Who the hell are they? Were they supposed to be famous writers? I've never heard of any of them."

"Probably Maine writers. In Maine, everybody is either an author or a character in somebody else's book. But please, please don't tell her I said that. She'd flip. That novel is her baby."

"Sure, boss." Joe saluted.

Both men looked up at the doomsday clock at the same time. The solitary hand was now approaching the two, well on its way to the school's final reckoning.

"I hate that thing," said Brisco.

Before Joe had a chance to comment, a buzz rattled the air.

"Shh!" Brisco put up a hand and listened. "Five buzzes. I wonder who that is?"

"Not me. I'm fourteen."

Brisco thumbed his chest. "Thirteen."

"Bully for you."

And the two men went their separate ways.

THIRTEEN
A COLLEGIAL VISIT

Early the next morning, Marcus was in the silo, sitting at his desk, gazing out the window and thinking of love—a powerful distraction from his heavy burden. Pacer reclined in his lap, squinting in his catlike way as Marcus absently scratched behind the tabby's ears. *It's a most unusual feeling,* Marcus reflected. What could he compare it to? The smell of a new Impala? The joy of a deal on a pickup? The grudging slap on the back from Mr. Bell when he made, yet again, Salesman of the Year? No, it was more than that, or at least different. He felt a door had been opened, a door marked Possibilities, and when he stepped through it, he was in a wonderland where all was right with the world and every one of his senses was heightened. Had life ever smelled so sweet, looked so grand, tasted so incredibly delicious?

Language had changed too. Bella was now his Harebell because that was the first flower he spotted after being transported by love under the bower. And to Bella, Marcus had become her MooMoo because a heifer being led along a nearby tote road had lowed during their tryst. It all seemed so right, so prescient, so serendipitous, so fated.

"My little Harebell," Marcus mused as he looked out over the campus. "My flower." This put him in a generous, creative mood. It occurred to him that nothing had yet been done to celebrate the gift of the campus community, including all the newcomers from the homeless shelter, the mental health institution, and the state prison. "We must bring this campus together if we're to come out of this in one piece." he said, rising from his desk. He sat down again, realizing he didn't have any place to go. He buzzed Hattie.

The secretary didn't like being buzzed. It made her feel like a servant. But the only other option was for Marcus to shout through the door, so she got up from her desk and plodded into the president's office. "Yes?" she said, her tone weary.

"Hattie," began Marcus, quivering with anticipation, "I've been reading in *The Handbook of College Reorganization* that a college president needs to occasionally arrange campus-wide events to rev up school spirit and make everyone feel included."

He didn't mention it also cautioned that true inclusion only slowed the wheels of administrative initiative and control. Be that as it may, he asked Hattie, "Do you have any special talents?"

Hattie paused to give the question thought. "Well, as a girl I could spit bubbles from the tip of my tongue. A good six feet, at least."

Marcus blushed. "Actually, I was thinking more in terms of maybe a musical instrument or singing or juggling—"

"Juggling? I'm not a performer in a sideshow. I'm a highly trained secretary. I can type sixty words a minute, take shorthand, and use one of those new word-processing computers if you would get me one."

"Hattie, I think there is an abundance of creative energy on this campus. I want to have a talent show. Everybody welcome. Faculty, staff, students. It will be a grand time and take people's minds off that clock for a while. So please, draft a flyer and distribute copies. I want everyone to feel included. We'll have the talent show two weeks from today. Have the grounds crew set up a stage outside, right in the middle of the green."

"What about the bison?"

"Timmy and Boss? They're welcome too!" He rubbed

his hands together with glee. "But I don't know if they'll want to participate. They're off grazing in the woods these days." He looked at Hattie, stars in his eyes. "So what do you think of this idea?"

"I think it's ludicrous. Absolutely ludicrous."

"But you do think it's an idea?"

"Yeah, it's an idea."

"Good! Then it's done. Two weeks."

Hattie didn't mind the sinecure. In fact, she relished it. What would the faculty think when she threw the flyer in their faces? In the middle of their war planning—and the school's death spiral—they were being asked to pull rabbits out of hats and dance like trained dogs. Maybe there would even be a spinning-plate act.

As Hattie exited the silo to see Stash Zakraski about the stage, she ran smack into Bella, who was on her way in, tra-la-la-ing like a schoolgirl. "Well, your step is light today."

Bella kneaded her hands in anticipation of seeing her MooMoo. "There's always so much to do. One has to keep moving, you know."

Hattie squinted and nodded. "I remember a time when you hated those stairs." She glanced at the silo. "But now it's like you're climbing the stairway to heaven."

"It keeps me fit."

Hattie took a step back and looked Bella up and

down. "Well, then I'd say you'd better keep climbing."

Bella glowered at the secretary. "That's harassing language. I could grieve you for that."

Hattie waved her off. "Oh, you can't grieve a damn thing. Anyway, don't you want to know about Brisco?"

In her ardor, Bella had forgotten about the parking issue. She immediately softened. "Thank you for reminding me. What did you find out?"

"Nothing," said Hattie, and Bella's expression fell. "I talked to Jim Burns, Hector Lopez, Diane, the whole kit and caboodle, but everyone is tighter than a clam. Either they're not talking, or they don't know anything."

Bella bit her lip. If what Hattie said was true, then she would have to go to the source and pry it out of Marcus.

Hattie spoke up, leveling her gaze at Bella. "Listen. The whole gang knows about you and Uncle Jumbo."

"Knows?" Bella took hold of her pearls and glanced skittishly about.

Hattie shook her head and let out a breath. "Well, I suppose it's your business. But I do know one other thing. Presidents come and go, but we're here for the duration, even if"—she paused to look up at the clock—"durations are not as long as they used to be." She turned her attention to Bella. "By the way, there's going to be a talent show. His idea, not mine. I look forward to seeing you up there, warbling or whatnot."

Bella's heart sank. "Are you serious?"

"Scout's honor," she said as she gave the appropriate sign, laughed, and continued on to Stash.

Bella rested her head in one hand. *What on earth will the faculty say when they hear this?* She gazed toward the top of the silo, and her heart rose again. "MooMoo," she murmured and began her ascent.

In the meantime, Brisco was standing in front of the Brain Shrine, talking to Jim Burns and Dan Stupak. "On board?" he asked after a long speech about teamwork and pitching in.

"Why not?" said Jim. "What do we have to lose?"

"Our jobs," Dan muttered without taking the pipe from his mouth.

Brisco shook his head. "It's bigger than that. If we hang together, we have the best chance of saving the school. We need unanimity if we're to push back against the president."

"Then we have to include everyone," said Dan.

Brisco threw him a questioning look.

"Spox," the biologist hissed through his turtle lips.

"That will be tough," said Jim. "Excluding Spox has become such a part of the culture here that it will be hard to suddenly slap him on the back and call him pally."

Brisco swallowed hard. "Still, Dan's right. Dan, can you run point on this? Can you reach out to Henny and make nice?"

"Sure, but no promises. My impression is that he can be pretty stubborn and hasn't wasted any time lamenting the love lost between himself and our happy little family. Since we never ask anything of him, he's used the time to advance his research."

After acknowledging the challenge, Brisco shook hands with each man and checked his watch. "Okay, let's synchronize. We're on for noon today. Remember: encourage everybody to attend. This will be an important meeting."

"Just like the last one," said Jim, snorting.

"I've told Joe Dolch to zip it," said Brisco.

Jim Burns chortled. "And I've told the sun to turn blue."

Just then Hattie breezed by.

"Why the hurry?" called Brisco.

Hattie backtracked to the group. It was delicious, absolutely delicious, to think of the bomb she was about to drop. "Oh, I'm on a little errand for Uncle Jumbo. I'll have some news for all of you later."

"Couldn't you give us a little preview?" Brisco asked.

Hattie scrunched her shoulders together. "Oh, I guess I could." She looked at each man in turn. "But I won't. You'll just have to wait." And then she sailed off.

Dan clamped down on his pipe. "She's impossible," he said through gritted teeth. "Has she forgotten you're tenured senior faculty?"

"She doesn't care," said Jim sadly. "It doesn't mean anything to her."

Brisco looked after the retreating secretary wistfully. "Twelve o'clock," he said, turning to his colleagues. "Please instruct all the troops to be there."

Back at the silo, Bella had finally arrived in Marcus's office, out of breath, her legs aching from the long ascent, her plantar fasciitis giving her particular grief. But those legs didn't have to bear all her weight for long, because Marcus swept Bella into his arms and nuzzled her with abandon. "My lovely Harebell! My flower!"

"MooMoo!" cooed Bella. "My cow."

The two snuffled and embraced and generally communed for the next fifteen minutes. "This is so unseemly," Bella remarked, but without conviction.

"Even used-car salesmen are entitled to a little happiness."

"Please don't refer to yourself as a car salesman. I'm in love with a college president."

Marcus closed his eyes and pulled her head into the crook of his neck. "All things must pass," he mused.

"Not this moment. It would be unfair for it to pass, because I've waited so long for it."

"Harebell!"

Hattie walked in without knocking.

Bella pushed herself from Marcus's arms and

straightened herself out.

"President Marcus," Hattie said in a businesslike manner, feigning obliviousness, "the faculty has called an emergency meeting about reorganization today."

"Emergency? Hmm. I don't know how that sounds. Is it a good thing? Are they going to support my plan?"

"I don't think so. Uh-uh."

"Well, I guess the only thing, then, is to wait and see. Did you distribute the flyers for the talent show?"

"I was going to, but then I thought it best to give them out at the faculty meeting when everyone's in the same place."

"Good thinking. That's what I call efficiency."

Pacer, prowling the desktop, meowed.

"Speaking of efficiency . . ." Bella fingered her pearls and cast a dark look at Hattie.

The secretary marched out and closed the door behind her.

Bella turned to Marcus and delivered an indulgent smile. "MooMoo, I need to dot an *i* in my faculty welfare report."

"Welfare is very important," affirmed Marcus.

"Yes, it is. And I'm so glad you think so, MooMoo. You see, I'm trying to justify all the handicapped-parking spaces on campus. We've had some fraud in the past and—"

"Fraud!" Marcus fetched Pacer from the desk and

clutched the tabby to his chest. "Oh, I don't like the sound of that."

"Neither do I." Bella limped a couple of steps closer to him. "So I'd just like to dot this last *i* by justifying the parking space for Brisco Quik."

"Ah. Professor Quik. Yes. I thought we'd cleared that up. He has a delicate condition, which has compromised one of his major life functions."

"Yes," said Bella, diverting energy to shoring up her smile. "I think you told me this once before. But I was wondering if you could give me something a little more specific to write in this nagging blank space on form USHHS-413(k)."

"Form 413!"

"K."

"Hmm. This does paint me into a corner. This information is supposed to be confidential."

"Yes," agreed Bella, "but I thought I might qualify as having a need to know."

"Oh. I'll have to research this one, I'm afraid."

Bella knew she was at an impasse. Best to shift gears, at least temporarily. "MooMoo, I'm concerned. It's that clock. I think it's weighing on everybody. I mean, when that hand has completed its circle—"

"Yes, yes, I share everyone's concern. That tocking is very loud, especially up here. A constant reminder of where time is taking us. Hattie said our student numbers are up. That's a huge help. If we can continue to move in that direction and get the reorganization off the ground, we'll at least buy some time, and maybe that hand can be turned back a bit. I'm counting on the faculty to come up with ideas. I read here in *The Handbook of College Reorganization*"—he seized the book from his desk and caressed its cover—"that presidents should encourage the faculty in this regard, so that the president doesn't have to think so hard. Perhaps I should try a more personal touch to inspire them. What do you think?"

Bella smiled. "If anyone can do it, you can. But please don't forget about me. I'll have my thinking cap on as well."

"I knew I could count on you, Harebell."

Bella blushed and gazed into Marcus's eyes. "I need to go," she said, stepping away from him as he looked longingly after her. She swooped in for a final peck before mouthing, *MooMoo*, one last time.

Hattie pretended to arrange papers on her desk as Bella passed by. "Well, life is an interesting thing."

"I have to go," said Bella, waving over her shoulder. She limped to the stairs, feeling as if she were stepping on a red-hot poker.

"See you at the talent show," said Hattie without looking up, "Hairball."

Bella bristled but was already making her descent. She didn't want to lose momentum by pausing to return fire.

In the meantime, Dan Stupak had ventured over to Henny Spox's space, a tumbledown shack some distance behind the Victorian, near an old cow path. There was a small, hand-lettered sign above the door: Institute for Invariant Semi-Tessellated Mathematics.

"Hmpf," huffed Dan dismissively. "Institute." He took a deep breath and gave a sharp knock at the plywood door with his pipe. No answer. He knocked again. Shave-and-a-haircut this time. Still no answer. Since the door was already ajar, Dan encouraged it to open a bit more. Then he lifted one stumpy leg and stepped over the threshold.

He had never been inside. So far as he knew, neither had any of the other faculty. It was a modestly appointed affair with a long workbench against the wall and several pieces of unusual-looking equipment, all with tiny, blinking, red and green lights, making the place look rather Christmassy. On a small, cluttered desk was a half-eaten egg salad sandwich lying in state on waxed paper.

"Hello!" called Dan. " The door was open, so I—"

Henny emerged from behind a metal cabinet, his bifocals perched on the tip of his nose, some papers in his hands. He glanced about. "Who are you?" he asked the ovoid figure hovering before him with red suspenders stretched to the snapping point.

Dan took the pipe from his mouth. "It's me. Dan. Dan Stupak. I'm one of your"—he could barely utter the word—"colleagues."

"Colleague?" echoed Henny, his expression searching. "Are you math?"

"No," said Dan, glancing over his shoulder to confirm the door was still open should he feel the need to beat a quick exit. "Bio."

"Bio?"

"Biology."

"Ah. Have we met before?" Henny barely opened his mouth when he talked.

Dan strained and squinted to make out what he was saying. "Met? Well, in a manner of speaking. I suppose so. You dropped some books on the way to class a few years back, and I pointed this out to you."

"Ah."

There followed an interlude of uncomfortable silence, during which Dan glanced about the room, his gaze coming to rest on a blackboard filled with unfamiliar symbols reminiscent of the alien markings from the UFO wreckage at Roswell.

Henny noticed this. "You . . . like math?" he inquired.

"Well, I wouldn't exactly say that," Dan said cheerfully, still examining the symbols. He'd become a biologist specifically because it wouldn't require him to confront mathematics, which had always confounded him.

He quickly looked to Henny. "But I have an appreciation for it. I wouldn't want to be taken for an intellectual malingerer."

Ma-ling, mouthed Henny.

"Be that as it may, I just thought I'd—"

"Would you like to see what I do? It involves fungus."

Dan considered this for a moment. No, he concluded, despite his mycological leanings he didn't have the faintest interest in Henny's work. In fact, he'd supported Cyrus's proposal to strike math from the curriculum. Did Henny recall Dan's connection to that affair? Was he toying with him now? Dan looked at Henny and attempted a smile, but the old mathematician only examined him imploringly.

"I'd be fascinated," said Dan, swallowing hard.

What ensued was an effusion of language that was opaque to the biologist. Henny may as well have been speaking Apache. Dan reminded himself he had a PhD, damn it, so he needed to at least feign some level of comprehension. He nodded, chirped an occasional "Yep," and added at the end of the lecture a coronating, "Fantastic," hoping to God Henny wouldn't cross-examine him.

But all the mathematician remarked was, "You are a quick study."

Dan beamed self-indulgently. He had, however, gathered the words *bot* and *nano*. But what in God's name did they have to do with fungus? His impulse was to retreat to the more familiar and reassuring shoal waters of his biology laboratory, where, if an experiment failed, at least he could account for what he had, or hadn't, done. And failing everything, he could still brew a decent cup of coffee on his distillation apparatus. But Henny was absolutely marinated in his work. Everything in the cluttered, paper-strewn room seemed geared to his research. In truth, the air of ambition in the place made Dan's skin crawl, and although he wouldn't admit it in so many words, he resented the mathematician's single-minded dedication to his work. Who did he think he was? What did he hope to achieve? And what did he expect Grover Cleveland College to do if he were to ever receive a major award? Acknowledge him? What, in fact, was he doing eating an egg salad sandwich?

"Er, Henny," he said, mustering a honeyed smile, "the faculty want you to come home."

There it was, then. No preamble, no stumbling about for the right words, no hemming and hawing. Dan felt a warm glow of pride in his ability to get to the point.

"Home?" Henny moaned, looking about. "This is home."

Dan followed the mathematician's gaze. "Well, yes, er, I can see that. But it's more like a subset of a bigger home." He immediately wished he'd chosen a word other than *subset*, for fear it might encourage more dreaded math talk.

But just then, when Dan thought he'd seen

everything there was to see in the claustrophobic shack, a door opened and a youngish, svelte but very shapely woman stepped into the common room. She had dark hair draped over one shoulder and a sultry, come-hither look in eyes which rested on high, broad cheekbones.

Henny beamed at her and reached out to fish her closer. Once they were standing together, he turned to Dan and announced, "This is YaYa."

The woman smiled sweetly. Closing her eyes, she nodded toward Dan.

The biologist adjusted his focus to get the couple in the same frame, remarking to himself on the juxtaposition of types: the aged, frazzled mathematician with the dewlapped face and this gorgeous, olive-skinned Venus who had just stepped out of her clamshell. "Nice to meet you," he managed.

The woman nodded again. "You too. Do you like working with Henny? He's a genius, isn't he?"

Dan removed the pipe from his mouth and examined the bowl for a moment. "Well, that's something to say, then, isn't it?" he stumbled. "There's certainly work to be done in such a rarified area of study, I'd say."

Neither Henny nor YaYa had a response to that.

Dan took this as his cue to back toward the door. Then he remembered why he was there in the first place. "Oh, Henny, please come to the faculty meeting today at noon. We'd love to see you there. Important matters will be discussed."

Both Henny and YaYa stared impassively at Dan, who continued to move toward the door, finally reaching the blessed threshold. "Very nice visit," he said. "Keep up the good work."

Two seconds later he was out again, gulping fresh Grover Cleveland air.

"How did it go?" Brisco asked when Dan arrived in his office. "Is he on board?"

"I saw him. I extended the invitation, but he didn't commit. You know, I had thought all these years that the shack was just his work space. But the guy lives there. He even had an egg salad sandwich."

Brisco nodded. "Well, I guess we should show a wee bit of compassion. I mean, it's got to be lonely."

Dan took his pipe in hand. "Oh, I don't think he's lonely, Brisco."

FOURTEEN
YAYA AGAIN, AND BELLA SWALLOWS HER PRIDE

Shortly before noon, faculty migrated from all points on campus toward the Victorian. Marcus alit from the silo and went off to visit Henny.

He arrived at the Institute for Invariant Semi-Tessellated Mathematics and gave a stiff knock. He was anxious to be apprised of Henny Spox's progress on his most interesting project, hoping there might be something in it to proffer the bank to forestall its seizure of the college.

It was YaYa who opened the door. She immediately brightened. "Don't tell me. You are—you must be—President Marcus Cleveland."

"Is it so obvious?" asked Marcus, throwing up his hands. "Do I know you?"

"I'm with Henny."

The mathematician sidled into the picture. "Ah, Mr. President! I see you've met YaYa."

"Not by name, no. I didn't know you had an assistant."

YaYa and Henny stepped aside, bidding Marcus enter.

"Calling YaYa an assistant is like calling a brain surgeon a mechanic. YaYa is much, much more. She is my right-hand woman, my second-guesser, my inspiration, my muse."

"That's quite a testimonial. Well, since you've said it all, I have no further questions. I can do no less than welcome YaYa to our happy family."

YaYa smiled with closed eyes and gave a slight bow.

Oh, how charming, thought Marcus. *She lends a touch of elegance to the college. I wonder if the faculty have met her? They would no doubt be charmed as well!*

Henny invited Marcus to take a look at one of his experiments. The two men walked to a bench topped with a riot of glowing tubes, blinking electronic devices, and percolating solutions. "This is it," said Henny, transfixed.

"It?" echoed Marcus.

"It," confirmed Henny.

"Tell me what it all means," said Marcus with alacrity. "I mean, in words a college president could understand."

That was all the encouragement Henny needed. He

launched into an enthusiastic—and largely unintelligible—effusion of jargon and oblique descriptions of his work. Marcus's expression froze into a mask of smiling incomprehension.

Sensing this, YaYa went over and began to translate. "You see," she said in a low, mellifluous voice, "Henny is incubating a species of fungus he found growing in the woods right here at the college. It's a most unusual species, because the spores are the perfect size and shape to be carried by his nanobots. But there's more. The fungus contains a cancer-fighting substance that has performed miraculously in the petri dish."

"Miraculously," repeated Marcus without taking his eyes from the apparatus's lights and bright colors.

"But there's one problem," said YaYa.

"Problem?"

"Yes. The fungus reproduces very slowly under laboratory conditions. Henny can't even propose industrial-level production until we can either make the organism produce more spores or find a large natural supply of the fungus itself. Unfortunately, it seems to be a very rare species."

"Rare," said Marcus, rubbing his chin. "But you said it grows here on campus, no?"

"Yes." Henny stabbed a finger earthward. "A very unusual find, and I've discovered only very little of it. It may have been living here for thousands, millions of years."

"Millions!"

"Yes," Henny said, "but I fear I scraped up the only vestige of it. I've never seen any more."

"Hmm . . ." Marcus considered, still rubbing his chin. "Perhaps you need a collaborator to help you in your search. Have you spoken with Professor Stupak? He seems to know something of the fungi." Marcus was recalling the destroying angel The Egg had unceremoniously crushed underfoot.

"Professor Stupak was here," said Henny. "But on other business. The faculty members are meeting at this very moment. They even invited me. But I don't know what they're talking about. Professor Stupak said only that it concerned important matters."

"Ah, yes," said Marcus. "I noticed the faculty migrating toward the Victorian. I understand they're meeting to discuss my reorganization plan. But they'll also be learning about the talent show."

"Talent show?"

"Indeed. Everyone is invited to perform. Why, you could contribute something, I'm sure," he added, bristling with enthusiasm. "Would you? Would you, please?"

"Well," Henny reflected, casting a glance at YaYa. "I suppose I could talk about this fungus."

Marcus made a humming sound. "I'm afraid to say that might not draw them in, Professor Spox," he said, but gently. "Perhaps you could offer something with broader appeal."

Henny nodded. "I will think about it."

"Good! Thinking at a college is to be encouraged, or so I read in this most wonderful book I'm consulting." Having had the final word, Marcus left.

In the meantime, Bella, after much consideration and self-recrimination, had decided to seek counsel regarding the ocean of love she was now plying. She was so confused. She knew she loved Marcus, but she also felt an ill wind rising at her back, as if the world were swelling in disapproval of her reignited passion. She was of two minds about this. On the one hand, she wanted to tell any detractors to kiss her ample buttocks. On the other, she recognized there was power in numbers and relationships had been plundered by the conjoined forces of onlookers who, for one reason or another, decided to take a destructive interest in other people's affairs. And destruction, in her case, would mean only one thing: the chicken farm.

But to whom could she go? She had no close friends. However, she refused to indulge in self-pity at this deficit, because she had learned through experience that college administrators were characteristically friendless. It was, someone had once told her, the nature of the job—something akin to the loneliness of command. Then she recalled the many occasions she had seen Hattie Sims in the company of some man or other. Once, in the local Shop 'n Save, she'd spotted her in the produce section, cooing and cuddling with a motorcycle type in a leather jacket while holding an eggplant in her free hand. Bella had partially obscured herself behind a display of dried flowers, observing their behavior to learn something, if she could, from two people who were clearly oblivious to the world around them as they dissolved in each other's attentions.

Could she? Would she? Was it possible for her to swallow her pride and approach Hattie for—gulp— something resembling advice? At first blush, she was revolted by the idea. and smarted at the possibility that Hattie might seize her approach as an opportunity to humiliate her. They had engaged in verbal repartee for so long, for so many years, that they knew no other way to relate to one another.

Still, Hattie was a woman, certainly an experienced woman. And there was no one else Bella could broach the delicate topic with. She was so confused, fearing she would soon have to choose between Marcus and her career. Didn't men eventually exit relationships? Didn't they tend to trade their women in for younger models? Oh, what did she know of such things! Unless one believed in the prophetic properties of chicken gizzards, such knowledge seemed almost impossible to come by, except by experience, and having no experience in matters of love, she felt hopelessly adrift on a sea of consternation and doubt.

Thus it was that she pulled herself together and marched to the grain silo. She stood at its base and gazed up at its heights. Then she and her plantar fasciitis began the slow, agonizing ascent.

Unbeknownst to Bella, Hattie wasn't at her station. She'd decided to visit Brisco, hoping to catch him in the lull before the meeting. When she entered his office in the Victorian, she found him pacing before his desk, talking to himself.

"Wouldn't it be nicer to talk to somebody who could talk back?" she said with a hint of playfulness.

Brisco gave a start, and his heart began to race. But maybe that was only because he was so worked up about the meeting. However, the cloud of sweet, sweet perfume that wafted in with Hattie didn't help. "You caught me at a bad moment. I'm beset with this reorganization. And that clock."

Hattie drew closer. "Why are you killing yourself over it?"

Brisco considered taking a step back in tandem with Hattie's approach, but his feet seemed anchored in place. "It's my nature. War is a stiff wind. If you don't lean into it, you'll be swept away."

Hattie drew an expression of pained concern. "This isn't war, Brisco. The war's over."

"No!" Brisco brought a fist down upon his desk.

"That's the problem. War created this school. We can't seem to live without it. See for yourself: this whole reorganization thing is nothing more than divide and conquer."

"But in the end, doesn't everyone, even the general, want peace?" Hattie couldn't believe she was being so clever with Brisco, when what she wanted to do was throw her arms around him and pry his mouth open with her tongue. "Look," she continued, "haven't you noticed that this reorganization thing hasn't split you faculty members up? It's driven you together into a clump."

Brisco paused to consider this. "Maybe that's why I can't seem to breathe." Then it hit him. "That's it!" He locked his gaze on Hattie. "You're right. This isn't divide and conquer. It's compress and smother."

"I didn't say that," said Hattie, who'd advanced two floor tiles toward Brisco and could now feel the heat of his breath. "But I'm willing to take credit for it," she said as, in a flash, she threw two tentacles around him and went to work on his mouth.

Brisco didn't give in so much as simply allow Hattie to indulge herself for a grand total of seven seconds before he slowly but firmly pushed her away and said, as if he were talking to Wanda all over again, "That's it."

"It?"

"Hattie," said Brisco slowly, "you're arousing emotions in me that I can't afford to have aroused."

Hattie braced her hands on her hips. Her impulse was to lash out, but she sensed it was not yet game and there was still some possibility of success here. "Well, at least you give me credit for arousing those emotions."

"Yes," said Brisco, poker-faced. "You get credit."

And with that, Hattie backed off and left the Victorian, not knowing exactly how she was supposed to feel.

When Bella had pulled herself onto the top step of the silo, she draped her arms over the railing to catch her breath. A few minutes later, Hattie, still smarting from her less-than-satisfactory encounter with Brisco, overtook her. She opted for a course of nonrecognition, if only to imply that she was as busy and important as anyone else on campus.

This interlude gave Bella a chance to collect her thoughts and settle on the best approach for eliciting advice from the secretary. It finally came to her, elegant in its simplicity: she wouldn't ask for advice at all; she'd maneuver Hattie into offering it in an unsolicited fashion and play the part of passive recipient of her wisdom.

"He's not in," Hattie finally said as she plopped down at her desk to shuffle papers. "He's talking to that kook Spox."

As Bella made her way into the office, a sharp pain seized her right leg.

Hattie picked up on this. "You hurtin'?" she asked,

more out of curiosity than concern.

"It's nothing. I'm learning to admit I'm not the woman I thought I was. In fact," she added reflectively, "I don't mind confiding in you that I have an awful lot to learn. About a lot of things."

Hattie arched her eyebrows. "Well, we all do, I suppose," she said, although she still believed she knew more than most people did.

"I heard about the tongue-lashing you gave the faculty," Bella said in a low voice. "I have to tell you there was something in me cheering you on."

"Even though you weren't there," quipped Hattie, intent on maintaining the upper hand.

"True," said Bella, ever nimble. "But like I said, I heard about it. It made me wonder about just who you are and what you must know."

Hattie narrowed her eyes and regarded Bella the way she might a shark that had been brought into the boat but was still flailing. "Know about what?"

"Oh, I don't know," mused Bella. "A lot of things. Life, the school, the ways of faculty, even ..." and here she hesitated before blurting out, "love."

Hattie sat back and began to power up. "That's quite a combination of things I know about. And it goes to show that faculty, for example, are another species."

"How's that?" fished Bella.

Hattie leaned forward, her palms resting on her desk

as if she were about to hold a séance. "Look, take biology professors, for example. They have tragic love affairs with their students. I've seen it time and again. And you know why? Because they talk about sexual reproduction—from germs to humans, like a song, and those young girls lap it up and want to know more—after hours, if you know what I mean.

"At the other end you have the mathematicians. They never deal with reproduction and handle their sexual repression by attending conferences and investing in vanity plates that say things like L-U-V-M-A-T-H.

"Now, in the middle you have the sociologists and psychologists. You ever notice how little they say at meetings? That's because they're sizing everybody up. But you can't keep all those observations bottled up inside you, so they become insufferable gossips.

"And then you have your English profs. They're the angry ones because, well, they have to read hundreds— no, thousands—of essays about abusive boyfriends and organ enhancement products. They have insecurity complexes, because they're using the classroom as an excuse for their own failure to write the sequel to *Gone with the Wind*, and it's made worse because they feel they're not educating their students but rather are being de-educated by them.

"Then there's the foreign language professors, like Hector Lopez. They're the romantics who get seduced by their students because they teach love poetry in languages students don't understand. Since their students don't learn to say a darn thing in French or Spanish, they look to improve their grades by other means. This makes the foreign language profs feel guilty, and they wind up talking to themselves in public."

After a pause for breath, Hattie darkened and clenched her fists. "The historians and political scientists, now, they think they know *everything* because they have that long view. And maybe they do know a lot, but this makes them snobs. Or maybe their hearts are just dead because they have absolutely no ability to live in the present. If you ask me, they're all impotent or gay or both. I mean," she said, looking up at Bella, her eyes suddenly pained, "I've always thought of myself as attractive." She clamped her mouth shut on this last word, sensing she'd played out too much line.

Bella had been holding her breath through Hattie's discourse. When she realized Hattie was done, she finally exhaled. "That covers a lot of ground."

Hattie sat back in her chair and glanced about, quickly composing herself as she ran a wrist across both eyes. "And that's only a start. You've still got the administrators."

Bella's eyes widened. *Pay dirt!* "You mean, there's more?" she probed, anxious to stoke the fire now that the kindling had caught.

"More?" exclaimed Hattie, now fully in control. "Are you kidding? If I had another chair, I'd tell you to sit down and listen."

"I'll stand," said Bella, bridling her enthusiasm.

Hattie leaned forward and held forth on chapter two. "You know, this isn't the first college I've worked at. Let me tell you, administrators are all alike. They take care of each other. The school could be slashing spending left and right, with faculty and staff being thrown by the wayside, students fleeing like mice, and programs being dumped willy-nilly. And you know what? After all the damage is done and the smoke clears, not one administrator has lost his job. In fact, he's given a raise! And there's more. When, say, a university president resigns, they actually keep him on, circling the campus like a dead planet, drawing a handsome salary for doing nothing. Nothing! They make up a position and call him something like university professor of interdisciplinary studies. You want to know the definition of incest? Well, there it is."

Bella considered that Hattie had forgotten she, too, was an administrator. But she had no illusions of being kept on should there be a sea change at Grover Cleveland. What if the school didn't die at the end of the semester but simply shrank? No, there would be no circling of the campus for her. It was the chicken farm for sure.

But all this was beside the point. Hattie hadn't yet

told her anything she needed to know. She'd have to prime the pump a little more. "Hattie, do you think it's wrong for a faculty member and a student to, well, become"—Bella dropped her voice and glanced about—"romantically involved?"

Hattie looked perplexed. Was there a tawdry professor/student affair on campus she didn't know about? The last one had been between a long-gone anatomy prof, Simon Glicks, and a sweet little thing who'd asked him to demonstrate the Heimlich maneuver in the privacy of his office. He obliged her, and the next thing anyone knew, the two were off to Bangor and Jim Burns was forced to teach the muscles and bones course—a legendary disaster still talked about by Grover Cleveland alumni.

"Well," Hattie said, "I'm not sure *wrong* is the right word. It certainly complicates things. But," she continued, as if trying to recoup lost ground, "what does one do when love begins to stir? I guess there are two choices: walk away from it or give in to it."

Yes, thought Bella, *that's the stark choice. That's exactly it*. But why would she even consider resisting the wave of love that had taken so long to arrive on the shores of her postponed desires? Maybe it was because, if she was any judge of which way the wind blew, the college, in a couple of months, would cease to exist. What then? Well, there were only two choices: back to the chicken farm or—and here the pilot light of hope burned a little more brightly—build something new with Marcus. Bella felt a weight lift from her shoulders. She was *safe*.

She looked up at Hattie and cast an earnest smile. "Thank you, Hattie. You're very wise. We should talk more often."

Hattie shrugged and smiled self-indulgently. "And there's so much more."

"I'm sure there is." But Bella had no need or desire to hear more at the moment. She felt she could enjoy smooth sailing now. She turned about and began her slow descent to ground level.

But Hattie pushed past Bella with the talent show flyers in the crook of her arm. "S'cuse me. I gotta get to that faculty meeting. I have something for them."

FIFTEEN
A GRAND PLAN

The meeting in the Victorian had more than a quorum of faculty, all milling about, chattering, grabbing at the sandwiches in the middle of the conference table. The adjuncts dutifully waited until the tenured faculty had completed their first assault before swooping in to gather the scraps.

Frannie Moore had resumed her place at the head of the room, prepared, this time, to hold her ground should Brisco try to usurp her position again. "Please," she said just above a whisper as she jabbed the air with her pen. "Please."

If Hector Lopez hadn't noticed Frannie moving her lips, the ruckus might have gone on forever. "Peoples!"

he called out in an uncharacteristic show of assertiveness, waving his hands. "Peoples!"

Brisco took up the slack. "Everybody!" he boomed.

But it was the entrance of Jiminy Schmitz, with Onan perched on his shoulder, that drew the assembly together, and everybody took a seat.

"Come in, Jiminy," said Brisco. "You're faculty, too."

Jiminy shuffled to a folding chair in a corner of the room. "I'm already in. Carry on."

Brisco stood up and intoned, "Now," as if he were going to launch into a major speech.

But Frannie, still holding her pen, poked the air in his direction. "Brisco, I'll open the meeting."

"All right, Frannie," he conceded, resuming his seat and crossing his arms, "but we need command decisions."

"Oh, Brisco," tsked Diane Dempsey, who was bent over a disorderly pile of student papers. "Please. This isn't the Battle of the Bulge."

Brisco opened his mouth for counterattack.

"Can we move on?" interjected Jim Burns, who was stretched out in a chair with his hands knotted behind his head.

Frowning, Brisco scanned the faces before him. "Am I the only one who knows this is war?"

Frannie had him now. "We're not going to have a war," she said, flapping her hands as if she were airing dust cloths.

"But we've *got* to have a war," pleaded Joe Dolch, grinning mischievously. "We've already paid a month's rent on the battlefield!"

Brisco spoke through gritted teeth. "None of you knows what the president is proposing to do."

The faculty looked at one another. "Do you mean the reorganization?" ventured Dan Stupak in measured tones, shifting his pipe from one corner of his mouth to the other.

"*Reorganization* no longer does justice to what's afoot," said Brisco. "I had mistakenly thought he was going to cut us up into warring factions. I was wrong, difficult as it is for me to admit."

"What's going on, then?" Scott Ott removed his watch and began to fiddle with it.

"What I see," said Brisco, "is an attempt to compress and smother us into a tiny core faculty, stripped of tenure, that will operate within a miniscule budget in an attempt to save some remnant of the school."

The adjuncts in the back of the room gasped.

"Core faculty?" Stupak said. "What does that mean?"

"It means the president's giving up. Whatever we're becoming—if we survive at all—will be a mere shadow of what we are now. The remaining faculty will be more caretakers than teachers and researchers."

"My God," said Vikram Chabot, thinking of his beloved Grover Cleveland College Press. "It's like that infernal clock is running the show. It's already at a quarter past the hour. So you're telling us that when time is up, either we'll be extinct or there will be a few of us milling around, nattering to ourselves for lack of students?"

"Ha!"

All heads turned to Jiminy. He prompted Onan to perch on his finger and addressed the bird. "They think it's that simple."

Onan chattered gaily.

Brisco called, "Jiminy, do you know something we don't know?"

Jiminy scratched under Onan's beak. The parakeet chirped and began to preen. "Of course we do. The president told us everything."

Silence. Seconds passed, but Jiminy didn't elaborate. Brisco threw Frannie Moore a glance and cocked his head, as if to say, *Well, you want to lead the troops, so lead!*

Frannie gave the table a few sharp raps with her pen. "Provost Schmitz, it would please the assembly to hear what you have to say."

Jiminy had sprinkled some cracker crumbs into his beard and was watching Onan peck them out. Finally, he said, "It's a grand plan."

"*Grand*, as in *great*?" asked Pete Blatty, quickly looking about for assurance that this was an appropriate question.

"I have a sinking feeling," said Brisco, shaking his head. "I don't think it means *great*, or else Marcus would have told us himself and not sent Jiminy to do his dirty work."

Onan, hopping about Jiminy's beard, seemed to be preparing a nest.

"Grand plan," repeated Jiminy. "Grand."

"Okay, okay," said Jim Burns, unknotting his hands from behind his head. "We know it's grand. Just tell us what it's about."

All attention was on Jiminy and Onan. The provost looked up with sparkling eyes. "I am the president's emissary. I have been to the mountain."

Joe Dolch leaned over to Dan Stupak and spoke out of the corner of his mouth. "He means the silo."

"This reorganization," continued Jiminy, "is the most inspired I have ever heard of. There's never been anything like it. It will save our beloved school."

Joe emitted another aside. "He sounds like a circus barker describing a freak show."

Brisco bounced out of his chair. "Jiminy, for Pete's sake, just speak in plain language and let us have it raw. Are you saying he's going to slice us up after all? And if so, in how many pieces?" He collapsed into his seat again.

Jiminy speared the air with a lean, crooked finger. "One."

The word reverberated through the room.

Onan hopped merrily about in Jiminy's beard.

Brisco, dumbstruck, gestured for Jiminy to continue.

"There will no longer be departments," Jiminy

explained. "No chairs, no directors, no deans, nothing like that. We will all finally be one. As I look at all of you, I see the lines of division fading away. You . . . we . . . all of us are about to become the Faculty of Humanity, united by a common phone."

Brisco felt his throat closing. "I told you. Compress and smother!"

Dan Stupak took his pipe from his mouth and examined it.

Hector Lopez leaned over to Pete Blatty for translation, pleading, "What does this mean? What did he say?"

Brisco finally recovered his voice, but in the heat of battle his courage and leadership once again failed him. Turning to the front of the room, he bleated, "Frannie, do something!"

Frannie began to speak but in tones so low it appeared she was talking to herself.

"But why?" piped up Pete Blatty. "Why this consolidation?" Turning to Brisco, he said, "You were right! He's making us small enough—"

"About the size of a golf ball," said Brisco. "And he's preparing to tee up and drive us into oblivion. Then it will be just a matter of closing the doors and throwing the bolts."

"Then we're looking at the end of . . . of Grover Cleveland College Press?" Vikram Chabot's fluffy ring of white hair was set off by his beet-red face.

Diane Dempsey clutched her pile of student papers. "Vikram, if the college goes, the press goes with it, of course."

Scott Ott cleared his throat as he clamped his watch back around his wrist. "I'd like some clarification of the plan. There must be some way to avoid all this. I'm willing to sit on a committee."

"It's clear," said Dan, gesturing with his pipe, "that the president views this as a done deal. In which case, I suggest we make a counterplan to demonstrate how we can reduce costs from our side and show him that compression of our ranks is unnecessary."

"I've got an idea," said Joe Dolch, leaning forward in his chair and sweeping the air with his hand. "We put up a sign outside that says, Place Under New Management. We'll set up a five-dollar meal that'll knock their eyes out. After we knock their eyes out, we can charge them anything we want."

"Oh, Joe," moaned Diane, as if she were at the end of her rope.

The meeting descended into general disorder.

"Where are the bison when we need them?" pleaded Joe.

At that moment, Hattie Sims entered the room bearing the flyers. "Looks like another well-organized meeting," she quipped. "Is it about the vending machine?"

"That's a good question," said Pete, looking around. "Maybe we should tackle one issue at a time. The vending machine first. Right, Brisco?"

"To hell with the vending machine," Jim Burns said. "To hell with reorganization. The ship is going down, and we're not even being given life jackets."

"We have to call the president to account," Dan said. "We need to have it from the horse's mouth. It's time to stop dancing around this thing."

There was a general murmur of agreement.

Jim Burns drummed the table with his fingers.

Hattie stood at the back of the room, waving the flyers over her head. "Excuse me, everybody!"

"More bad news," said Joe Dolch.

"I bring tidings of joy," she announced.

"What did I tell you?"

Hattie circulated the flyers. "These are self-explanatory."

Brisco took one and leapt to his feet. "A talent show!"

"Yes," said Hattie, continuing her rounds. "Uncle Jumbo thought it would give us a sense of community." Turning to Dan Stupak, she asked, "Will you be dancing or singing? I hear you do a Jimmy Cagney imitation to beat the band."

A shared feeling of confusion and indignation flared among the faculty—except for Pete Blatty, who thought the idea of a talent show intriguing, although he knew better than to voice this.

Frannie gestured insistently with her pen. "It's clear," she began. But when nobody paid her any heed, she mustered the energy to push a copy of Morrison and Boyd's mammoth *Organic Chemistry* onto the floor, where it landed with a loud clap. This brought the faculty around. "It's clear," she repeated, "that there is a general lack of receptiveness."

"Unanimous!" shouted Jim Burns through cupped hands.

Frannie emitted a sick smile. "Unanimous. A unanimous lack of receptiveness to the idea of a talent show."

"I'm wondering if the students might be interested?" Pete fidgeted in his chair. "Maybe it is a way to bring the campus together."

Silence. But not in response to Pete's comment. Another player had entered the room. He stood just inside the threshold in his white bicycle helmet and well-worn Carhartt jacket. He looked from face to face, his own expression deadpan. "I was invited. Is this the meeting?"

He was, of course, too late. Passions had already carried the day, and the faculty rushed past Henny as a wave, in frantic competition to get to the phone in the pigsty, to call Marcus and demand an explanation.

SIXTEEN
A NOVEL IDEA

Diane Dempsey sat in her office in the Victorian. She was strangely serene about the looming closure, perhaps because she saw this as the kick in the pants she needed to wrest herself from her inertia and see what possibilities existed for her in the wider world.

She was by no means incapacitated by the acceleration of events. She wanted to work on her novel, but the muse was mum. However, her students had plenty to say. The semester was young, and already they were asking about extra credit. Another batch of English comp papers had come in, and they were, in a word, execrable. In light of the turn of events, Diane suddenly realized the poignancy of the assignment—"Is Grover Cleveland a Beautiful Place?"—and felt a tear well in her right eye. That tear ran when she read through the papers and saw that not one student thought it was. But this wasn't the problem. They wrote about everything under the sun except beauty, with a single exception: one student had quoted "Ode on a Grecian Urn," using it as a springboard for a rambling, stream-of-consciousness description of sunsets he'd seen in Newark, New Jersey, ending with, "'Beauty is only skin-deep,' that's what I always say," as if he'd fathered the aphorism.

"Oh, God," Diane sighed. She pushed the papers aside and gazed dolefully at her manuscript baking on the windowsill, speckled with spider shit. It had been so long since she'd worked on the novel that she'd lost the thread. She'd have to read it from the beginning to connect with the story line again and regain her momentum. Would she ever succeed? Who was she, anyway, to think she could write a book? Was there any record, beyond the school, that she even existed, except for an obscure gloss in a now-defunct community newspaper about her graduation from eighth grade—a brief mention that she'd won the Perfect Attendance Award?

She rose from her desk, ascended the stairs to the first floor, and looked out a window onto the college green. She saw students lying in the still-warm sunshine of the Maine autumn as red and gold leaves drifted down from the maples. The students seemed absolutely oblivious to the impending extinction of their world, and she wondered what had motivated them to attend Grover Cleveland College in the first place. How, in other words, had they stumbled upon this backwater without the draft to impel them here?

One couple sat back to back, oblivious not only to the school's crisis but to each another. The young man fiddled with a handheld game as the woman did her nails. Was this what relationships had become? Were those two even aware of one another except as a means of lumbar support?

Diane could remember her own undergraduate days in the sixties. Everyone seemed to have a paperback in his back pocket. After English class, she would chase down Professor Nagely—handsome Professor Nagely!—and plead for his insights into Dylan Thomas's *Under Milk Wood*, whose prose had mesmerized her. In the evenings, she and a clutch of other students would sit barefoot on the floor of her dorm room and ply the waters of *The Dharma Bums* while gobbling fistfuls of homemade granola, the girls braiding each other's hair. *Oh, where have they gone, those days, those friends, those impulses to acquire as much language as possible and then sit in wonder at the variety of it, the many ways in which it could be used and how it garnished the mind?*

Diane descended to her basement office again. A few

moments after she sat down, there was a knock at the door.

A young female student with straight black hair and small, intense green eyes laden with black mascara, walked in. She was chewing a large wad of gum, snapping it every few seconds. "Professor Dempsey? Do you have a moment?" she asked in a kittenish voice.

Diane nodded and attempted a smile. The student sat opposite her. She held a corrected paper, and Diane feared she'd come to challenge her grade.

"Professor Dempsey," said the student in a voice that was almost too sweet to bear, "I wanted to thank you for your comments on my paper. They were very helpful."

Diane sat up a little straighter. She mustered an expression of passing interest. "They were meant to be," she said, smiling more naturally now.

"In fact," said the student, "you've inspired me to become a writer."

Diane's heart sank. So it was worse than she'd feared. Another student who wanted to be a writer. As if that were the purpose of English 101: to turn out polished authors ripe for the Pulitzer. "Whom do you read?"

The student brushed hair away from her eyes, but the black curtain immediately fell back into place, making Diane feel she was stealing glimpses of something forbidden.

"Nobody yet," said the student with a snap of her gum. "But I want to start now. That's why I'm here. Do you have a recommendation for me?" Snap!

A recommendation? thought Diane. *Only one? Well, who should it be? Ayn Rand or Danielle Steel?* Lord of the Flies *or the Bible? My God . . .*

"I've heard," squeaked the student, "that many great writers never read a book in their lives."

Diane sat back in her chair and gripped the armrests. "I think it would be difficult to name one. Can you?"

The student shook her head. "Nope. Anyway," she continued, offhandedly, "I'm interested in becoming a poet."

Diane felt a hand tighten around her heart. If ever a land were inhospitable to poets, it was modern America. Frost, Sandburg, Williams, and Plath had been the last gasps of a culture that had replaced meter with malls and now perennially squatted in front of the boob tube watching sitcoms and political nincompoops celebrating their lobotomies. She hadn't heard a real poet in years, their efforts having been supplanted by so-called poetry slams, where illiterate—or sometimes über-literate—idiots hurled themselves at the microphone and screamed about the indignities they'd suffered at the hands of their parents. It all made her head spin. When she finally dispelled these wayward thoughts, she was surprised to see that the young student was still sitting before her. The only word Diane managed to muster was, "Why?"

"Well," said the student, with a double snap of her gum, "it rhymes and all that. And it's short, so I think I could handle it. Do you know," she said, leaning forward, "what the shortest poem in the world is?"

Diane looked positively sick. She slowly shook her head.

"'Adam had 'em.'" Snap! "And do you know what the title of that poem is?"

Diane shook her head again, gripping the armrests like a passenger in a doomed aircraft.

"'Fleas,'" said the student with a bounce. "Isn't that interesting?"

Diane turned and gazed at her manuscript again, with its curled edges and discolored pages. Time and tide had no intention of waiting for her. Whenever she despaired of completing her book, she made the mistake of marking time by reading one of the greats. At the moment, she was in a horrific funk because she felt she'd never be able to write like Nabokov. She turned back to the student. "Read *War and Peace*. It's a good place to start. Come and see me when you're done."

The student wrote down the title. "Sounds like fun," she said with a sparkle in her voice. "Thanks for the advice. I'll show you some poems when I'm done." And with that, she was up and out the door.

Diane turned to her desk. She began to shuffle her students' papers. She was in a state of approach/avoidance about correcting them. Then she noticed the flyer for the talent show. She didn't know what to think of it, coming as it did in the midst of calamity and growing rancor. But for some reason, she hadn't had the visceral reaction the rest of the faculty had. Was this really something they should resist?

Diane smiled. She remembered, as a young Boston miss, trudging through the snow to her clarinet lessons with Mr. Toptopchev, an elderly Polish man who rented a claustrophobic space in the back of Carapelli's shoe store just off Beacon Street. Can you imagine? A nine-year-old girl sitting alone with a strange old man behind a closed door in a dimly lit room? It would never happen today, in a nation of suspects. But Mr. Toptopchev was the sweetest man with an Old World way about himself, despite his ragged tweed jacket and seedy loafers, one of which was torn open at the toe. He'd called her Little Deluxe. The only times there had been any physical contact at all was when Mr. Toptopchev gently aligned her skinny fingers on the tone holes. Then, at the end of her final lesson when she was fourteen and on her way to high school, Mr. Toptopchev had leaned forward and, in the presence of her parents, planted a fleeting kiss on the crown of her head. "Little Deluxe," he said for the last time. Three months later, he died, alone, in the rooming house he'd called home for years.

This recollection brought tears to Diane's eyes. She still had the clarinet, which for some reason she kept in her office. She pulled the dusty case off the shelf, opened it, and ran her hands over the dark, shiny grenadilla wood. Inspired, she assembled the instrument. The taste of the reed transported her back to her girlhood, to that dank little room in back of the shoe store. What was that piece Mr. Toptopchev had taught her that she had come to love? "Piece No. 6" by Geminiani. She blew soulfully into the black tube. The keys were sticky and clicked as she worked them. But slowly, surely, the melody emerged in plangent tones. Of course, Diane's rendition would have put a chill down Geminiani's—and Mr. Toptop-chev's—spines, but to her ear it sounded like heaven. With every note she played, she dispelled the rancor of faculty assemblies, the poverty of her students' performance, the uncertain future of the college, and the frustration of her unfinished novel. She played, and like the piper of Hame-lin, she led her concern for all these things into oblivion.

SEVENTEEN
A WALK IN THE WOODS AND A SURPRISE VISITOR

Henny followed the stampeding faculty out the door, taking up the rear at a measured pace. The revelation of the talent show had upended the meeting from its original intent, so when Henny approached his colleagues as they competed for the phone in the pigsty and asked about reorganization, nobody knew what he was talking about. The old resentments resurfaced, and Henny was made to feel most unwelcome.

"Go back to your equations," said Jim Burns as he waited in line for the phone. "Let us handle this."

Henny shrugged and headed back across the green. Along the way, he ran into Marcus and Pacer taking their daily constitutional about campus.

"Henny," Marcus sang out with arms spread wide.

This brought a smile to the mathematician's face. He pumped a thumb over his shoulder in the direction of the pigsty. "A lot of disorder in there. Confirmation of chaos theory."

"Oh, that's just the way of faculty meetings, or so the book I'm reading tells me. I'm sure they'll hash things out."

"I think they're trying to get in touch with you."

"So I've heard. I'm sorry I've been out and about so much. I never did get to make my important announcement to the faculty, but I understand the cat's out of the bag now. Do you see how having one community phone has brought people together?"

"Cat?" said Henny.

Marcus waved the issue aside. "Let's not dwell on it. Tell me now, how is everything going with your nan . . . your nano—?

"Nanofungibots."

"Ah! I see the name has lengthened since last we spoke. May I take that as a sign of progress?"

"Little by little. The limited supply of fungus is still a problem."

"As it always is," Marcus pondered. "As it always is. Have you given any further thought to a collaborator?"

Henny threw Marcus a helpless look. Who would want to collaborate with him? Who else on campus shared his rarified interest in nanoparticles and fungi? "I haven't thought about it."

But Marcus had been thinking about this for some time, as if the school's days weren't numbered and the doomsday clock were doing nothing more than keeping time. He'd love to see Grover Cleveland become a center for advanced research of some kind, and it didn't really matter in what. "I've been thinking of Professor Burns. Are you familiar with his mucus work?"

Henny stared blankly at Marcus. He wasn't sure he'd ever uttered the word *mucus* in his life. But now here it was, hovering between the two men. "No, I have not been keeping up with the literature in that area."

"Well, speaking of literature, Professor Burns is writing a book on the topic. It's projected to make quite a splash in research circles. I wouldn't be surprised if it became the standard work in its field. It would certainly draw attention to our dear college, and with attention would come, I hope, a little support in our time of trial."

"Trial?"

"Yes. And I think I've already mentioned Professor Stupak," added Marcus, recalling once again the incident with the destroying angel. "He seems to know quite a bit about the fungi."

"Yes," said Henny impassively.

Marcus moved off on another tack. "I'm on my daily walk. Would you like to join me? I find that walking clears the mind, inspires creative thinking, and takes us places we might not otherwise go."

Henny had promised YaYa he'd return to the institute after the meeting, but since he hadn't really attended the meeting, he had time on his hands and decided to go with Marcus. In fact, he was flattered to be asked. The two men ambled away toward the forest path, with Pacer taking up the rear.

In the meantime, Brisco Quik had once again seized the helm from Frannie Moore and, through force of personality, reconvened the disrupted faculty meeting in the cramped pigsty. It seemed the natural thing to do, since no one was answering the silo phone, several faculty members having taken a turn trying to get through to Marcus. "So it's unanimous," Brisco announced. "We will boycott the talent show."

There was a mumble of agreement, but then Jiminy Schmitz spoke up. "Oh, I don't know." He reached into his pocket to check on Onan.

Brisco focused on the provost. "You don't know what, Jiminy?"

Jiminy thought for a moment. "Well, if you think contributing to the show is, well . . . There are birds I've known that . . ." The provost scratched his head and stared into the distance. "I seem to have lost my train of thought."

"I understand that, as both administration and

faculty, your loyalties are divided," said Brisco charitably. "But by gum, we'd like to have you in the trenches on this one."

All eyes were on Jiminy, who looked from face to face. "I've also been wondering about the vending machine."

"Brisco directed me to query possible suppliers," piped up Vikram Chabot, waving from the margin of the gathering. "I'm happy to say we have a vendor. The machine will be electrical as opposed to mechanical. It will be oversized, and will have juice as well as pop."

Frannie Moore, in a bid to regain her posture, murmured, "But we still need to vote."

"We shall, we shall," said Vikram, raising his bushy eyebrows in synchrony with his speech. "But even the committee hasn't voted yet because we haven't had a quorum."

"Well then," said Dan Stupak, "you don't have a vendor after all."

"Well, we have a vendor we're going to vote on."

Brisco was incredulous. He wasn't a psychologist, but he knew denial when he saw it. His colleagues seemed irretrievably lost. Instead of tackling Moby Dick, they were pursuing a red herring. He made halfhearted efforts to rein them in, but it was no use. Unwilling, or unable, to face the dissolution of the school, they comforted themselves with something they thought they could manage. The rest of the meeting was dedicated to parsing the question of the vending machine, while the silo clock continued its incessant tocking, its solitary hand about to obscure the four. Feeling divorced from the proceedings, Brisco quietly slipped out the back door. Grim and resigned, he headed for the Victorian.

A short while later, he was in Jim Burns's office, stewing. Pete Blatty was present as well, as were Dan Stupak and Joe Dolch, who sat with his feet up and tossed an apple from hand to hand.

"So here we are," said Brisco, pacing. "We're effectively reorganized, and not a shot was fired from our end. It's a bloodless coup. 'Faculty of Humanity'! What the hell is that supposed to mean?"

Pete spoke from a corner. "Maybe it will work out. Who knows?" he asked in an attempt at consolation.

Brisco glared at him. "Goddamn it, Pete, *I* know! And whether it works out or not, you're missing the point. Administration is not supposed to impose sea changes like this. There's a process."

Pete nodded. "Well, maybe you're right."

"You're goddamn right I'm right." Turning, he prodded, "Aren't I, Dan?"

"Sure, Brisco. You're right. The way I see it, the president has reduced us to a mere appendage. We'll be disposed of, and the physical school will be replaced by a Walmart."

Brisco seemed to fold into himself, crossing his arms. Then he unfurled. "You know, I don't really care if I lose my job. It's not my job I'm worried about. Or yours or yours or yours," he added as he pointed from man to man. "I'd quit if I thought it could save the school." As he said this, he pictured himself and Hattie driving away together, their car disappearing over the horizon.

For lack of anything relevant to say, Dan uttered, "But what about the talent show? Have you seen the hubbub outside? The students are all worked up. They've got rock bands, a bushel of poets, a juggler, two plate spinners, an escape artist, and they're even training the bison to do tricks."

"Well, I don't care about that either."

"*Eye*-ther," corrected Joe.

"Eye-ther," conceded Brisco.

"*Ee*-ther," said Joe.

Brisco turned to Dan. "So what are you trying to say?"

"That we can't boycott the show. We still have a school and a faculty. At least for the moment. We have to be there. We can't alienate the students. We have to support them if we ever want them to support us."

Brisco worked his jaw. "Damn that Uncle Jumbo. Isn't that what Hattie calls him? Uncle Jumbo?"

"That's what she says."

"Well, it looks like he's got us by the cojones," Brisco lashed out with a finger. "But look here—we'll go to the damn show, but the faculty is not to participate, okay?

We've got to draw a battle line somewhere. I mean, where is our self-respect?"

Jim nodded. "That's reasonable. I certainly have no intention of getting onstage and making a fool of myself. What about you, Pete?"

The musician swallowed and cleared his throat, fixing his gaze on the apple, which coursed between Joe's hands like a metronome. It was difficult for Pete to resist a talent show. He had so few performance venues as it was. But he was outnumbered—and by personalities far stronger and more assertive than his. "Well, okay. But I have students who want to perform. I can't discourage them."

"No, you can't," conceded Jim.

Deep into their forest walk, Marcus and Henny talked of many things: the teaching life, the inquiring mind, the existential query of whether to repair or replace broken consumer electronic devices, and, of course, fungi.

As the men came to a broad clearing, Henny's expression brightened. "You see," he said, spreading his arms, "how the treetops lean in, shading the clearing? It's dark, warm, and moist. Perfect. But do you see what's missing?"

Marcus peered into the glade, his small, active eyes scanning, searching, studying. "I'm stumped. It's a lovely place, but what is missing?"

"Fungi," pronounced Henny. "This place should have a lot of it. But it doesn't have any."

"Curious! Maybe we could plant some."

Henny smiled charitably. "No, that's not the way it works. Fungus chooses its own spot. You never know where it will come up. There was a case in New Jersey where it started growing under a man's driveway. The thing is, the driveway had been paved for years. The fungus had simply been waiting for exactly the right conditions. When it did begin to grow, it was unstoppable. It broke through the asphalt overnight."

"Remarkable!"

"There are many such stories."

The two men spent a good long while standing at the edge of the clearing, staring in wonder at the fungusless expanse.

In the meantime, preparations for the talent show went on unabated. Diane Dempsey was still in her wistful mood, which accompanied her, like a following mist, as she entered her English comp class in Quonset #3. Nineteen souls sat, or slumped, in their desks. Normally, Diane would begin with a full-frontal assault on the deficiencies of their work, but this time she just leaned back against her desk and scanned the entities arrayed before her, the milk-faced as well as the unshaven ones from the homeless shelter and the mental health institution. Even the murderer garnered a cursory glance. Finally, she asked, in a low voice, "Who here is still a virgin?"

The students froze, apoplectic.

Diane, oblivious to their paralysis, went on with a personal statement. She began with her materially effuse but emotionally barren childhood and, from there, moved on to her less-than-satisfactory adolescence, her ostracism for her bookish ways, and even the morsel that she had a sprawling mole she'd never had the courage to have removed from the inside of her left thigh. This emanated from a woman who'd always insisted on being addressed as Professor and, out of a sense of propriety, retreated to the bathroom to blow her nose. The catharsis gobbled up thirty-seven minutes of class time, after which Diane waved at the students, said "Well," and then told them she was sure their work was good and that any grade they assigned themselves would meet with her approval.

The class thawed enough to applaud, and Diane, for the first time in their recollection, smiled. She felt an unfamiliar thrill. So this was what approbation felt like!

On the ensuing days, the campus was a hive of activity. Marcus had stumbled onto something, as all talk was about the talent show, which meant very little work got done in the classrooms. Even Brisco saw a silver lining, which he exploited in The Political Nature of College. Walking into that class one day, he sensed the mood. "Form small groups and write a statement about the role of talent shows in enhancing community on campus. Go on. Get to work." Then he stepped out for a cup of coffee.

The campus took on a circus-like atmosphere, with students doing handstands on the green or walking a tightwire between trees. Jugglers with Hacky Sacks and batons sprouted like dandelions. Small musical ensembles, including a triangle quintet, erupted here and there. And Timmy and Boss, moaning miserably, labored under one young woman's attempts to bring them to heel, each command accompanied by a crash of the cymbals she'd borrowed from Pete Blatty.

Marcus, holding Pacer in his arms, gazed upon the scene from his perch in the grain silo. "Isn't it wonderful?" he commented while Hattie passed through his office. "Look how everyone has come together. I tell you, that handbook isn't beyond reproach, but the chapter on community building was spot on."

"Yeah, sure."

Marcus turned to Hattie. "Are you planning on offering something at the show?"

"Who? Me?" She chortled. "Uh-uh. Nobody's gonna get me to stand on that stage, grinning like a baboon."

"Oh, Hattie," mourned Marcus.

But his attention was soon captured by the appearance of Bella, who'd just conquered the last of the ninety-two steps. Half bent with exhaustion, she hobbled on her bad foot.

"Harebell!" sang Marcus as he flew to her.

Bella, looking self-conscious in Hattie's presence, waited until the secretary left the room and then fell into Marcus's arms.

"Did you have a long climb?"

Bella lifted her head from his chest. "I would climb the Great Pyramid for you. I would've been here sooner, but I just arrived on campus and my new parking space is quite a distance away."

"I know, Harebell. I know." Marcus patted the back of her head. "But as you know, Brisco's handicap stirs me deeply. I mean, it could be any of us. Just think—he will never pass on his genes to little Quiks."

Aha! thought Bella. *So that's it. A male problem.* She ventured, "Oh, MooMoo, I'm not criticizing your decision. Just for the record, though, Brisco has never expressed a burning desire for children."

Marcus shrugged and laughed. "Who knows what the future will bring? Butt Oligny, one of the salesmen at the dealership and a confirmed bachelor, had twelve. He said they were cheaper by the dozen. Did you ever hear anything so funny? Cheaper by the dozen!"

Bella tried to laugh too, but her foot was killing her.

Marcus dragged her toward the window. "See, Harebell? Those students, all working together, getting ready to perform in the talent show. This is Grover Cleveland at its best."

"Yes, MooMoo." Bella sighed. "I see."

"Will you be performing?"

Bella pushed herself back from Marcus. "Performing? Me?"

"Why, yes. This show is open to everybody. Students, staff, faculty—even Timmy and Boss will be doing their part."

Bella searched Marcus's eyes for some hint of irony. But they only sparkled, as they always did when he was in love with an idea. Then she found an exit.

Pulling herself close to her hero, she said, "I'd much rather sit next to you. To me, you're the greatest show on earth."

"Harebell! My flower!"

While Marcus was spooning, a brilliant black Cadillac slowly cruised onto campus. It stopped first here, then there, as if sniffing about. Finally it came to rest at the base of the grain silo. The driver alit and opened a rear door.

An ashen but fit and bolt upright figure in a crisp, charcoal-gray suit emerged. He gazed up at the summit of the grain silo, then signaled to the driver.

The driver entered the building while his master waited below, staring up at the clock, which issued a particularly strong tock of recognition.

EIGHTEEN
THE METAMORPHOSIS

"Mr. Bell!" gushed Marcus, like a child happy to see a favorite teacher. At the driver's bidding, he'd made the long descent to ground level and was now standing before Harlen Bell, shifting his weight, his joy percolating. "That's a beautiful Cadillac," he observed with the authority of the veteran salesman he was. "Heated seats?"

"What else? It also has a memory. When I get in, the seats automatically contour to my preprogrammed anatomical specifications."

Marcus threw his arms around himself. "Wonderful," he breathed.

"Yes, wonderful. But what about you?" He gave a few

quick, birdlike glances about campus. "So this is where you fled to."

"I wouldn't exactly say *fled*. It was more of a calling."

"Yes, yes," said Mr. Bell, waving his thin hand in a breezy manner. "But the question is, is the place better off since your arrival? Have you improved it?"

Marcus managed a weak smile. "Well, we are in a process—"

"Ah! So the answer is no." Bell lowered his voice. "Is there someplace we can sit and chat in private?"

Marcus glanced up at the silo. "My office is at the top. I'm afraid there's no elevator, though."

Harlen Bell gasped. "That absolutely will not do."

Marcus nodded. "Sorry, Mr. Bell. But I have a place we can go," he said and led his former boss to the Brain Shrine.

Harlen Bell was aghast. "This looks like a pigsty," he exclaimed, covering his nose.

"Well, it certainly was a pigsty. But look here and see what we've done with it." Marcus led Mr. Bell to the catafalque hosting the presidential artifact.

Harlen Bell drew his face close to the glass vessel and squinted. "Why, it's brains! How awful."

"Oh, no, no," Marcus objected gently. "Not just any brain. It belonged to Grover Cleveland."

"The president?"

"Yes. My great-uncle brought it here."

After a last gander at the organ, Harlen Bell straightened up and averted his eyes. "Well, it's macabre. Of all things."

Marcus led Mr. Bell past the offending object, helping him to step over the sleeping student sentinel.

"One of your scholars?" sniffed Mr. Bell.

Marcus made no reply. He escorted his old boss to a couple of folding chairs in the back of the shrine. "I sometimes come here to think."

Mr. Bell snorted.

A few uneasy moments ensued, during which Harlen Bell looked Marcus over. "So," he finally said, "tell me how the school is doing, if you will."

Marcus was not good at prevarication, so he yielded. "Truth to tell," he said, kneading his hands in his lap, "the school is bankrupt and heading for closure by the end of the semester unless we come up with a plan."

Harlen Bell seemed fortified by this news. "Well," he said, throwing up his hands, "do you have a plan?"

"Nothing specific yet. I'm trying to boost morale so that the faculty might come up with something."

"Come up with something? Who do you think you are—Mr. Micawber?"

Marcus didn't recognize the Dickens reference, so he peeped, "Was he a customer?"

Harlen Bell feigned deep disappointment. "So you've failed, is what you're saying."

Marcus raised a finger. "Not yet," he said with a

note of triumph, as if not having yet failed were an accomplishment in itself. "Tonight, for example, we're having a talent show. I'm hoping it will inspire everyone to persist and maybe bring some outsiders to campus who might want to assist us in our time of need."

"So that's it," said Harlen Bell, narrowing his eyes. "You're going to ask me for money. Cash. Dollars."

It hadn't occurred to Marcus to ask Mr. Bell for anything. And he thought it best not to point out that it was Mr. Bell who'd come to Grover Cleveland unbidden. "No, not at all. I'm just happy to see you."

Harlen Bell sat back and let his long arms hang down beside him. Then he folded himself forward again and struck a saccharine tone. "Marcus, look. This place isn't for you. You were a successful car salesman. Do you know how deeply hurt I was when you left? I felt as if my own son were abandoning me."

This was news to Marcus. He'd always had a certain respect for Mr. Bell because of his business acumen, but the idea of him as a father figure was alien. "I didn't mean to hurt you."

"Well, you did. Profoundly," he said, revealing his teeth and a viscous rope of spit, then added, "But I'm forgiving by nature. If you'll come back now, you can pick up exactly where you left off. Same hours, same commissions."

Marcus felt himself listing toward his former boss. He could envision himself rising from his chair and then, trancelike, following Mr. Bell to the waiting Cadillac with its heated memory seats. But just then, when he was most vulnerable to the seduction, Marcus became aware of the tocking of the doomsday clock. He pursed his lips and spoke softly. "I can't, sir. You see, it's not only the school that I have a debt of honor to. I'm also in love."

"Love!" screeched Harlen Bell, as if Marcus has said "Plague." He pulled at the loose skin of his face. Leveling his gaze at Marcus, he launched the last of his weapons. "You're a bad, bad man. And a stupid one."

Marcus absorbed these salvos impassively. He considered whether Mr. Bell might be at least partly correct. He was sure he wasn't bad, but could he be stupid? Or at least arrogant to assume that he, an uneducated man, could aspire to captain anything so complicated and challenging as a college? He finally gave the only answer that seemed honest. "Oh, I'm not a bad man, Mr. Bell. But I'm willing to consider that I may be a bad college president."

"Bah!" Harlen Bell rose from his chair. "You're hopeless." His impulse was to say *useless*, but that wasn't true. If it were, he wouldn't have made the long drive to Maine. "I offer you opportunity, and you slap my hand away. I'm humiliated."

Marcus knocked his own chair over as he struggled to get up. "I am so sorry. I never meant to be ungrateful."

Harlen Bell sought his own way out of the Brain

Shrine, marching past the honored relic and stepping over the slumbering student. He snapped his fingers at the driver, who threw the rear door open. He folded himself into his memory seat, so beautifully contoured to the anatomical specifications of his scissorlike body. Through the open window, he grimaced at Marcus. Then he looked up at the doomsday clock. "What good is that thing with only one hand?"

Marcus followed his gaze. "It tells us how much time we have left."

Harlen Bell smiled. "Well, don't come crawling to me when this place goes belly up. But to show you how magnanimous I am, I'm willing to give you the last word."

Marcus thought this decent of Mr. Bell. He put a finger to his lips and thought for a moment. Finally he came up with, "If you'd like to make a contribution to our cause—"

The tinted window rolled up.

Inevitably, the talent show arrived. Stash Zakraski had worked long hours with some student help to erect a temporary stage in the center of the green, fronted by concentric arcs of folding chairs. One couldn't have asked for a more beautiful evening. The air was still and unseasonably warm, the sky clear and adorned with the evening star and a rising gibbous moon. Shortly before seven, the seats began to fill. Even a respectable number of townsfolk had come out of curiosity. Under Cyrus Cleveland, nothing like this had ever taken place. There had been no need: he'd presided over a seller's market, thanks to the draft.

At precisely seven thirty, Marcus appeared. He stumbled through the sea of chairs and clambered onto the stage while a student-operated spotlight followed his every clumsy step. Finally, standing in a pool of light in the middle of the stage, he straightened his jacket, gazed out at the crowd of not entirely friendly faces, and cleared his throat. He glanced down at Bella, who sat in the front row, smiled at her, and took heart.

"Greetings," he said, which was as far as he'd gotten in writing his speech, as Mr. Bell's surprise visit had upended him from the task.

As soon as he uttered this, Bella's hands came together, which stimulated a smattering of tepid applause.

"Thank you!" sang Marcus, and the words flowed from there, as he knew they would. "This is the first time Grover Cleveland College is presenting a talent show."

"Tell us who you are!" yelled out one of the townsfolk.

Marcus smiled in embarrassment, pulled a handkerchief from his pocket, and mopped his forehead. Then he introduced himself, which drew no applause whatsoever. His train of thought had completely jumped the rails. He instinctively looked to Bella, who made rolling motions with her hand. "Oh, yes," stammered Marcus. "Roll on, roll on!"

Robert Klose

A female student in a Gypsy dress—lithe, barefoot, and with flowing auburn hair—drifted onto the stage to introduce the acts, which were legion and followed one another machine-gun style. A young man played the guitar and sang a lament about what the world would've been like had he never been born. A young woman in a nun's habit did a liturgical dance. Three white students in blackface and a black student in whiteface sang a made-up tune, barbershop quartet style, about the austerities inflicted by their student loan burdens. One of Pete Blatty's piano students played the same four bars over and over for fifteen minutes while Pete sat riveted, listening for the slightest mistake.

As the acts avalanched onto the stage, Brisco seethed. He sat with his arms folded across his chest, breathing as if gasping for air. He kept glancing at the other faculty, who actually seemed to be enjoying themselves. Jiminy sat up front, waving his index fingers, as if conducting an orchestra. Only when an unfamiliar figure ascended the stage was Brisco's attention seized. He noted a young woman with a nice figure and a foreign look about her. She displayed something he would actually characterize as grace.

YaYa turned to face the audience, which acknowledged with a closed-eyed dip of her head. Then she held up a sheet of paper and read. From the cadence, it sounded like a poem. In fact, it was a poem—an ode to Henny Spox. It detailed his origins, his path to becoming a genius, the brilliant ideas that had occurred to him over the years, and how he was shunned by his colleagues at Grover Cleveland. It was at this point that YaYa began to sob, continuously cupping a hand over her mouth, as if muting a trumpet. The audience was rendered silent by the recitation. Only Jiminy seemed happy with the output, smiling away as he continued to conduct.

Marcus sat next to Bella in the front row with his hands folded in his lap. He didn't know whether YaYa's mounting hysteria was part of the recitation or a genuine loss of control. Perhaps it was simply what poetry had become. Finally, the ordeal ended with YaYa repeatedly stamping a foot as if she were killing a cockroach. Then she left the stage, sobbing into one hand, and disappeared into the night.

No one could have been prepared for what happened next. A woman ascended the wooden steps and crossed the stage. She was attired in a full-body tiger-stripe leotard and hot-pink patent-leather stiletto heels. Her hair, dyed flame red, flowed over her shoulders and down her back like rivulets of lava. She was holding a clarinet and dragging a garden hose, whose nozzle she set down on the stage. After locating the keys and tone holes with her slender fingers—the nails having been painted gloss black—she addressed the audience in a smoky voice. "The object of teaching is not the crude transmission of information but rather to help the student find his or her way. Some-times, as professors, we find that we are talking to our-selves. If only we would listen! Then we might learn we are our own best teachers. In this light, I have rediscovered something I'd thought was long lost, but now I know it was simply lying dormant. Yes." She nodded. "My soul. My musical muse. It now wishes to speak. To you."

There was a shared sense in the audience that this juncture warranted applause, but no one moved a muscle. All eyes focused on Diane, who continued her soliloquy.

"I will not be playing any of the Rychlík pieces for solo clarinet," she announced.

This didn't disappoint the audience, none of whom, including Pete Blatty, knew Rychlík had written solo pieces for clarinet, much less who Rychlík was.

"Nor will I treat you to Mozart, who adored the instrument. Instead, I would like to play a composition of my own, inspired by a happy childhood memory. I call it 'Heavy Fog at Block Island for Clarinet Alone.'"

Marcus incited the applause. In the distance, Timmy and Boss bellowed as if they, too, were filled with anticipation.

Diane began by talking into the bell of her instrument, quoting from *The Grapes of Wrath*: "Before I knowed it, I was sayin' out loud, 'The hell with it! There ain't no sin and there ain't no virtue.'" Then she clicked the keys wildly while distending her tongue in concentration.

The effect, for Brisco, was of ants crawling all over his

body. But his arms remained crossed, as if welded together.

After several more paragraphs of Steinbeck, the first movement ended.

In the second movement, an *andante rubato più mosso*, Diane put the clarinet in her mouth and intoned, in the deepest voice possible, "Hoo, hoo, hoooo," before ascending in a glissando screech that loosened Brisco's arms so he could clap his hands over his ears.

The mood of the music darkened considerably as the third movement, "Aqua Regia," began. Diane got down on her knees and removed the clarinet's mouthpiece, connecting the garden hose directly to the instrument's barrel. She opened the nozzle and plumes of water spewed out of every tone hole, glistening in the spotlight. Pete Blatty interpreted this as an updating of Handel's *Water Music* and leapt to his feet, followed by his passel of music students.

The fourth movement, a *fuga del diavolo*, saw Diane moving across the stage on her knees, blowing the restored but dripping clarinet with manic abandon, the notes flying like cinders from a crackling fire. Her hands danced all over the instrument, springing madly about, as if she were trying to subdue a wild animal. No one—not even Pete—could follow the complicated, seemingly random, and certainly irreproducible progressions and regressions. The music finally rose to a crescendo of squeaks, flutters, and quacks before Diane, without warning, collapsed on the stage.

Marcus, with tears in his eyes, struggled to his feet. He faced the audience and, repeatedly pumping a thumb over his shoulder at Diane's body, said, "This is what I'm talking about. Have any of you ever seen such a thing? This college is a gold mine of talent. And if we access this talent and give it direction, our dear school will have a brilliant future!"

That was it. There were no other acts, as Timmy and Boss could not be coerced into performing. Four male members of the intramural volleyball team carried Diane's body from the stage. Others volunteered to fold and stow chairs. Faculty members hobnobbed.

But Brisco was conspicuous by his isolation. After all the other chairs had been put away, he remained seated, his arms once again across his chest, nibbling furiously at his lips, and listening to the blood pound in his ears. He threw an accusing glance at Pete Blatty, who quickly looked away. Then he moved his laser focus to Jim Burns, who shrugged and skulked off with Dan Stupak and Scott Ott.

Only Joe Dolch walked over to Brisco. He looked down at the brooding figure. "I was going to ask her to play a tune if she got near one," he joked. "Hey, you'd better beat it. I hear they're gonna tear you down and put up an office building where you're sitting."

Brisco glared at Joe.

"Oookaay," said the chemist as he drew away.

Once everyone was gone, Stash Zakraski turned off the lights, and Brisco was left sitting there, before the empty stage, in darkness.

NINETEEN
BRISCO ALONE AND A SEXUAL CONSIDERATION

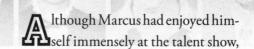

Although Marcus had enjoyed himself immensely at the talent show, he'd not forgotten Mr. Bell's visit. His recriminations sharpened his mind and gave him renewed focus on the steadily approaching X hour. And should he forget this, the doomsday clock was there to remind him.

Despite the solitary hand of the clock having arrived at the five, a peculiar calm now settled over Grover Cleveland College. An impartial, prescient observer with the eye of God might have called it a time of introspection and self-possession. Or perhaps it simply had something to do with the advancing autumn and the effect of cooler evenings, the growing transparency of the surrounding woods as the leaves departed the trees, and the hard morning frosts that made the still-green grass crackle underfoot. Students attended classes, the faculty taught, Marcus—accompanied by loyal Pacer—read and dreamed in his silo redoubt, staff worked away at the cogs of the college machine, and Timmy and Boss fattened on whatever flora they could find in the woodlands, preparing for the winter ahead. There were, at least for the moment, no more faculty meetings, no more calls to arms, no more frantic consultations with Jiminy Schmitz. Norman Rockwell might have painted this pastoral moment as part of an Americana series.

Brisco, for his part, continued to seethe. The reason: the absence of war. But how could this be? This was the question he repeatedly asked himself as he paced about his office in the Victorian. Had people lost heart? The will to act in their own interests? Was he mired in a nest of cowards? Didn't they realize how close they were to seeing the doors locked and the lights extinguished, whereupon they would begin their diaspora to who knew where? He could only surmise that the others, by pretending all was well, were hoping the problem would simply go away.

How different he was from his so-called colleagues! He had known war. Well, he'd known about war. He'd been a Navy corpsman during the incipient years of Vietnam but hadn't had the honor of seeing combat. Rather, he'd been relegated to shore duty at

Naval Hospital Beaufort in South Carolina, emptying bedpans and delivering meals on plastic trays to complaining dependents and demanding retirees.

He'd asked for a transfer to Indochina, but the commanding officer, a good old boy with a Charlie Brown head, had consistently denied that request. "Son, you got yourself a cozy little stint here," he'd drawled. "There's thousands of sailors over there who'd give their left nut to swap places with you. Why do you want to trade a warm bed for the hard ground of the Fleet Marine Force over there in gook land?"

And so Brisco had whiled away his four years doing his monotonous duty. In his free time he took courses by correspondence, surprising even himself by earning an associate degree in political science by the time of his discharge. For lack of anywhere else to go, he returned to Maine, saw an ad in the local newspaper for a political science instructor at Grover Cleveland, and the rest was history. All his colleagues knew was that he'd served in the military in wartime, but the way he told the story, one might have assumed he'd personally led a division of Marines to the gates of Hanoi, to the brink of victory, before being ordered to turn back by compliant generals whose hands had been tied by incompetent, yellow-bellied politicians who didn't know squat about war.

What had the campus become now? An oasis of indecision and apathy. Resigned to defeat! Brisco, in his frustration, kicked the wastepaper basket against the wall, made fists, and pivoted about, first this way then that, as if he were under attack from all sides.

"Come on!" he growled. "Come on!" But he was perfectly alone, the only sounds his heavy breathing and the buzzing of the season's last bumblebee as it repeatedly banged against the window in a bid for freedom.

Brisco grabbed a copy of *The Grover Rover*, rolled it up, and hauled back. But at the last moment he relented, opened the window, and the bee banged along until it found the opening and flew out into the sunshine.

And what of Hattie? Brisco felt a burgeoning obligation to her, to at least acknowledge her interest in him. But his preoccupation with the college had rid him of any hankering for romance, let alone sex. His mornings were now bereft of those once-vigorous waking erections. Perhaps he really needed that handicap placard after all. He'd loaded up on pornographic novels in a bid to rekindle some degree of ardor but had no time to read them. "I am so sorry, Hattie," he wanted to say. But what would she think he was sorry about?

In the meantime, Dan Stupak was visiting Jim Burns in his office. Jim was seated at his desk, running his hands through his hair while Dan stood over him, puffing away on his pipe.

"I've neglected my research," Jim lamented, shaking

his head. "All because of Brisco and his panic attacks that suck all of us into these incessant meetings that accomplish nothing."

Dan sniffed. "The fate of the school really is at stake, when you look the thing dead in the eye. But what fascinates me more than the question of where I—all of us—will wind up, is the psychology of it all. I mean, we have a couple of months to go before they come with the padlock, yet we're behaving like a man who doesn't know he's terminally ill. The problem is that this isn't a public institution. We don't have the state to appeal to. There isn't even a board of trustees. Marcus owns this school. Cyrus gave it to him. I guess he can do whatever he wants with it."

"Maybe resignation is our only choice, then." Jim's face was taut. "In which case, Brisco is pissing into the wind and getting all of us wet."

"There, now." Dan's pipe seesawed as he spoke. "You're getting yourself all worked up. How close are you to completing your book?"

"It's done," Jim said, patting the manuscript with its title page in black, forty-eight-point font: *Mucus and Its Precursors*.

"Then why so glum, chum?"

"Because Vikram is hedging about publication. I can't believe it. He said he was interested. Now he doesn't seem to want to even look at it."

"Maybe he's busy packing. I mean, it takes a good

year to put a book out, right? Our hourglass runs out in a couple of months."

"I've thought about that. But it would still mean something to me if the book were in press, even if the plug were pulled before publication. It would at least give me a selling point when I approached another publisher."

"Have you stayed on Vikram's good side? Editors can be temperamental."

"As much as anybody can. It's that damned red eye of his. You never know what he's thinking. It's like that Edgar Allan Poe story."

Dan smiled, and his pipe stood up at a jaunty angle. "You're not going to cut him up and stash him under the floorboards, are you?"

Jim exhaled through his nose. "I don't think Vikram has a good side. He seems to take pride in rejecting anything that isn't reminiscent of that book on the blackfly, which he seems to see as the gold standard."

"Maybe it's your title."

Jim stared down at the manuscript. "What's wrong with it? It tells the reader everything he needs to know."

Dan took the pipe from his mouth and made a jabbing motion with it. "That's exactly the problem. If the cover tells the reader everything, why would he want or need to open the thing and actually read it?"

"Your point?"

Dan tapped his pipe against his hand. "A wise man once

said the main job of a writer is not to write; it's to promote."

"I'm not a promoter," said Jim, who nevertheless found himself listening to Dan with guarded interest.

"My God," said Dan in a rare show of emotion, "think of yourself as a realtor who can make a fixer-upper sound like Valhalla. You have this manuscript that's taken you five years to write. Are you willing to chuck it all because of Vikram's red eye? And there's a bigger consideration. If it's a success, it could help the school immensely."

Jim managed a fleeting smile. "Maybe you're right. I'd be happy to donate at least some of the royalties to the school. Maybe I'm just distracted, that's all."

"Distracted?"

Jim waved him off. "It's nothing. I guess I'd better start promoting."

"That's the spirit," chirped Dan as he turned to leave. "See you around, pal."

Jim hadn't told Dan everything or really anything, for that matter. It wasn't the book that was bothering him so deeply. Or the impending closure of the school with its uncertain aftermath. It was the talent show. Or more to the point: Diane. That . . . that tiger-stripe leotard, her suggestive moves, the flame-red hair—all of it had stirred something deep within him. Ever since his divorce seven years ago he'd felt, well, desexed, like a gelding relegated to the monotony of pulling a plow. Life had gone on, but it was bereft of sparkle, gusto. He had become J. Alfred

Prufrock, going through the motions, wondering what he might do to improve himself, but always inertia had won out. He thought he might have low testosterone, but he lacked the motivation to have a simple blood test. It had gotten to the point that he envied Timmy and Boss their sexual tension.

But now, well, how could he have known he would respond so powerfully to Diane's performance? To her appearance? She'd made herself into a seductress, a vixen, an imp that had attached to him and was egging him on until he was almost blind with passion. But, by God, he was fifty-two years old! It didn't make any sense from an evolutionary point of view. He'd spent years, decades, telling his students that, as far as nature was concerned, their bodies were no more than delivery vehicles for their genes. The whole point was reproduction, at an early age, after which nature had no use for the body and people were on their own, so good luck! But there was one flaw with this reasoning: why, then, did humans continue to feel passion as they aged? He'd just read an article about nursing-home patients who snuck into each other's rooms at night for the express purpose of copulation. One of them had been a ninety-six-year-old woman with a walker.

And so he burned, like a sixteen-year-old who couldn't keep his hands off himself, tossing under his covers, red-faced with heat. But what could he do about it? He'd made an avocation of ridiculing and shortchanging

Diane for her overly cautious nature, her peacemaking, her dull, snobbish commentaries, her prudishness, her conservative dress. It would be impossible for him to approach her without at the same time disgusting her. He was the enemy, and she knew it.

But then again, she was single. She must also have feelings, desires. Maybe she burned as well. Jim pulled a small mirror from his desk drawer and examined himself. The hair on the top of his head was still brownish, but on the sides it had grayed. He had bags under his eyes. Maybe he should try cucumbers. He glanced back at his manuscript, and it suddenly hit him: this was his in. He would bring it to Diane and ask her advice. He would humble himself, cower, praise her superior knowledge of all things literary. By virtue of his neediness, he would make himself irresistible.

In the meantime, Marcus was once again under the bower with Bella. The only thing separating them from coition were a few thin layers of fabric. Otherwise, they clutched at each other and rolled first this way, then that, like two dung beetles in embrace.

"MooMoo," managed Bella in a moment of respite, "I'm worried about falling behind on my duties."

Marcus could barely catch his breath. He finally swallowed and heaved a mighty sigh. "Be careful about getting too much satisfaction out of your duties. The talent show was a great success, and everyone deserves a little break. Don't you feel that the campus has become much happier?"

"Yes, yes," agreed Bella, panting. "There is a certain calm now. People aren't running about so much. There haven't been any emergency meetings. But maybe that's because people feel powerless to change things, to alter the direction we're headed. Or maybe they're not having meetings because they fear another rampage by the bison."

Marcus pushed himself to a sitting position. "Timmy and Boss? Why, they're as gentle as kittens. Henny and I visited them in the big forest glade the other day. They're grazing like two lambs."

Bella smiled and nodded. "I know, MooMoo, but rutting season is never far away."

Marcus pinched Bella's cheek. "I know, Harebell, but the college green is nicely cropped, isn't it?"

"Well, I suppose."

"You worry too much," Marcus said and lunged for her.

She inserted her hands between them. "I can't help worrying about the college. Time is getting so short. MooMoo, what do you think we should do?"

Marcus sat up. "I can't help but hope something will turn up. With all the faculty activity on campus, I feel the law of averages is on our side and some breakthrough will rescue us."

Bella considered that Marcus might be withholding

something more solid than vague hope. "Please forgive me for being so direct, but I think the faculty is looking to you for the solution."

"I wonder," reflected Marcus, "if there has ever been an instance where a college president has single-handedly rescued his school. It seems to me that, with so many people involved, a team effort is the only solution. But still, what we need is a great idea. Just one. Don't you think? I only wish *The Handbook of College Reorganization* weren't so mute on the subject."

"Hello in there!"

Bella yelped and pushed herself away from Marcus.

Both of them looked up and saw Hattie squatting at the entrance to the bower, flush with delight, as if she'd discovered a leprechaun. "So that's where you two have been!" She resumed her businesslike demeanor. "Listen, President Marcus, you've got a situation."

Marcus crawled out from the bower and stood, brushing off his clothing. "Situation?" He reached down to help Bella to her feet.

"Take a look at this." Hattie shoved a paper into his hands.

Marcus placed a hand on his chin and read the missive. "Hmm? What's this? Hawaiians?"

Bella gently took the paper. "Let me, Moo . . . er, Mr. President."

Hattie rolled her eyes.

Bella read. A moment later her face lit up. "This is wonderful! A representative of a group of Hawaiian recidivists is coming here next week, to Grover Cleveland College, to present us with a special award 'For the efforts of President Grover Cleveland on behalf of the Hawaiian Kingdom.' Don't you see? This could be the salvation we've been waiting for. They could be bringing a sizable sum of money." Embracing Marcus, she added, "Oh, MooMoo, you were right. I'm so sorry I doubted you."

"I still don't understand," said Marcus, looking from Bella to Hattie.

Bella smiled at her beloved, willing to forgive him anything. "Hawaii was once independent, you see. The United States overthrew the queen and annexed the islands. President Grover Cleveland tried to stop it. He's a hero to them."

"A hero!"

"Yes." Bella handled the letter as if it were the Magna Carta. "This is big. It may save all of us and put the college back on the map. Oh, MooMoo!" And, Hattie or not, she threw herself into Marcus's arms.

The big man laughed contagiously.

Hattie was the only one not laughing. "I'll get the leis ready," she said sourly as she left.

After a final embrace, Marcus and Bella also parted. Bella limped off to her office to prepare a press release, while Marcus returned to the silo to look up the meaning of *recidivist*.

TWENTY
CONVERSION

The doomsday clock was at the six now, its tocking undiminished. In fact, to many it seemed to be growing louder, more insistent. Maybe this visit by the Hawaiians was only the first of many boons to come, cheating the clock of its grim objective. After all, Marcus considered, he'd never heard about a college closing. So why should Grover Cleveland be the first? The odds, in his mind, were against it.

The news of the Hawaiians' visit reignited the campus. In light of the impending Maine winter, the idea of a tropical Pacific breeze was intoxicating. Marcus immediately asked the Student Government Association to organize a decorating effort to welcome the visitors from the land of aloha.

In the meantime, Jim Burns had screwed up his courage and was marching across campus toward Diane Dempsey's office in the Victorian, holding his manuscript out before him, as if preparing to appease a god. The closer he came, the brighter the flame of his passion grew. On the way, he ran into Joe Dolch, his arms laden with books.

"Look at this," complained Joe as he walked alongside Jim. "The dog days of the twentieth century and I'm still carrying books and papers. Somebody should invent a small, handheld device for all of this."

"One day they will," said Jim absently, licking his lips, his eyes fixed on the Victorian.

"You really think so?" said Joe, hustling to keep up. "Even when you consider lab manuals, handouts, overheads?"

"One day you will be a dinosaur," said Jim flatly.

"What's eating you?" asked the chemist, blinking behind the smudged lenses of his horn-rims. "Why are you staring like that?"

"I'm on a mission."

"Oh, no, not another mission. Did you hear the prez wants the faculty to develop a strategic plan for the school? He says he has certain visions he wants to be included: a faculty buddy program, monthly faculty sleepovers, pizza Monday mornings. How in God's name is any of that supposed to save the place and our sorry asses?"

"They're not visions," said Jim, still staring at the Victorian, still plodding ahead. "They're hallucinations. Now leave me alone."

"Alone?" Joe froze in his tracks, shifting his books while Jim receded. "Who are you, Greta Garbo?"

But Jim hadn't heard him.

As Jim entered the Victorian, Dan Stupak was leaving. "Hey, Jim," he said as he lit his pipe. "You change that book title?"

"Yes," said Jim mechanically as he walked past his colleague and allowed the door to slam shut behind him.

When he got to Diane's office, the door was open and she was sitting with a student. She'd shed the tiger-stripe leotard for skin-tight jeans and a low-cut yellow top with a V so deep it revealed a small, newly minted, purple butterfly tattoo low on her left breast. Her marcelled waves of red hair still flowed down her back.

Jim pulled out his shirt to hide the evidence of his arousal and hovered on the threshold, clutching his manuscript. The student, a goth clad in black leather adorned with rings, studs, chains and badges, was complaining bitterly about a grade he'd received on an essay submitted before Diane's new policy about self-assignation of grades. This struck Jim as strange. He'd assumed goths considered things like grades and assignments, along with the rest of established culture, meaningless. But this student was in the middle of a full-court press.

My God, he's crying, Jim thought.

Black mascara ran down the student's cheeks. "I just don't understand why I got a D. I mean, I know I didn't finish reading *The Grapes of Wrath*, but I knew what grapes were and I looked up the word *wrath*. It means anger, right? So I wrote my essay about being angry about grapes. What I'm saying, Professor Dempsey, is that I was being honest about my feelings."

Diane inclined toward the student, her face awash with sympathy. "Let's take another look."

Jim watched as she scanned the paper. "Yes, yes," she reflected. "I see what you mean. These are your feelings, and they're honest feelings, good feelings." She handed the paper back to the student. "Would you feel better if I gave you an A?"

The boy was dumbstruck. "Well, er, that's a big change. Are you serious?"

"Of course," said Diane as she pulled out her grade book. "Look here. I'm changing your grade from a D to an A. And don't ever let anybody tell you that your feelings are invalid."

The student jingled as he pulled himself to his feet. "Thank you so much," he said, wiping his eyes with his hand. "You're a great teacher."

Diane nodded. The student jingled past Jim and loped down the hall and out of the building.

"He's happy now," said Diane as Jim entered her office.

"Happy, yes. But did he deserve such a precipitous grade change?"

"Sit down, Jim," said Diane breezily as she slouched back in her chair.

He swallowed hard and took his place, sitting like a schoolboy with his manuscript plopped in his lap and his hands under his thighs. He'd never seen Diane like this. Her posture was normally bolt upright and severe, her hands folded before her. But now she was reposing like an odalisque. Blood pounded in his ears.

"Jim, I've found the secret."

"The secret?"

"Yes," said Diane as she threw her hair back. "The secret. I was getting really ill from all the tension of grading and then having the grades challenged, not to mention all the political tension on campus, the incessant meetings, and of course the approaching death date of the school. I finally decided everything is valid. Everything they write. So why not give them all As?"

Jim arched his eyebrows. His impulse was to cry out in horror or indulge in a belly laugh, but then he remembered his mission and decided instead to swallow. "That, er, sounds like a real breakthrough."

Diane glanced about as she processed her colleague's

comment. "Yes, yes," she finally said with gravity. "That's exactly what it is. But it's not an original idea. When Robert Frost was teaching, he often misplaced his students' papers. When they finally asked him how they did, he would scratch his head and say, 'Oh, yes, you got an A. Very fine work.' And look at the number of poets he inspired."

Jim hadn't heard a word. What was that perfume she was wearing? It was infecting him, tempting him, its molecules streaming into his nostrils like a flight of swifts down a chimney.

"So why are you here, Jim?"

"Hm?"

"You look out of it. Now share."

Jim took a deep breath. "I've been unfair to you for years, decades—"

Diane put up a hand. "No. I will not recall the past. There is no past. There's only the moment. As far as I'm concerned, I've never known you until today, until now." She seized his right hand and pressed it between both of hers. "James, it's nice to know you. My name is Diane. How are you?"

That was the trigger. His manuscript flew apart as he became like a fluid and washed over Diane, toppling her to the floor. He had the presence of mind to kick the door closed as he flailed. To his delight, she didn't resist. He was lost in a sea of appendages, as if he were wrestling an octopus.

"Yes, yes," she moaned. "The moment! The moment! Seize the moment!"

Jim had achieved his objective. And he had no concerns about his performance, because the new Diane gave only As.

TWENTY-ONE
ALOHA AND A CEREBRAL AFFRONT

Marcus was up in the silo watching an episode of *Hawaii Five-0* when Hattie walked in. "I think I have the flavor of the place now," he said as he clicked off the TV. "Very lush, very green, very pretty."

"Yeah, just like Maine," cracked Hattie. "Well, they're here."

"Who?"

Hattie rolled her eyes. "The Hawaiians." And then, "Where's Hairball?"

"Here already?" Marcus erupted to his feet and straightened his jacket. "I thought you said they were coming tomorrow."

"Yeah, that's what I said yesterday. Tomorrow is today."

Marcus shifted his eyes and thought for a moment. "Well!" he said, rubbing his hands together. "If they're here, they're here."

"No truer words were ever spoken." Hattie sniffed. "Are you ready? Do you have a few words to say?"

"I'll take care of that," came a voice from the doorway. It was Bella, leaning against the jamb, breathing hard. She was wearing a pretty print dress—light blue sprinkled with tiny red roses. "I'll brief the president." She limped into the office.

Hattie snapped her gum and smiled. "I know you will," she said, leaving the room.

"Harebell," sighed Marcus.

Bella flew to his arms. "This will be a brilliant day for you. The Hawaiians have come a long way just to honor us. This will make the evening news. The man's name is Kahananui. Akamu Kahananui."

"Oh, my. That's a mouthful. I hope this isn't too big a fuss."

"This college needs a fuss," said Bella, nestling into his chest.

"I like your spirit," Marcus said. And then, tenderly, "Harebell."

"Everything is arranged. We've set up a small event area in front of the Victorian. Have you seen the campus?

There are leis and pineapples everywhere. One of the students will play the ukulele."

"I can always count on you."

Bella removed herself to arm's length, holding Marcus's hands. "Did you read the briefing I left for you?"

"Briefing?" echoed Marcus.

"I told Hattie to put it on your desk. A little background about the history of the Hawaiian annexation and President Grover Cleveland's stand against it."

Marcus rubbed his chin. "I have to admit I haven't examined my desk for some time. To tell you the truth, sometimes things show up that I'm not in a mood to see."

Bella blanched. "Oh, MooMoo," she admonished him. Then she smoothed his lapels. "Just thank them for the honor. And remember what President Cleveland said. That the annexation of Hawaii was a perversion of our national mission."

"Perversion! Strong language."

"It's time to go." Bella advanced toward the spiral stairway ahead of Marcus.

But he reached out and restrained her. "Let me go first. That way, if you stumble, I'll break your fall."

"MooMoo!"

As Marcus began his descent, Hattie signaled to Bella. "Are you going to ask me about Brisco?" the secretary whispered. "Because I didn't find out anything."

"Well, I did," said Bella, happy to not have to honor

her obligation to Hattie now.

Hattie looked hard at her coconspirator, her eyes begging for elucidation.

But Bella just shrugged. "Don't worry about it."

Hattie seethed. Now there would be no guarantee of just-cause protection, leaving her wondering when she would no longer be needed, no matter how indispensable she thought she was. "I can still be of help," she said feebly, having apparently forgotten that in a very short while all considerations of protection or job security would be moot.

Bella turned and headed down the stairs. "Not at the moment." She cast a wave over her shoulder. "Toodle-oo!"

Of course, Brisco still had her parking space, for the moment at least, but she'd kept Hattie in her place.

Just as Bella had said, the campus was awash in leis and pineapples. A stoned male student wandered barefoot, plinking tinny notes from a plastic ukulele, casually making his way across the campus green toward the Victorian. A strikingly handsome, dark-skinned man, accompanied by a pudgy young man with bangs, holding a manila envelope, stood before the collected faculty, staff, and a smattering of students.

Marcus shuffled through the crowd, with Bella limping close behind. Jim Burns was standing up front, holding hands with Diane Dempsey, who kept tossing her red tresses back as if she were auditioning for a shampoo commercial. Henny Spox was there in his solitude. Onan chirped on Jiminy's shoulder and nibbled his earlobe. Pete Blatty signaled to the ukulele player to come closer, while Dan Stupak tamped Borkum Riff into the bowl of his pipe. Joe Dolch stood next to Dan, head and shoulders above most of the crowd. Scott Ott, a cigarette plastered to his lower lip, fiddled with the microphone. Only Brisco Quik was conspicuous by his absence.

Bella introduced Marcus to Mr. Kahananui. She looked on as the Hawaiian put his arm around Marcus's shoulder and conferred with him for several minutes. Then she turned and tapped the microphone. "Can you hear me?" The microphone crackled and squealed, which sent OK Ott running for the controls.

"The dog days of the twentieth century," muttered Joe Dolch, "and they still can't get a microphone to work."

OK Ott turned from the control box to Bella. "There. Try it now."

"Honored guests," intoned Bella.

Crackle. Squeal.

"President Marcus, faculty, staff, students . . ."

Joe Dolch leaned over to Dan Stupak. "She forgot the bison."

Bella went on to give a little historical background of the Hawaiian annexation, for Marcus's sake as well as the crowd's. She concluded with, "This is a gala day for Grover Cleveland College!"

"Well, a gal a day is enough for me," cracked Joe. "I don't think I could handle any more."

Marcus stepped up to the microphone. "That was quite a speech, Bella," he said and laughed.

"Why is he laughing?" asked Dan.

"Because it was quite a speech," said Joe from the corner of his mouth.

"No one was more surprised than I when I heard about our visit from Hawaii," continued Marcus. A camera flashed, and the ukulele player struck a chord. This threw Marcus off, and he cast a helpless glance at Bella.

She mouthed, *Perversion*.

"Oh. Oh, yes," stammered Marcus. "The visit from Hawaii is a perversion of our mission."

Bella frantically signaled to the ukulele-playing student, who began to strum and pluck. Then she hurried in front of Marcus and took the microphone. "Yes, Mr. President. You are right that the late, great President Grover Cleveland called the annexation of Hawaii a perversion of our national mission. On that note, I think our guest has a few words to say."

The tall, handsome Hawaiian man with the mane of thick black hair and pronounced native features stepped up to the mike, accompanied by a wave of applause. He flashed a brilliant smile and said, "Aloha."

An effusion of alohas erupted in response.

"Very good," said Mr. Kahananui in a sonorous

baritone. "You actually know two Hawaiian expressions now, because *aloha* means both hello and good-bye. But we don't want to say good-bye just yet."

The crowd chortled amicably, charmed by the manner and poise of this exotic visitor. They listened as he went on to recount, from the Hawaiians' point of view, the events leading up to the Hawaiian annexation, the sad end of Liliuokalani, the last queen of Hawaii, and the attempts of Grover Cleveland to right the wrong. When he had finished these remarks, the ukulele player launched into "My Little Grass Shack."

When the music ended, Mr. Kahananui reapproached the mike. "But what is gratitude without substance? Out of a sense of admiration and appreciation for the efforts of President Grover Cleveland to restore our independence, we think it fitting to support the mission of the school that bears his name. In this light," he said, receiving the manila envelope from his assistant, "we have here a check for the endowment of a dedicated chair—your first, I am told—to be held by a professor who embodies the qualities of diligence, rationalism, scholasticism, and perseverance in the face of adversity."

Frannie Moore stood on her toes but was still invisible in the sea of bodies. She'd always felt herself to be diligent, if nothing else, in leading the Faculty Assembly.

Dan Stupak felt the blood rush to his face. Perseverance, he felt, was his middle name. For years, he'd offered high-quality instruction in the face of ever-diminishing budgetary support.

Jim Burns squeezed Diane's hand. This award would certainly be enough to subsidize, if need be, the publication of his book on mucus, which he'd retitled *Naked Heat*.

Hector Lopez was totally lost. He had not understood any of those last words and wasn't even sure he could pronounce *scholasticism*.

Bella felt sick. *An endowed chair? Whose money will that be? The school's? The professor's who occupied the chair?*

"On the advice of your president," continued Mr. Kahananui, "I am happy to announce that this endowed chair—The Grover Cleveland Chair in Applied Academics—will be held by Professor Henny Spox."

The faculty emitted a collective gasp, like a communal asthma attack. Not one of them could bring one hand up against the other, but ample applause was provided by students and some of the staff as well as Marcus.

Bella was paralyzed. Just as the applause died down, there was an ululation from the back of the crowd. All heads turned to see a now-familiar, shapely, animated woman storming toward the microphone. A moment later, she was the center of attention.

YaYa began to weep even before she said a word. "Yes! Yes!" she sobbed while raising a fist in the air. "Finally. At long last. Oh, you'll never know how that man—that genius—suffers. You have the brain of Grover Cleveland in a jar, but what good is it? Henny's brain should be in a jar for all to admire, if not worship. If any of you had an ounce of decency, you would thank God Almighty that he is here among you. I wish I could explain the sense of the man and how he has striven to be the best he can be. But how could any of you understand? You're willing to stage marches to free Cambodia from hegemonic interests. I even once saw a hunger strike on campus, after which the students pigged out on pizza. Where is the virtue there if you know you've got a warm bed coming if only you'll sleep out in the cold for a night to prove a point?" YaYa dropped her head into her hands and sobbed. "Oh, why can't we all just get along!"

YaYa's performance had riveted the crowd, including Henny, who stared with the rest of them. Finally, he began to work his jaw. "Did I win something?"

Bella gently maneuvered YaYa out of the way and took the microphone. "Professor Spox," she barely managed, "we . . . we congratulate you."

"That's a good thing, no?" said Henny.

YaYa continued to sniffle, her shoulders heaving with emotion.

"Yes, very good," said Marcus. Turning to Bella, he asked, "Isn't it?"

Bella nodded slowly. Her face was grim, but duty was duty. Leaning into the microphone, she muttered, "Perhaps Professor Spox would like to say a few words?"

Hands fluttered again. Henny Spox looked about, said, "No," and walked off toward his institute with YaYa in his wake.

Mr. Kahananui looked perplexed, but he was practiced in dealing with unexpected turns of events. He stepped to the microphone and said, "Well, I'd sure like to see that brain."

Marcus, recalling YaYa's comments, thought he was talking about Henny Spox's brain and wondered how such a thing could be arranged. But then he understood. He assumed the mike. "Yes, why not? Let's have a procession to the Brain Shrine."

The entire crowd moved off as a unit and swarmed toward the shrine. The Hawaiian man walked alongside Marcus. "You're fortunate to have such an important piece of history. How did you come by it?"

Marcus didn't have the slightest idea. He'd never thought to ask. He turned to Bella, who leaped to his rescue. "After President Cleveland's autopsy, it was transported cross-country in one of the very first Model Ts. Then, somehow, it got lost. Twenty years later, someone found it behind a beer keg in a Milwaukee warehouse, and the rest is history."

"That's quite a story," said the Hawaiian.

"Yes, it is!" exclaimed Marcus, fascinated by the tale.

The procession reached the Brain Shrine, which had been tidied up nicely for the visit. Spruce boughs had been laid at the entrance, and the explanatory plaque had been polished. Despite budgetary restraints, the eternal flame had been ignited for the event, and the student sentinel, as per custom, had fallen asleep. The only thing missing was The Brain, along with its repository jar.

A shudder passed through the crowd, which erupted into animated speech.

Bella hobbled about the catafalque that had held the relic. "Who could have done such a thing?" she pleaded.

Marcus hummed disconsolately. "Not a good thing," he finally said. Turning to the Hawaiian, he asserted, "I'm sure it hasn't gone far."

Mr. Kahananui smiled diplomatically. He checked his watch and adjusted his tie. "Well, when you find it—and I'm sure you will—please send me a photo, preferably with all of you gathered about it. It would give me something to remember the school by."

"Excellent," Marcus said. "Will do."

And with that, the two visitors from the far islands of the Pacific left.

As the crowd dissipated, Marcus turned and stared at the vacant catafalque. "I'm trying to reason this out," he said, mostly to himself, with Bella standing next to him. "We had a brain. Now we don't. This means it's disappeared. Since it was dead, it couldn't have wandered off by itself. This means someone must have taken it."

"MooMoo! What a wonder to see your Holmes-like

mind at work, eliminating the impossible to arrive at the correct conclusion."

In the meantime, a figure skulked along the margin of the college forest, hunched over a bundle clutched close to its body. After the crowd dispersed, the figure set a new trajectory—directly for the Institute of Semi-Tessellated Invariant Mathematics. No one would ever think to look there, and perhaps Henny Spox would turn out to be a valuable, if unsuspecting, ally.

TWENTY-TWO
SANCTUARY AND A DARK CLOUD

Jim Burns walked across campus hand in hand with Diane.

Her face was raised to the sun. "I'm happy you're not afraid to display affection for me in public."

It struck Jim that he'd never thought of the campus as public. The school had always felt like a bubble to him—a blister on the fickle finger of fate that went largely unnoticed by the world at large. He glanced at Diane. "If we're going to have a fling, I guess we'll need witnesses."

Diane chortled and threw her hair back. "Oh, Jimmy," she said, noting his uncharacteristic remark. "I think I've loosened you up." She smiled. "Tell me how your book is doing."

Jim became animated. "Vikram has decided to go ahead with it. In spite of the school's circumstances."

"Jimmy! What changed his mind?"

"The new title. I laid the book down in front of him, and that red eye of his began to pulse like a laser. He said even if the school goes under, he had a plan to start a press of his own, and since my book would already be in the pipeline—"

"That's the ticket. The title must have grabbed him. It will be published, people will buy it, and even if they don't find it interesting, they'll just shelve the book rather than trouble themselves to return it. And you'll profit from the sale. It's perfect."

Jim Burns attempted a smile, not sure what to make of the backhanded compliment. "But I'd like people to enjoy it," he said meekly, searching Diane's face for affirmation.

"Enjoy schmoy," she said with a wave of her hand. "You'll be published. Who cares if anybody reads it?"

Jim peeped, "I do."

In the meantime, Brisco had made his way with his precious bundle to the Institute for Semi-Tessellated Invariant Mathematics. Huddling against the door, he looked furtively about and gave a stiff rap. After a few moments, he knocked again. "Come on, come on," he growled as he juggled his clumsy burden. Then he heard the latch, and the door squeaked open. A woman's face appeared in the crack. "What do you want?" she asked, her voice rife with suspicion.

"Sanctuary," said Brisco, as if this were the password that assured entry.

The woman seemed to freeze at the door, but after a few moments, she opened it and Brisco stumbled inside.

He glanced about the cluttered room like a frightened bird. Hurrying over to a table, he cleared a space among a mass of papers and set his bundle down.

"Don't touch a thing!" commanded YaYa, her hands to her face.

"Oops," said Brisco. "Too late. I just had to put it down."

He straightened up and continued to look about, noting the instrumentation, papers, books, and a blackboard covered with equations. This was a real working space, and Henny Spox was clearly a very busy man. But who exactly was this attractive woman, her eyes sparkling with self-possession and intelligence?

"I saw you at the talent show," he finally said. "I like people with conviction. Are you Henny's daughter?"

YaYa squared her shoulders. "I am his companion."

Brisco liked the sound of that. He had actually expected her to say *girlfriend*, which had a fleeting quality about it. But *companion* spoke of durability, the willingness to stick with someone through thick and thin, like a buddy in a foxhole. For a moment, he considered whether Hattie were companion material. Or did she just want bragging rights to having conquered him?

YaYa stood before him, one hand nesting in the other. "What do you want?" she repeated.

Brisco steeled himself. "I need a place."

YaYa slowly shook her head. "I don't understand. For what? And why here? Henny does not like to be disturbed."

"I won't disturb him. The college is about to die, and nobody cares. It will take a strong hand to turn things around. The president is clearly not up to the task. I need a place to think out my plan."

YaYa turned her attention to Brisco's bundle. "What is that?"

Brisco also considered the bundle. "Our only hope."

YaYa let out a sigh. "We don't have a lot of food. Food isn't important here. But I do have pumpkin seeds from the garden and honey that we make from African bees. Sometimes there's egg salad."

Brisco was actually a steak-and-potatoes man, but he knew he wasn't in a position to demand or bargain. "Whatever you have."

"Sit."

In the meantime, Hattie stood before Marcus's desk, slapping a hand on a mess of papers she'd thrown down. "Don't you see?" she pleaded. "The students have got a whiff of what's going on. They're going back to the shelter and the nuthouse. We can't pay the bills. Oh, yeah, I know there was this blip when those buffaloes showed up, but that's all over. Got any more tricks up your sleeve?"

Marcus had no choice but to pay attention to Hattie. He sat in his chair, looking up at her, rubbing his chin. Pacer leapt onto the desk, arched his back, and hissed at the secretary, who cast a wary eye at the feline.

"I'm sure something will turn up," Marcus said. "That endowed chair helped, didn't it?"

"Yeah. It helped Henny Spox. But what the hell good is it when the school is closed and they put up a Burger King where you're sitting?"

There had been nothing in *The Handbook of College Reorganization* about increasing or even sustaining student numbers, so Marcus was at sea on this one. He couldn't figure it out, though. It didn't make any sense. Besides the bison, there was Henny's research, the famous blackfly book, the coming triumph of Jim Burns's book on mucus, the talent show, the visit of the Hawaiians, the NEA recognition, and the occasional presidential brain. Yet, if Hattie was right, all of this had done nothing to staunch the exodus of the student body and sustain the school's cash flow. In a very short time, then, the bankers would arrive with their hands out. What on earth would he tell them?

Marcus thought hard for a long moment. Then he focused on his secretary, standing before him expectantly, her arms crossed. "Where do we stand on the vending machine?" he asked as he gathered Pacer to his chest and scratched behind his ears.

Hattie shook her head, sending her broad curls first this way, then that. "It's going to take more than orange Fanta to turn this place around. If you want my advice, it's time to man the lifeboats." Then she stormed out.

Marcus was alone. He swiveled in his chair and looked down on the campus. "Cyrus," he pled softly, as if he could channel his uncle's spirit, "what would you do? What should I do?" Of course, Marcus couldn't imagine what Cyrus might do, because he'd never really known the man. All he knew was that he himself had answered a call to service. But for the first time since arriving at Grover Cleveland, he was laden with doubt about his own abilities. He'd falsely concluded that his experience selling cars would be good preparation for a college presidency.

In the chapter of *The Handbook of College Reorganization* titled "The Fix is In," the author divulged that most college presidencies were arranged by a small number of insiders. Yes, there was advertising in national and professional periodicals, a selection committee was convened, and the college community was allowed and even encouraged to cross-examine the candidates, but this was all pro forma. The next president had already been chosen by the powers that be, and all the preliminary theater was designed to dupe the suckers into thinking they actually played some role in the selection process.

Marcus now realized it hadn't been much different with him. He had gotten the call, responded, traveled to Grover Cleveland, and made that first inaugural grope up the silo's spiral stairs, past the conga line of mourners waiting to see what was left of Cyrus. If there had been a true selection process and people's feelings and preferences had been taken into account, would he really have been considered Grover Cleveland material? For the first time since accepting the position, Marcus was forced to face reality: the school was on the brink of collapse—on his watch.

Next door, Jiminy Schmitz stood before Hattie's desk, bent and exhausted from the long climb.

Hattie was speechless. Jiminy had never been to the top of the silo before. "You . . . you want to see him?"

"See who?"

"Him. President Marcus. That's why you're here, right?"

"The president's name is Marcus?"

Hattie squinted. "Which president are we talking about?"

Jiminy reached into the pocket of his careworn sport

coat and pulled Onan out. He stroked the parakeet's head with a bony finger, and the bird trilled. "I'm actually here for my pension," he said without removing his focus from the budgie. Then he carefully repocketed his pet.

Hattie stared at him, bereft of emotion. During her tenure at Grover Cleveland, no one had ever asked about his pension. The faculty had been static for years, except for the occasional death. She sighed. "Why?"

"Sea level is rising," the provost said, "and I might as well have my life jacket."

Hattie smacked the table and cackled. "Finally, someone who sees reality and knows what he wants! Provost, if I had your pension in my purse, I'd give it to you right now. The truth is, the school has not paid into your pension fund for years. There's not much more than the little you've contributed from your own pay."

Jiminy nibbled on the tuft of beard bordering his lower lip. "Hmm…" he pondered. "What does that come to?"

Hattie stood up, scanned a high shelf, and removed an old ledger lying on its side. She took a Kleenex and wiped the dust from the cover before opening it. "Here," she said as she jabbed a page. "Five hundred and sixty-two dollars and seventy-three cents." She looked up at Jiminy and laughed as if she'd just read the punch line to a particularly funny joke.

Jiminy rocked on his heels for a few moments before

saying, "I'll take it."

Hattie had no idea how to disburse the money, but she didn't want to look incompetent, especially in front of the provost, so she riffled through a few manila folders and pulled out a piece of paper with some lines and boxes on it. "I'll file this form for you and keep you apprised of its progress as it moves through the system," she said mechanically, giving the impression she'd done this a hundred times.

"What system?" chirped Jiminy.

"Don't worry. I'll make sure it goes through."

"Well, I guess those are all the apples we're going to pick today."

"Do you want to see him while you're here?"

"See who?"

"Him. President Marcus."

Jiminy scratched his beard. "Oh, I suppose so," he said, like a man reluctantly agreeing to view a display of Tupperware.

"Just go in," said Hattie. "I don't think he's all that busy."

Jiminy gave Hattie a cursory salute.

Jiminy found the president sitting with Pacer on his lap, lost in thought.

When Marcus saw him, his face lit up. "Provost! This is a pleasure. Long time no see. Did you enjoy the talent show?"

Jiminy actually recalled the show. "I was like a kid at the circus. I thought it was great fun. And I didn't hear a harsh word from anybody. It was a real crowd-pleaser."

Marcus beamed.

Pacer leapt from his lap and onto the desk, where he began to prowl.

"Yes," Marcus said. "I only wish more people had contributed to the donation bucket."

"Sad. Very sad," said Jiminy, who hadn't thrown in a nickel himself. "I've come to say good-bye."

Marcus's face dropped. "Good-bye? Are you going somewhere?"

"It's my time."

Marcus became disconsolate. He leaned forward and whispered, "You're dying?"

Jiminy thought for a moment. "No, I don't think so. Not yet."

"Well, that's the bright side, then."

"The truth is, I think I've done all I can for the school. It's time for someone else to fill my shoes." Even as he said this, Jiminy searched his recollection for something he might have accomplished. Some small contribution. He decided it would come to him if he stopped thinking about it so hard.

Pacer arched his back and hissed at Jiminy.

"There now, Pacer," admonished Marcus. "That's no way to treat an administrator. Show some respect."

But the cat continued to bare its teeth in a grotesque smile.

"I don't know what's gotten into him," said Marcus. "He's usually very gentle."

"Maybe it's this," said Jiminy as he pulled Onan from his pocket and perched him on his forefinger. Like a sprung trap, Pacer leapt, seizing the bird in his teeth and continuing out the door in a smooth arc of mammalian prowess.

All Marcus could manage was a blunt "Hupp!" while Jiminy stood there, frozen, his finger in the air, as if expecting the bird to re-alight.

"I-I'm so sorry," blurted Marcus. "How unfortunate! I will reprimand Pacer severely," he said, making a chopping motion with his hand.

Jiminy thawed and reanimated. "Such is the way of the world." He sniffed, wiping a tear from his eye. "Life is short; death is certain." And then, after a pause, "I'll say good-bye now."

Marcus watched as the provost shuffled toward the door. "I'll recommend you for emeritus!" he called after his colleague.

A minute later, Hattie came in. "I just saw the saddest man in the world," she said, shaking her head. "Poor man." She handed Marcus a sheet of paper with crude lettering. "Not to change the subject, but we've got a situation on our hands."

Marcus took the leaf and examined it. Aloud, he read, "I have The Brain. Unless a vending machine appears on campus in three days, I will destroy it. Believe me."

"The gall!" exclaimed Hattie. "Who would steal the brain of a president?"

"There, there," Marcus counseled as he patted the air. "Look at the bright side. At least we know what happened to it."

Hattie threw her hands up. "Well, Captain, what now?"

Marcus's eyes flew between the paper and Hattie. "Please forward this to the Vending Committee. They'll see the urgency and act accordingly, I'm sure."

Hattie took the note and shook her head. "You dream. But sure, I'll give it to the committee. Why not? It'll give them something to do," she said and left the office.

"Ah, Pacer," Marcus said as the cat leapt onto his desk. "We were all alone when the call came to serve. I fear we will soon be alone again. Perhaps that's the way things are supposed to be for us. At least you won't have to pack a bag."

The feline meowed, and as he did, a small, blue feather flew from his mouth and floated gently to the floor.

TWENTY-THREE
THE EVE OF CONVOCATION

Henny Spox didn't bat an eye when he returned to the institute and found Brisco hunched in a dim corner, spooning pumpkin seeds and honey from a bowl, his jaw working mechanically as he eyed the mathematician. Henny offered a cursory hello and turned immediately to some papers that had accumulated on his desk. Brisco felt a sting of remorse for the role he'd played over the years in marginalizing Henny, but he couldn't bring himself to say anything that might sap the strength he needed for the battle ahead, so he continued to chew.

YaYa came through the door and flew to Henny. She rubbed his back, whispered something in his ear, and then stood by his side as he continued to paw his papers.

Finally Brisco piped up. "Did you deliver that note for me?"

YaYa turned to him. "I put it in campus mail. The president should have received it by now."

"Good, good," mumbled Brisco as he scooped another spoonful of seeds. "Then we've crossed the fail-safe point."

YaYa threw him a blank look and turned back to Henny, who finally dispensed with his papers. "I'm haunted," he said, incongruously.

"Speak to me," said YaYa with intense concern.

"When President Marcus and I took our little walk a while back—did I ever tell you how fond I am of him?—we stumbled upon this glade in the woods. It seemed like an excellent place for fungi, but there wasn't a mushroom or mold to be found. This has been bothering me. I think I need to return there. I am drawn."

YaYa patted his back. "I don't like it when you're bothered."

"Ach," said Henny with a wave, "you shouldn't be so preoccupied with me."

"Hush," said YaYa, placing a hand over his mouth. "You are my life, my center, my still point."

"YaYa."

Across campus, Marcus had rendezvoused under the

bower with Bella.

"It's been so long," she panted as she clutched at him.

He grabbed her hands and looked her dead in the eye. "We must control our passions for the moment, Harebell. I'm afraid there's no easy solution for the crisis we're in."

Bella had never heard Marcus speak with such focus and dread, although she felt a pulse of relief that the school's dire circumstances were finally garnering his attention. She was the one accustomed to staring reality in the face and taking charge in the midst of tumult, for fear that she would be blamed for any failures and— gulp—wind up back at the chicken farm. But now she was bearing witness to an unfamiliar show of strength in the man she loved.

"This is my greatest trial yet," said Marcus as he held Bella at arm's length. "Despite my best efforts, we're losing more students and hemorrhaging red ink. I've been forced to confront the numbers. There isn't enough money to pay the faculty. What will I do when the end of the month arrives? What would Cyrus do?" And then, finally, "What will the bank do?"

Bella knew exactly what Cyrus would have done. He would have written a heartfelt letter to Richard Nixon congratulating him on his conduct of the war in Vietnam and urging him to stay the course. He would have pressured Maine legislators to open the floodgates on state-sponsored student loans. He would have found private benefactors. Then he would have beaten the bushes for students, warning them of the alternative should they not plop into a desk at Grover Cleveland College posthaste.

But this was peacetime, and there was no draft to send masses of warm bodies running to the embrace of Grover Cleveland. A parsimonious legislature was making it tougher to get a student loan. All the philanthropists Cyrus had known were either addled or dead, and even the alumni were crying poor mouth. Bella felt the sweat pooling under her arms. Once again she was seized by familiar doubts. When the college failed, as now seemed inevitable, would Marcus spirit her away? Or would he retreat into some dark emotional recess where even she wouldn't be able to reach him? Ultimately, would he hop the next bus to New Jersey and beg his old boss for a job on the wholesale lot?

"I received a ransom note today," said Marcus.

"A ransom! Has there been a kidnapping? Oh, MooMoo!"

"Be calm," said Marcus, patting her arm. "Someone has The Brain and is threatening to destroy it unless a vending machine appears on campus by Saturday."

"Who is it?" insisted Bella. "Who has The Brain?"

"The note wasn't signed," said Marcus, biting his knuckles. "But I directed that the Vending Committee be charged with averting this calamity."

"The committee!"

Marcus's face flushed with anxiety. "Was that the wrong thing to do, Harebell?"

"I wouldn't say *wrong*," said Bella. "But it might not be expeditious. The committee is chaired by Brisco Quik, and he seems to have disappeared from campus.

"Disappeared?"

"Yes. And even if he were here, my fear is that he would refer the issue to the Committee on Committees, which would then pursue the question of whether it's contractually permissible for the Vending Committee to fast-track the issue."

"I wasn't aware the faculty had contracts."

"They do. But they're only symbolic, instituted years ago to represent a wishful goal. They aren't binding, because there is no union to pursue contractual issues. Cyrus wasn't very fond of contracts, much less unions. But even the illusion of having one can slow things down, I'm afraid."

Marcus blinked. "Chapter sixteen of *The Handbook of College Reorganization* talks about executive privilege and power. It's a frightening chapter because the consequences of a college president's unilateral action can be dire. There was the case of Serendipity College, where the faculty rolled the president up in a rug and dumped him into Umbazooksus Stream for naming the new library after his mistress."

Bella blushed and looked away. Then she slowly turned to Marcus again. "It's okay, MooMoo," she said softly. "There are no rugs on campus."

"A small comfort. But any comfort will do at the moment. Any port in a storm."

In the meantime, Jim Burns and Diane Dempsey strolled along the edge of the college forest, holding hands, Diane's red hair blazing in the intense autumn sun.

"It's funny," said Jim, "but with the bison at large, I've avoided walking here. I was afraid they'd charge out and trample me."

Diane laughed like a macaw. "Oh, Jimmy!" she sang. "You have such odd fears. Relax. I'm here with you. I'll subdue the beasts if need be."

Oddly, Jim took comfort in this, and they continued to walk.

"A penny for your thoughts," prompted Diane.

Jim shrugged amiably. "You know, I thought once my book was out of my hands, I'd be beset about the end of Grover Cleveland. I know it's coming, but it's like those four steps you go through when you've been told you're going to die. I'm past denial and anger, and I never had anything to bargain with, so here I am stranded on the shores of acceptance. What about you?"

Diane actually sniffed and wiped a tear. "If this were almost any other place, we could count on the engineering department to bring in the big grant money. But as an English prof, well, what can I do? I dream, Jimmy. I dream."

Before he could ask what she was dreaming about, he spotted a student making her way into the woods. "Isn't that your aspiring poet?"

Diane placed a shielding hand over her eyes. "Yep. Many poets have sought inspiration in the forest. Maybe she'll find her muse there."

They watched as the student dipped her small feet into the understory and hopped into the woods like a nymph.

How could Jim and Diane have known that the student had already found her muse, her inspiration, in a member of the faculty? He sat on a stump in a small clearing, looking anxiously about. The student came up behind him and placed her hands around his eyes. "Guess who!"

Hector Lopez quickly reached up and grabbed her wrists. "You scare me!" he said in a harsh whisper.

The student swung her lithe body around him like a pole dancer and landed—plop!—in Hector's lap. She threw her arms around his neck and planted a moist kiss on his lips. "Someday I'm going to teach you how to French. You've got a lot to learn."

Hector's heart raced. "We must be careful, Amber," he said, glancing furtively about. "Someone will see."

For all his years at Grover Cleveland, Hector was

strangely ignorant of many of the traditions of the academy, such as the dirty little faculty-student affair. At forty-two, he was only now, for the first time, plying these sweet waters, tasting this ripe fruit, this taut-skinned peach ready to burst at the slightest touch. "*Dios*," he finally breathed. Amber, still with her arms around his neck, pulled back. "Is that a good *Dios* or a bad *Dio*s?"

"I-I don't know."

"It's time you got bred," she said as she pulled him to the ground, making the undergrowth crackle. She straddled him and began to recite Dylan Thomas as she rocked. "'If I were tickled by the rub of love,'" she sang. She stopped her gyrations for a moment. "I just learned that one," she said, staring down at Hector. "You like it?"

"I-I—"

"'A rooking girl who stole me for her side.'" She rocked.

"Am—?"

"'This world is half the devil's and my own.'"

"*Dios*!"

Brisco had put the word out: there would be a Convocation of Concerned Faculty, a summit meeting, an emergency session, a crisis council, to save the school from falling victim to the president's failed and halfhearted initiatives to save it. Brisco stormed about Henny's institute, raving.

Henny struggled to pretend Brisco wasn't there. "Quieter," was all he said whenever Brisco's volume got to be too much.

For YaYa it was like living with a chimpanzee. She finally approached him. "You will have to be quiet. You are disturbing Henny."

Brisco threw himself into a worn, overstuffed chair and bit his fist. "I feel so constrained. It was a mistake to ever leave the Navy."

There was a knock at the door.

YaYa sighed and turned to Brisco. "You have opened a flood. It used to be so calm here. So peaceful." She went to the door.

Hattie nodded. "I remember you from the talent show," she said, pointing at YaYa. Then she glanced at Henny and snapped her gum. "Oh, I get the picture. Say no more."

YaYa looked at Hattie blankly. "I wasn't going to say anything."

Hattie huffed. "Well, to each his own. Anyway, I'm here to see him." She nodded toward Brisco.

YaYa stepped aside, and Hattie trotted in. YaYa and Henny left the room.

"Brisco, hon," Hattie said, "you got your convocation. In the Victorian at four this afternoon. I don't know what good it's gonna do, though. Jiminy has already jumped ship, and the students have all but formed a caravan leaving campus. This place is for the history books now. The bank's not going to have a stick of trouble throwing it in the back of a truck and hauling it away."

For the first time, she seemed to notice Brisco's sorry appearance. Her heart swelled with pity and affection as she regarded his unshaven face and rumpled clothing. She went over to him and ran a hand through his matted hair. "You've been putting me off. I don't like it, Brisco. I want to go away someplace with you. Where I can take care of you." As she said this, she felt vulnerable, exposed. She'd always worn cynicism like a second skin, and here she was stripping it off in front of a man who didn't even seem to notice she was a woman. "Come on," she said, running her nails down to his scalp. "You're looking for a solution that isn't there."

Brisco stared darkly at the floor. "There's always a solution."

Hattie rolled her eyes. "You make a rotten optimist," she said, withdrawing her hand and taking a step back.

"I'm a realist," said Brisco. "I really believe we can be saved."

Hattie gave up. "Shoot. You can't even get a vending machine," she said as she turned to go. "How you gonna get a new population of students? How you gonna get money?"

Brisco looked up at her. "You don't understand. It's symbolic. Of our inertia. We have to start somewhere.

If we can get the vending machine, then maybe we can do anything. Even save the school. Anyway, it's in God's hands now."

Hattie threw him one last look. "God?"

"Yes," said Brisco. "I am God."

Hattie's eyes widened. "You are confused. A piece of advice, since you didn't ask: don't say that at the meeting."

Hattie left, and a pall fell over Brisco. He sank into himself and pondered the options. Spotting the *Bangor Daily News* on the floor, he picked it up and began to aimlessly page through its contents, his gaze landing on the Help Wanted ads. Heating contractor, electrician, heavy equipment operator, surveyor's assistant, phlebotomist. He realized with despondency that he couldn't do any of those things. He was a prisoner of the academy, unable to function in any productive way outside its walls. It was as if the school had birthed him and someone had forgotten to cut the umbilical cord: he still drew oxygen and sustenance from Mother, and it was too late to do anything about it.

But this realization focused his mind. Didn't this mean he *must* save the school? If he could get the vending machine, the other faculty would rally to him for his show of leadership. Most had been here all their professional lives, too, and were just as dependent on Grover Cleveland as he was. Surely they would understand this. Surely they would seize the opportunity to follow him when he called for emergency measures to stave off collapse.

He leapt up from his chair, picked up The Brain, and made for the door. "I'm going," he said to the ether. "I'm going now."

TWENTY-FOUR
THE GREATEST SHOW ON EARTH

At the convocation, there quickly developed an air of grim resignation now that faculty were all in one place, once again confronting the issue of the school's extinction.

Dan tried to lighten the mood. "I've been through these crises a thousand times," he said, philosophically, as he chewed on the stem of his pipe. "We always seem to come out of it in one piece."

"That's very nice, Pollyanna," said Joe Dolch, smiling. "Can I quote you on that?" He jerked his head toward Jim Burns, who'd just entered with Diane. "The campus scandal," he said, wiggling his eyebrows. "And it's about time we had one."

Dan stared at the couple. "I heard Vikram's going to put Jim's book out."

"And I'm going to put the cat out," Joe said.

Brisco, looking as if he'd just come off a three-day bender, skulked through the door, clutching The Brain to his chest. Arched over his burden, he hobbled through the crowd to the head of the room, set The Brain on the front desk, and withdrew the cloth cover. There was a collective gasp.

Joe leaned over to Dan. "I always knew Brisco had the brain of a hundred-and-fifty-year-old man."

Even Dan couldn't suppress a chuckle at that one.

"So!" Brisco addressed the gathering. "Here we are."

"Is that a motion?" asked Joe, loud enough for everyone to hear.

Brisco threw him a scathing look.

"Can we get the show on the road?" begged Pete Blatty in an uncharacteristically assertive tone, earning him an approving nod from Jim Burns.

Brisco glared at Pete. "*Et tu, Brute?*"

"Well, uh," said Pete, making himself small, "all I was saying is that some people might want to hear what you have to say." And then, looking anxiously about, "Right?"

"I have The Brain," said Brisco, stating the obvious. "I took it because I, for one, am fed up with administrative inertia and ineptitude. In the words of Theodore Roosevelt, 'I have only a second rate brain, but I think I have a capacity for action.'"

There was a minor rumble of discontent. Which brain was Brisco referring to, his or the late president's? The mention of TR was, in fact, irritating because Grover Cleveland had been a staunch Democrat, and at Grover Cleveland College it had always been considered bad taste to invoke the Rough Rider or, for that matter, any Republican.

Frannie Moore cleared her throat. "What are you trying to say, Brisco? Why are we here?"

"Tomorrow is Saturday. If there is no vending machine on this campus by tomorrow, I will destroy The Brain."

"My God Almighty!" Hattie exclaimed, having abandoned all hope of getting into Brisco's pants. "People! There are bigger fish to fry. In fact, there's only one big fish. We might not even be here by tomorrow. There's no more money. We're broke. This is it!"

The faculty looked at Hattie, the child claiming the emperor had no clothes. This was the big one, then. Colleges had indeed closed before—it wasn't as if they were exempt from the basic laws of economics. The initial shock of Hattie's pronouncement gave way to a general collapse into animated, intense, aimless commentary from all corners. Even the adjuncts erupted.

"Maybe there's something we can do," spouted Pete, anticlimactically.

"At this stage of the game?" Jim Burns sniffed. "We've been on life support for so long we thought the body would never die."

"If only Cyrus were here," Pete said. "He'd know what to do, wouldn't he, Brisco?"

Diane turned to Jim Burns and whispered, "Isn't this wonderful?" Then she licked his ear.

Brisco was still riveted in place, next to The Brain, observing the general disorder. They had, indeed, long ago grown too dependent on the assumed wisdom of administration to resolve every issue. Well, he was going to show that the faculty was capable of action, of resolve, of resolution. Once the vending machine was in place, success would beget success and the bigger fish, as Hattie put it, could then be fried; the school, in fact, saved.

But these considerations weren't enough to rescue the meeting, let alone the college. As per tradition, it was sprouting wings and flying off for parts unknown. Brisco saw this and decided that for once he wouldn't waste energy trying to push water uphill. He seized The Brain and hurried out of the room, leaving behind a confused, milling, chattering mob.

Despite the swirling storm, the inbound planet-killing asteroid, the rising floodwaters, Marcus decided to take a walk. Alone. He kissed Bella good-bye in the bower and disappeared into the woods. It wasn't long before he stumbled upon Hector and Amber, locked in an embrace.

"Oh, excuse me!" said Marcus. "I hope I didn't disturb you. Actually, I'm just passing through."

Hector froze with fear and embarrassment, while Amber, clutching him, smiled sweetly and batted her eyelids.

"I-I," stammered the Spanish prof.

"Carry on," said Marcus with a cheerful wave as he continued on his way.

Eventually, he came to that unusual clearing he'd visited with Henny some weeks back. Only now, Timmy and Boss were grazing, or rooting, or otherwise scraping the ground with focused intent. In fact, they had been digging for some time. The glade resembled something of a field in the process of being de-mined, with sodden clumps of dirt everywhere.

"Oh, bad behavior!" Marcus said as he shooed the bison.

But they remained where they were, with Boss lifting her head for a moment and offering a snort.

"Oh, what will Professor Spox say?"

In fact, Henny was himself en route to the clearing. Brisco's sojourn at the institute had thrown him off-kilter. He felt he couldn't think within the confines of those walls at the moment, redolent as they were with the lingering aroma of formaldehyde and an unwashed Brisco.

Henny, too, passed Hector during his transit. When

the Spanish prof saw him, he quickly withdrew his hand from beneath Amber's halter and shot to his feet, where he stood at attention. Henny threw him a glance and continued on.

When Henny arrived at the clearing, he saw Marcus up to his ankles in dark, damp earth, trying to dislodge Timmy and Boss.

Henny, too, was struck by the upheaval of the glade. He kicked at the earth and then bent down to examine it with an eye practiced in observing the very, very small. "Hmm...." he hummed as he picked up a clump and kneaded it. Then he brought it to his nose and took a whiff. "Musty."

Marcus plodded over to the squatting genius. "Professor Spox," he sang out, wiping the sweat from his forehead with a checked bandanna as big as a dish towel. "Look what they did to this lovely field!"

"It's a godsend," said Henny, his voice full of emotion. He rose, still kneading the dirt in his hand.

"A godsend?" echoed Marcus.

"A miracle."

Marcus smiled amiably and shrugged. "I'm afraid you've got this old brain at a disadvantage."

"Here." Henny held the soil sample up between them. "Smell."

Marcus placed his ample proboscis close to the clod and inhaled deeply. The bristles of his mustache fluttered.

"Ah," he said with profound satisfaction. "Very fresh. But, no offense intended, musty."

"Yes, musty. That's just it. This earth contains fungus. And if I'm not mistaken, that's what drew the bison here. Please help me."

"I'll do anything I can! Just direct me."

The two men traipsed all over the glade, bending at intervals to sniff handfuls of earth. "Tell me if you *don't* smell anything musty," Henny called.

"Will do!"

Over at the grain silo, Brisco muscled The Brain up the spiral stairs, pausing every so often for breath. A bullhorn hung from his belt. The Brain was surprisingly heavy, saturated as it was with formaldehyde. It was like lugging a bowling ball. And then there was the heavy glass jar to consider. Sitting on a step to catch his breath, Brisco cranked his head and gazed up toward the distant landing. In a moment of lucidity, he asked himself if all this was worth it. Did it really matter if a vending machine ever arrived on campus? But once again, he concluded that the vending machine itself was no longer the point. This was about commitment, following through. It was like picking a scab—once you started you had to keep going. And so he hoisted The Brain and resumed his ascent.

Brisco's isolation in the silo gave him a bird's-eye view of the commotion that had erupted on campus.

Something had happened in the forest. Something that, at the moment, only Henny and Marcus were privy to. Timmy and Boss were the first wave. They came thundering out of the woods, bellowing, and ran roughshod over the green, knocking down benches and planters. After stampeding through the fading flower bed that Stash Zakraski had so lovingly planted, they charged off in the direction of the Quonsets.

Then came the second wave: Marcus and Henny arrived on the scene, briskly for men of their years. At that moment Bella was hobbling on her bad foot along the edge of the green, her hands in her hair at the sight of the destruction wrought by the bison.

When she saw Marcus, she was alarmed at his distress. "MooMoo!" She pumped her arms, propelling herself to her lover. When she reached him, they joined hands. "I love you!"

Marcus replied, "Where can I get a bullhorn?"

A cry erupted from atop the grain silo. Marcus and Bella looked up and saw a figure supporting some object at the edge of the window ledge. He was also holding the bullhorn he had brought with him. As he raised it to his mouth, it squealed and buzzed terribly, reverberating through the campus.

"It's Brisco Quik," said Bella. "And he's got The Brain!"

Brisco got the bullhorn under control. Then he began

to recite his list of grievances, all of them directed at Marcus and how he was running the school into the ground.

"He's unhappy," said Marcus as faculty, staff, and remaining students streamed out of the buildings to gather on the green.

Like a long, plaintive song of woe, Brisco poured forth his screed: the loss of individual phones, the reorganization, the inane talent show, the bison, and yes, the vending machine, on which he focused most of his indignation. "For the love of sweet Jesus," he thundered. "Someone do something! Disband the committees! Act now—apologize later!"

Frannie Moore, all but consumed by the crowd, was aghast. "Disband the committees? My God!"

The crowd had swelled until the green was studded with bodies. Even Hector and Amber had unclamped and emerged from the woods to see what the hullaballoo was about. Unaccustomed as the campus community was to anything resembling excitement, everyone simply stared up at Brisco, waiting to hear what he had to say next. But all he did was shove The Brain a little farther out on the window ledge.

"Professor Quik," bellowed Marcus as he stepped forward, waving.

Brisco raised the bullhorn. "Is that you, President Marcus? I can barely hear you."

"Yes, it's me," Marcus roared through cupped hands.

Bella clutched his arm. "Oh, be careful, MooMoo!"

"There, now," he said, patting her shoulder. "I think this will turn out well." Looking back at Brisco, he called, "Throw me the bullhorn."

Brisco blustered, "What?"

"The bullhorn! The bullhorn!"

Brisco held the instrument out before him, seeming to consider the request.

"I think he's going to do it." Marcus turned to two male students standing nearby. "Please catch the thing if he drops it."

The students ran off to the base of the silo. A moment later, the bullhorn was on its way down.

Marcus smiled and looked at Bella. "He's done me a terrific favor."

Once he had the bullhorn, Marcus addressed the crowd. "Follow Professor Spox and me to the forest!" Pointing the way, he led the foray into the woods while Brisco raved in the grain silo above.

The campus community—faculty, staff, students— swarmed behind Marcus and Henny. Practiced in incuriosity but enamored of the element of surprise, no one asked where they were going. An infectious air of adventure and giddiness reigned, serving as a sort of fuel, propelling the happy group.

The band eventually arrived at the clearing. After a

brief consultation with Henny, Marcus turned to them and raised the bullhorn. A series of ear-piercing squeals split the still autumn air before the president's voice rang through.

"Now, everyone," Marcus began, "please join hands in a circle around the perimeter of this glade but only where the earth has been overturned. Please don't trespass on the glade itself. Now quickly, quickly!"

Everyone streamed in two directions, skimming the border of the upturned earth and joining up again to form a vast, irregularly-shaped arena.

Henny broke ranks to walk to its center. With his arms stretched wide, he turned completely around until he had the full picture. "Amazing." Looking at Marcus, he announced, "If I'm not mistaken, we have discovered the world's largest living organism."

"What the hell is he talking about?" asked Jim Burns.

Diane squeezed his hand and laughed. "Oh, Jimmy, just go with the flow."

Marcus tramped out to the middle of the glade and stood next to the mathematician. "Go on, Professor Spox," he said, handing over the bullhorn. "Explain."

This was Henny's moment. With YaYa part of the circle, looking on with unremitting love, he commenced a soliloquy on his work, this discovery, the impact it would have on the college, and other things that qualified as little more than footnotes. In short, the exact species of fungus he'd been searching for had been growing right there, on college property—or rather, under it—for who knows how long, perhaps thousands of years. Not only that, but Henny was convinced that all the miniscule, musty fibers threading through this ground belonged to one individual, genetically unique fungus, making this, indeed, an organism of immense size—perhaps, as he'd said, the largest organism on earth.

Bella's mercantile instincts immediately kicked in. She didn't give a hang for the implications for Henny's research. She envisioned the advertising campaign that would ensue: "Grover Cleveland College: Home of the World's Largest Living Thing." She realized this would nudge The Brain to the periphery of significance, but so be it. And the implications for her own future were also crystal clear. With new life breathed into the campus, the prospect of returning to the chicken farm would evaporate forever. And then there was her MooMoo . . .

Jim Burns confided morosely to Diane, "Life will become unbearable. Henny Spox will be the patron saint of the school. Do you know how difficult it will be to make believe he doesn't exist?" Jim's deeper, unvoiced fear was that his mucus book would be eclipsed by this fungus.

Diane gave his ass a squeeze. "I think it's wonderful," she sang. "It's different. I like it."

If not for the wonders of Diane's body, Jim would have immediately dropped her hand and marched off.

But all he could do for the moment was bite his tongue and focus on the night to come.

Dan Stupak was philosophical. "Well, Joe," he said, "one cannot quarrel with success. I have to admit I see wonderful possibilities here."

Joe laughed. "Why, Dan, you sound like you're falling in love."

Speaking of which, Hector and Amber quietly broke ranks and skulked off into the forest again to pick up where they'd left off. Their escape, however, was interrupted by the roar of an engine.

Everyone in the circle turned to see an all-terrain vehicle in erratic flight, bumping and smoking its way through the woods, hauling a refrigerator-size cargo on a trailer. The driver was wild-eyed, spinning the wheel to retain control as he maneuvered around trees and over rough ground. Several people might have been struck if they hadn't been alert and jumped out of the way as the ATV barreled through the circle and continued into the glade, its wheels rutting the damp earth.

It finally came to a stop in the middle of the clearing, next to Marcus and Henny.

"This is unexpected!" Marcus said with delight. "I thought you'd retired."

Jiminy climbed out of the ATV and stood unsteadily on his thin legs. "My last act. As emeritus, I felt I had nothing to lose." He'd also concluded he hadn't, in fact, made any significant contribution to the campus in all his years as provost.

What he had delivered, of course, was a vending machine, already stocked with soft drinks. It was a vintage contraption, purely mechanical but seemingly in good shape. "Yard sales are wonderful," he said and then divulged that he'd spent half his pension on the thing.

Frannie Moore stepped daintily among the clods of earth and approached the threesome. "This is clearly a usurping of the committee's charge."

"The committee be hanged," said Jiminy. "The deed is done."

"Indeed it is," said Marcus. "Indeed."

Wild, sustained applause erupted from the gathering. Marcus smiled as he looked about, wondering if the approbation was for the discovery of the fungus or for the vending machine. *No matter*, he concluded, acknowledging the show of honest emotion and enthusiasm, both of which boded well for the future of the college.

After letting the cheering run its course, Marcus spoke paternally to the crowd, urging them to return to the school, strive to do well, and not forget to scavenge firewood for the winter ahead. When he was done, everyone dispersed and filtered back to campus.

Bella hobbled closer to Marcus and embraced him unashamedly. "This is your finest hour."

Marcus regarded her warmly. "It is?" And then, after

a moment's consideration, he said, "I suppose so!"

Brisco watched disconsolately from the silo as faculty, staff, and students washed back onto campus. Without his bullhorn, he was mute. He was also the only member of the campus community who had no idea what had just transpired. But he perceived the energy and positive vibes of the chattering crowd below. A few minutes later, when he saw the ATV bumping onto campus with its precious cargo, he felt vindicated and the wind departed his sails.

But his desperation, once abated, was succeeded by the simmer of loneliness.

Winter came. It was a time of incubation for all the hopes, desires, and faith that had been so recently invested in Grover Cleveland's future. Finally, after long months, the unrelenting cold and uncommonly deep snow abated, and after a brief mud season, spring returned in typical Maine fashion: it exploded. Croci broke through the last crust of ice, pines dropped their pollen in billowing yellow clouds, blackflies swarmed, and the surrounding forest turned an electric green. Most importantly, the fungus's great promise had been confirmed.

Bella wasted no time. With her typical diligence, she'd lined up all the media outlets in planetary order, coordinating press releases and helping to write hyperbolic copy, such as "President's Brain Upstaged by

Fungus." Camera teams from around the world swept onto the campus, bleating word of the spectacular find. The students themselves, in their communications home to family and friends, provided crowning propaganda, and the immense fungus, lovingly dubbed Max by a vote of the student body, soon exceeded the bison as a major point of interest. It even received a visit from the Soviet ambassador, an avid mushroom enthusiast.

Once Henny had confirmation that the fungus was the exact species he needed for his work, grant money poured in and a new building—the first new building ever erected on campus—appeared: the Institute for Nanofungirobotics. Post-docs and fellows and adjunct researchers precipitated out of the ether and soon peppered the campus, lending it a Harvard-like air of presumptuousness.

Small as it was, Grover Cleveland College had become the navel of the universe. Student numbers swelled as the applicant pool skyrocketed. For the first time since the Vietnam War, admissions standards were imposed and Hattie Sims, who'd been promoted to Director of Admissions, derived obscene pleasure out of drafting letters that read, "Although we are happy that you considered Grover Cleveland College for your higher education needs, we find that you have not met our rigorous academic standards and so must, regretfully, deny you admission." In short, she became the consummate professional. The years with Jiminy had exhausted her capacity for dealing with the bizarre, and she deemed it in the best interest of her ego and her mental health to concentrate on her new position, forget about Brisco or any man associated with Grover Cleveland College, and ply the more promising off-campus waters for romance.

As a result of the surge in the student population, course offerings multiplied. This promoted the balkanization of the curriculum to include such titles as Yankee Women's Studies, Lumberjack Poetry, Concepts in Black Hospitality, and Experiential Learning in Conjoined Twins. In short, there was soon something for everybody.

For the first time, nongovernmental financial aid was available, most of it endowed by newly self-appointed Grover Cleveland College hangers-on. An annual award of five thousand dollars came from Friends of The Brain. Henny himself endowed the Spore Scholarship for "a student specializing in mushrooms, molds, and itches." The Aloha Scholarship was created by yet more Hawaiian recidivists.

Frannie Moore left teaching to become the new financial aid director and dwelled quietly alone in her small corner office in the basement of the Victorian, disbursing awards with her usual care, concern, and diligence, with no Brisco Quik to challenge her quiet authority. She essentially disappeared from public view, giving rise to a rumor among the student body that hers was the name of a highly efficient software program.

Now that cash flow was once again established, the bank was easily won over and eagerly granted Grover Cleveland College a reprieve pending financial arrangements to resolve its debt. Soon the school was not only able to make its back payments and meet its current financial responsibilities, but it was going above and beyond the call of duty by catapulting salvos of money toward the principal.

Brisco, of course, never shoved The Brain out of the silo. Instead, he released his tenuous hold on reality, grew out his hair and beard, ceased to change his clothing, and moved into Jiminy's woodshed. He reclaimed the bullhorn, however, and periodically blared pronouncements that Marcus found so insightful and prescient, if unorthodox, that the president felt there was no other option than to name Brisco provost.

In return, Brisco became an admirer of the president and chastised anyone who came to him with a complaint or otherwise said an unkind word about the college's leader. Last, having dispensed with his car, he magnanimously returned his handicapped space to Bella, who acknowledged the gesture with grace and gratitude.

The monstrous fungus, of course, was the gift that kept on giving. The more Henny harvested, the more it grew. It not only fueled Henny's research, but it was sold to institutions all over the world, creating a steady flow of cash for the college's growth and almost any boondoggle that crossed someone's mind.

One of the major beneficiaries of the largess was the Grover Cleveland College Press. Newly flush with mazuma, Vikram Chabot didn't hesitate to publish Jim Burns's mucus book. As Diane Dempsey had predicted, the title alone was the propellant. The first print run of *Naked Heat* sold out immediately and rocketed to number ten on the *New York Times* best-seller list for nonfiction. Vikram vigorously enforced a no-returns policy, so that—once again, as per Diane—when buyers realized what lay beyond the title, there was no possibility of getting their money back. Some raged, others silently seethed, but most quietly retained the book, assuming literature had simply entered a new phase of expression that was, for the moment, beyond their comprehension.

"I'm happy," said Marcus one day as he strolled across campus holding Bella's hand. "I'm so happy!"

His bliss had diminished only briefly that very morning when he'd opened the paper and seen an obscure article titled "Legendary Car Dealership in New Jersey Goes Under." *Well*, said Marcus to himself, *I suppose I made the right decision after all*. And he'd spared a moment to shed a gentle tear for Mr. Bell.

He and Bella were no longer circumspect about their relationship. There was no need to be. In the new, heady atmosphere of the school, where every heart's desire was being satisfied, Marcus could do no wrong. Bella walked proudly in love beside her man, the two immense bodies moving about the campus like royalty, dipping their heads in greeting, pausing to accept the compliments of passersby.

"I wish Uncle Cyrus could be here to see all of this," said Marcus as the two of them enjoyed the sight of the maples' tender first leaves and the yellow explosion of forsythia. "Here we are, in the full flower of spring, and the campus itself is blossoming beyond anyone's wildest dreams."

"Cyrus was a genius, MooMoo," said Bella dreamily, "because he picked the right man to succeed him."

Marcus blushed. "Are you talking about me?" he asked coyly.

"Who else?"

Marcus glanced up at the silo. The clock's hand was on the nine. "Curious. That hand does not seem to have moved in a very long time."

He had no way of knowing, of course, that Scott Ott, in a bid to make some small contribution to the school's morale, had climbed the face of the silo in the dead of night, months before, when all seemed lost, and had stopped time in its tracks with the insertion of a well-placed chisel.

The two headed off toward the Brain Shrine, where the organ had been reinstated and the eternal flame burned steadily in the still air while a student sentinel dozed in a dim corner. Right next to the catafalque on which The Brain rested was the red-and-white vending machine, chock-a-block-full of soda pop. Marcus inserted his coins and pulled a handle. There was a rattle of bottles and then the reward of an ice-cold orange Fanta. He held the drink for a moment, and his eyes welled with tears as he regarded it.

"Oh, MooMoo, why are you crying?"

Marcus sniffed and then smiled. "Oh, it's nothing. I was just thinking. The idea of small things that began with Professor Burns telling me about his mucus book—which, by the way, is selling briskly, I'm told. Anyway, he was right. So was Henny Spox. Small things, small steps, small wonders. And now this machine. We fought so long for it, and now, hot and sweaty as we are from walking, I hold this cold bottle in my hand, and it's not the drink itself that satisfies me so much as the anticipation of it. The idea of it."

Tears flowed freely from Bella's eyes. "MooMoo, I've never heard you talk like this."

"I don't think I've ever felt like this. Or maybe I have. Maybe we all have. You know that feeling, the one we've just experienced, when spring was about to happen? The snow is gone, the sun is warm, and the buds are still clamped shut? All as preamble to something wonderful, something so fresh that you felt it would be different from all previous springs? Or that dream where you're hanging off the edge of a cliff, about to let go, wondering if you can fly? And then, when you do let go, you find that you *can* fly? It was that moment before spring, and before flight, that made you feel you were really alive, because you were full of anticipation for what would happen next."

All of this was too much for Bella. She took the bottle from Marcus's hand, placed it on the ground, and pushed him deep into the Brain Shrine, onto his back, oblivious to the snoring sentinel. It was their deepest and most protracted love experience yet, and as they loved, a mockingbird alit and twittered its song, a bullhorn trumpeted an inanity in the distance, Pacer prowled, the bison bellowed, quarters rattled into the vending machine, and the world, in Marcus's mind, felt suddenly smaller, if such a thing were possible.

ALSO BY ROBERT KLOSE

Nonfiction
Adopting Alyosha: A Single Man Finds a Son in Russia
Small Worlds: Adopted Sons, Pet Piranhas, and Other Mortal Concerns
The Three-Legged Woman and Other Excursions in Teaching

Juvenile
The Legend of the River Pumpkins

For extra content

For extra content

For more information
about other great titles from
Medallion Press, visit

medallionmediagroup.com

Medallion Press has created
Read on Vacation for e-book
lovers who read on the go.

See more at:
medallionmediagroup.com/readonvacation

MMG SIDEKICK
Do you love books?

The **MMG Sidekick** app for the iPad is
your entertainment media companion.
Download it today to get access to
Medallion's entire library of e-books,
including **FREE** e-books every month.
MMG Sidekick is also the only way to
get access to TREEbook*-enhanced
novels with story-branching technology!